All these years later, she was more beautiful than ever.

From the first time Forest had met Avery, she'd seemed to take an instant dislike to him. Even now, she seemed prickly.

Her mood probably had nothing to do with him and everything to do with losing her grandmother and Hazel trying to push them together. He wished he could take her to dinner or coffee or somewhere that they could sit down and get to know each other better.

"You're leaving tomorrow?" he asked.

"Yes."

"May I help you with the house?"

Anger flashed in her eyes. "I told you I'm not ready to put the place on the market and I have no idea if or when I will. Cool your jets, okay?"

He took a step back away from her.

"I wasn't asking for the listing," he said. "I meant is there anything I can do to help with the maintenance of the house while you're away."

Her mouth opened and then closed and her cheeks colored. "Oh. Um, no. No, thanks. I, uh, I need to go."

She disappeared inside, leaving him with the question *Why do you dislike me so much?* lingering in his mouth like a bad taste.

Dear Reader,

Welcome back to Tinsley Cove! *Holiday at Mistletoe Cottage* is the second book in The McFaddens of Tinsley Cove series.

I love the holidays. To me, it really is the most wonderful time of the year. I love picking out the tree and unpacking the ornaments and decorations. Each one is like rediscovering an old friend or reliving a cherished memory. I've had some of our decorations since I was a child. This book was inspired by a wooden advent calendar that's been in my family for years.

When Avery Anderson returns to Tinsley Cove, North Carolina, in December after losing her beloved grandmother Bess, her plan is to put Gran's affairs in order as fast as possible and get out of town. Tinsley Cove, where she lived for three years when she had to move in with her grandmother, was never her happy place. She redoubles her goal after running into Forest McFadden, who was the most humiliating date of her entire life. Forest, the oldest McFadden brother, and the newly elected—and youngest—mayor of Tinsley Cove, hasn't changed a bit. He's still infuriatingly good-looking and insufferably nice. When a Secret Santa delivers an advent calendar fully loaded with twenty-four holiday-themed challenges, Avery finds herself getting into the holiday spirit (despite herself) with Forest's help. As Avery finds herself under the mistletoe with the sexy mayor, will she finally find the place that feels like home?

I hope you'll enjoy Forest and Avery's story as much as I loved writing it. Please look for book three in the series next summer. In the meantime, keep in touch. I love to hear from readers.

Warmly,

Nancy

Holiday at Mistletoe Cottage

———

NANCY ROBARDS THOMPSON

HARLEQUIN
SPECIAL
EDITION

Recycling programs for this product may not exist in your area.

ISBN-13: 978-1-335-59437-2

Holiday at Mistletoe Cottage

Copyright © 2023 by Nancy Robards Thompson

For questions and comments about the quality of this book, please contact us at CustomerService@Harlequin.com.

Harlequin Enterprises ULC
22 Adelaide St. West, 41st Floor
Toronto, Ontario M5H 4E3, Canada
www.Harlequin.com

Printed in U.S.A.

Nationally bestselling author **Nancy Robards Thompson** holds a degree in journalism. She worked as a newspaper reporter until she realized reporting "just the facts" bored her silly. Now that she has much more content to report to her muse, Nancy loves writing women's fiction and romance full-time. Critics have deemed her work "funny, smart and observant." She resides in Florida with her husband and daughter. You can reach her at Facebook.com/nrobardsthompson.

Books by Nancy Robards Thompson

Harlequin Special Edition

The McFaddens of Tinsley Cove

Selling Sandcastle
Holiday at Mistletoe Cottage

The Savannah Sisters

A Down-Home Savannah Christmas
Southern Charm & Second Chances
Her Savannah Surprise

Celebration, TX

The Cowboy's Runaway Bride
A Bride, a Barn, and a Baby
The Cowboy Who Got Away

The Fortunes of Texas: Rulebreakers

Maddie Fortune's Perfect Man

The Fortunes of Texas: The Secret Fortunes

Fortune's Surprise Engagement

Visit the Author Profile page
at Harlequin.com for more titles.

This book is for everyone who believes in the magic of the holidays.

Chapter One

Tinsley Cove, North Carolina
Saturday, September 30

"Your grandmother was such a good friend," said the woman with the cake carrier and foil-covered nine-by-thirteen pan.

She'd said her name not two minutes ago, but Avery Anderson had zoned out.

It started with an *H*. Was it Helen...or maybe Hattie?

So many people had stopped by Mistletoe Cottage since Avery had arrived in Tinsley Cove two days ago, she was having a hard time keeping them straight. She remembered some of the callers from the year she'd lived in the small beach town a dozen years ago. Others, if she'd even met them, had been relegated to the file in her memory labeled "better off forgotten."

"Bess was so lovely, such a valued member of our

community," the older woman continued. "I cannot fathom what we'll do without her. I was with her just a couple of days before she passed. She showed me her wish list of all the things she wanted the two of you to do together when you came for Christmas. She was so excited about spending the holidays with you."

Avery forced a smile to stop the ugly cry that was threatening like a storm cloud. Now was definitely not the time to lose it. Not in front of a stranger.

"Thank you. Gran and I were very close. Hearing you say that means a lot." After an awkward pause, Avery asked, "Would you like to come inside?"

"Oh, no, this is just a drop-and-run, dear. I'm sure you have a lot to do while you're in town, but you'll need sustenance while you're here."

Avery was sure she hadn't met this one before. Wait, had she said her name was Hannah? No, that didn't sound quite right, whoever she was she and her grandmother must've been good friends if she knew how dogged Gran had been about Avery being here for Christmas.

As the tears welled in Avery's eyes, the woman thrust the food at her. Miraculously, Avery managed the transfer without dropping anything. "That's a chicken spaghetti casserole. Heating instructions are right here." With a pearl-pink polished nail, she tapped on the index card taped to the foil. "There's salad mix in this bag. And this is a lemon Bundt cake."

It was Tinsley Cove's version of tea and sympathy, and it usually involved at least a three-course meal. Avery was starting to run out of refrigerator space. What was worse, she was leaving tomorrow to go back to New York. She had no idea what she would do with all this food.

Once word got out that Avery was in town, the feeders had deployed. It seemed ungracious to refuse their offerings.

"Thank you," Avery said. "I appreciate it."

"How long did you say you'd be here?" the woman asked.

I didn't say.

"I'm leaving tomorrow."

"Is that so?" The woman frowned and eyed the food as if she was second-guessing her generosity. "Well, Bess has a deep freeze in the garage. You should be able to repackage and store everything you don't eat in there. When will you be back?"

"I'm not sure yet."

As a photojournalist with *World International* magazine, Avery traveled a lot. She'd been scheduled to fly to Dubai to photograph a business magnate when the call came in from the hospital.

A nurse had asked if Bess Loughlin was her grandmother. She'd said Gran had suffered a stroke and was in the ICU, and that Avery should come as soon as possible.

She'd called her boss, Barry Orr, from the airport. He had assured her that another photographer would cover Dubai for her. Avery should take as long as she needed.

By the time Avery reached the hospital, Bess was gone.

Avery hadn't even had the chance to say goodbye.

She bit down on her lower lip to stave off the ugly cry that was hovering closer.

The woman with the *H* name was still talking and Avery was nodding as if she was hanging on every word, but she couldn't focus. It felt as if she'd been pulled up and out of herself, and was floating above, watching everything unfold as if it was happening to someone else.

Gran had sounded fine when they'd talked last week. In fact, her grandmother had seemed full of energy as the two of them discussed plans for Avery's annual Thanksgiving visit. That's when Gran had pressed Avery about Christmas.

"I don't want anything else for Christmas except for you to visit," Gran had said. "Why don't you see if you can get your boss to give you six weeks off and you could stay through the New Year."

"I don't know if that's possible, Gran, but I'll be there for Thanksgiving."

Then Gran had belted a few horrendously off-key bars of "All I Want for Christmas Is You" and Avery had laughed along, ending the conversation with "I'll see what I can do."

She couldn't bring herself to disappoint Gran, but Avery knew she couldn't take off that much time. Her boss had dangled the carrot of adding a photo editor to the staff. The person who got the job would essentially be second in command at the magazine. She was up for the promotion. While it would be a drastic lifestyle change—more office time and less travel—she'd been living out of a suitcase for too long and part of her wanted to have a more normal life. Maybe. She hadn't decided if she really wanted it, but she still wanted to be a contender. That meant it was crucial that her boss saw that she was dedicated to her job. Since she wasn't married and didn't have kids, it was easy for her to make herself indispensable by stepping up at the holidays when most of her coworkers wanted time off.

Now she would be able to work Thanksgiving, too. Because there would be no Thanksgiving. Not for her. Not this year or ever again.

It seemed wrong to think about work and promotions at a time like this, but work was all she had left. That's why she intended to spend the rest of the day getting Gran's affairs in order, and she would fly back to New York tomorrow.

"Avery? Are you okay?"

Avery's attention snapped back into place. "I'm so sorry—I have a lot on my mind. What were you saying?"

"If you're looking for a florist, Daisy from Daisy's Flower Emporium on Main Street does beautiful work."

"The florist's name is Daisy?"

"Yes, and I know she would be honored to help you with flowers for Bess's funeral. When were you planning on holding the service?"

Avery stared at her blankly. She'd arranged for Gran's ashes to be sent to New York, but she hadn't thought much beyond that.

"I'll let you know," she said.

The woman tilted her head to the side, as if Avery had given the wrong answer.

"Well, please keep us apprised and if you need anything at all don't hesitate to call. My phone number is on a piece of masking tape on the bottom of the cake carrier. You are not alone in this."

It was a nice sentiment, but the truth was, she'd never been more alone in her entire life.

Avery adjusted her grip on the handle of the round, plastic container and shifted the warm casserole dish, which was starting to feel heavy and cumbersome.

"Thank you," Avery said.

"Such a loss. Such a sad, *sad* loss." The woman shook her curly, gray-haired head, then dabbed at her eyes with a tissue she'd pulled from the pocket of her blue cardigan and blew her nose before returning the tissue to her pocket.

The absence of sunshine on this humid, silvery gray afternoon made it feel as if the earth was mourning the passing of Bess Loughlin. It had rained earlier and steam rose from the pavement, leaving the air thick with moisture, like pent-up tears.

Avery turned at the crunch of tires on the crushed-seashell driveway next door, where a white BMW had rolled up. A moment later, a tall guy with dark hair wearing a tan trench coat who had the broadest shoulders Avery had ever seen unfolded himself from the car.

Before Avery realized she was staring, the guy turned around and caught her.

Ugh. It was Forest McFadden.

Her stomach bottomed out and she took a step back toward the door.

Of course it's him, dummy.

He'd bought the house next door to Gran a few years ago. Last year when she'd visited for Thanksgiving, he'd been driving a Mercedes-Benz. Avery hadn't recognized the BMW. And she hadn't realized his shoulders were *that* broad, she thought as she tried to make herself small behind the food containers.

From the way Gran told it, you would've thought

that royalty or an A-list celebrity had moved in next door. She used to joke that one of these days she was going to invite that handsome Forest McFadden over for dinner while Avery was there at Thanksgiving, but she'd never done it.

Thank goodness.

Probably because Avery's visits were so short and Gran didn't want to share her time. Or maybe Gran sensed that Avery didn't want to be forced into an awkward setup, no matter how benign or platonic.

It was silly to hang on to hurt feelings after all these years. Really, she didn't even think about Forest when she wasn't in Tinsley Cove. But what had happened—the way he and his friends had made her the butt of a cruel joke at a time when she was hurting and vulnerable—had been a life lesson in trusting people.

It was ironic that once again, when she was hurting and vulnerable, square-jawed, broad-shouldered, cock-sure Forest McFadden had a front-row seat.

People grew up. People changed. Or at least one would hope they did. It didn't matter now. Avery's life was in New York. She had no time for Forest.

The bearer of the cake and casserole—was her name Hope?—turned and followed Avery's gaze.

"Oh, look! It's Mayor McFadden." She lifted her arm and waved high in the air. "Hi, Mayor!"

"*Shhh! No, no, no.* Don't do that."

The woman didn't seem to hear her because she had been drawn into his tractor beam as he waved back.

"You're living next door to the most eligible bachelor in Tinsley Cove." The woman's eyes sparkled.

"Hello, Hazel," he answered.

Ahh! Hazel. That's right.

Avery had known it started with an *H*, but as she watched Forest make his approach, the name of Gran's friend became the least of her worries.

"Have you met Bess's granddaughter, Avery?"

"I really do need to go," Avery murmured. "Thank you for the—"

Hazel's hand snaked out and caught Avery's arm, securing her in place.

Avery pulled free and took another step back, butting against the closed door. If she'd had a free hand to turn the knob, she would've disappeared inside, leaving the two of them to talk, but she didn't. She would've had to set down the cake. He'd be on the porch by the time she opened the door and turned to pick it up again.

Reminding herself that the opposite of love wasn't hate—it was indifference—she steeled herself to prove exactly how indifferent she felt about this phony, phony man.

As he ascended the porch steps, Avery could see that underneath his beige trench coat, Forest was wearing a suit with a white button-down shirt and an ice-green tie that made his hazel eyes look maddeningly green. With his dark hair, full lips and face that had gotten even better-looking over the years—*damn him*—she could see how people like Hazel would be drawn to him.

Hazel, you've been bamboozled, girl.

"I do know Avery," he said. "Hello. It's been a long time."

Her cheeks flamed and she hated herself for it.

Yes, it had been a long time, but when translated into humiliation years, it had not been long enough.

Clearly, she was more exhausted than she realized because she was suddenly woefully self-conscious of her jeans with the ripped knees and the oversize ivory fisherman's knit sweater that was fraying a bit at the right cuff.

Gran had knitted her that sweater. She imagined it was like a big hug from her.

"Forest." She gave a curt nod.

"I'm sorry about your grandmother," he said. "Bess was a wonderful woman."

"Yes, she was." Avery tilted up her chin. "Thank you."

When Avery's parents had been killed in a car accident the summer before Avery's senior year of high school, Bess Loughlin had taken in Avery without a second thought, looking after the only child of her only child. Even though they barely knew each other when she'd come to live with Bess, by the time Avery left for college in the spring of the following year, they had bonded in a way that had them leaning on each other in their grief and helping each other through the loss.

Of course, it also meant attending a new high school in her senior year, and entering close-knit Tinsley Cove High, with its cliques and closed circles.

Avery adjusted her one-handed grip on the still-warm casserole dish, pushing it against her hip.

"Let me help you with that," Forest said.

"No. It's okay. I was just going inside."

He took the dish from her in one swift move.

Don't pretend to be nice to me.

"I was just about to ask Avery what she intends to do with Mistletoe Cottage," Hazel said.

"I don't know." Avery's voice was terse.

"Well, if you decide to sell, Forest is your go-to guy," Hazel said in a singsong voice. "Sandcastle Real Estate is the best in town. You do know he and his family have their own TV show, don't you? It's called *Selling Sandcastle*. They've made the entire town famous."

So Hazel is a fangirl. Surprise, surprise.

Avery forced a smile. "Congratulations, that's quite an accomplishment."

"Thanks." Forest shrugged. "I don't know if I'd call it an accomplishment, but it's an interesting experience."

"You're too modest." Hazel was looking at him in wonder. "The show was renewed after its first season and it has put Tinsley Cove on the map. That translates to good tourism revenue and—" the woman elbowed Avery "—skyrocketing property values. Forest, aren't you getting ready to film season two?"

He nodded. "We start in December."

"Maybe you can feature Mistletoe Cottage on the show?" Hazel volunteered.

"If not that, I can think of a handful of buyers who would be interested. We could get you a good price."

Avery held up a hand. "Gran has only been gone a few days. It hasn't fully hit me that she's…" Avery choked on her words, then cleared her throat. "I have no idea what I want to do with the place."

Hazel's hand flew to her mouth and her eyes brimmed with tears. "Honey, I'm so sorry. That was thoughtless of me. I did not mean to be indelicate."

Avery waved away her words. "It's fine. I just need some time."

Hazel put a hand on Avery's shoulder. "Of course you do."

"In fact, they say you shouldn't make any major changes for the first year," Forest added.

"He's right, dear," Hazel said. "You should listen to him."

He probably had everybody in this town under his spell. Easy to do when you were the big fish in the small Tinsley Cove pond.

"I know you have a lot to do," Hazel said. "I'll get out of your hair. Please let us know about Bess's arrangements."

The woman turned to go but stopped on the top step.

"Avery, are you single?"

Hello? Hadn't she just apologized for being indelicate?

"I work a lot," she said. "I'm sort of married to my job."

"Well, how about that. Forest is a workaholic, too, and he's single. You kids have a lot in common."

Forest knew the best way out of an awkward situation like this was to laugh it off and keep the mood light. "Hazel loves to play the matchmaker, don't you?"

"Well, you know that my Howie and I will have been married for sixty-five years next July. I just want everyone to be as happy as we are. They say there's a lid for every pot and when I see two perfectly eligible pots standing in front of me…"

She waggled her penciled-on eyebrows.

"If we're both pots, I suppose that means our lids are out there somewhere." Avery looked as uncomfortable as Forest felt. "Or not. There's no crime in being single. Thanks again for stopping by, Hazel."

"Oh, I don't know," Hazel said. "I believe one never knows if they're the pot or the lid until they find their match. Then, I suppose it doesn't matter, does it?"

Okay, enough of this.

Forest was certain that Hazel meant well, but it was the last thing Avery needed as she was trying to come to terms with her loss.

"Hazel, there's a city council meeting tomorrow—will we see you there?"

"You bet I will. The zoning for that new apartment complex is supposed to be on the agenda and I have plenty to say about it. By the way, Avery, if you're leaving tomorrow, maybe you could just give my dish and cake carrier to the mayor and he could bring them to the meeting tomorrow night? Normally, I'd say no hurry in returning them, but since you don't know when you'll be back, I might need them."

"I'm going to be in and out running errands today," said Avery. " I'll leave them inside the garage. That way you can grab them when it's convenient for you, Forest. I'll leave the side door unlocked. Would you please lock it after you pick up your things?"

"Sure, if that works best for you," said Forest. "I'll grab them before the meeting tomorrow and lock up."

Forest and Avery watched as Hazel tottered down the porch steps, clutching the banister.

"May I help you to your car?" Forest called after her.

"I'm fine." Hazel waved him away without a backward glance. "Help your lovely neighbor inside with the food."

With that, Avery opened the front door and set the cake carrier on the floor in the foyer.

When she reappeared, she held out her hands to take the dish. "Thanks for holding on to that for me. I can take it from here."

He remembered clearly the first time he'd seen Avery Anderson sitting by herself on the patio outside of the school cafeteria. With her long, wavy blond hair and dark brown eyes, he thought she was the most beautiful girl he'd ever seen. She'd seemed more sophisticated than the girls in Tinsley Cove, if not a bit shy. It would've been difficult to move to a new school in your last year of high school when everyone was anticipating college and wanting to be anywhere but there.

All these years later, she was even more beautiful than he remembered.

Right away, Avery seemed to take an instant dislike to him. Even now, she seemed prickly.

Her mood probably had nothing to do with him and everything to do with losing her grandmother and Hazel trying to push them together.

He wished he could take her to dinner or coffee or somewhere that they could sit down and get to know each other better.

"You're leaving tomorrow?" he asked.

"Yes."

"May I help you with the house?"

Anger flashed in her eyes. "I told you I'm not ready to put the place on the market and I have no idea if or when I will. Cool your jets, okay?"

He took a step back away from her.

"I wasn't asking for the listing," he said. "I meant is there anything I can do to help with the maintenance of the house while you're away."

Her mouth opened and then closed and her cheeks colored.

"Oh. *Um*, no. No thanks. I…need to go."

She disappeared inside, leaving him with a question lingering in his mouth like a bad taste—*why do you dislike me so much?*

Chapter Two

Alone in the house, Avery wandered from room to room, the emptiness echoing in her aching soul.

The task ahead of her seemed daunting. She would have to sort through everything in the house and decide what to keep or toss and what to donate.

The house was comfortably cluttered. Most things had a place, but her gran hadn't been obsessive about keeping things organized. That's why the place had always been so comfortable. It was too bad, that Avery hadn't found as much comfort outside the sanctuary of Mistletoe Cottage the year she'd lived with her grandmother.

She shook off the thought. She was leaving tomorrow, and while she hadn't wanted to commit to Hazel and Forest, most likely, she would be forced to sell the place. Even though she traveled a lot, her job was based out of New York City. She couldn't afford to keep this place and the two-bedroom Chelsea apartment that she shared with her roommate, Val.

Even so, she didn't have to make that decision yet. There was a lot to do before this place would be ready to sell, but in the meantime Avery needed to get back to New York so she could do her job and make money. Who knew, maybe she'd get lucky and win the lottery.

In the meantime, she needed to find Gran's will and then get organized so she could accomplish all the things that needed to be done before she left.

She'd do a room-by-room inventory and see if she'd missed anything on the mental list she'd started about what absolutely needed to be done first. Some of it could be done long-distance. Those tasks would be relegated to the bottom of the list. She really should write it all down, even though she didn't want to because that made her gran's passing all too real.

Reluctantly, Avery pushed open the door to Gran's office and sat down behind the antique desk. She took a moment just to observe the way everything appeared on the surface, exactly the way Gran had left it, as if she had only stepped away and would be right back.

An agenda calendar was lying open to this week's page, while scant stacks of file folders were fanned out on the desk beneath a cadre of ink pens and the twist-up yellow pencils that Gran had always favored. A few days' worth of accumulated mail was scattered about, along with scraps of paper with notes scrawled in Gran's handwriting: *return library books by Sunday. Take in car for oil change on Tuesday.* A random telephone number was written diagonally and appeared to have been jotted in a hurry.

The normalcy of it all made Avery's heart ache. She

didn't want to touch anything. Maybe if she didn't, if she left it all exactly as it was, by the time she got back to New York, Gran would call and tell her there had been a crazy mix-up. She was fine. She would insist that they make both sweet potatoes and mashed potatoes for Thanksgiving, because what other time could you get away with two types of potatoes in one meal? Except for Christmas. Christmas absolutely called for two kinds of potatoes. And had Avery asked her boss yet if she could have vacation from Thanksgiving through the end of the year?

"Gran, I'd ask him right now if it would bring you back."

Avery blinked away the tears, then gathered the mail into a neat stack and placed it on the corner of the desk.

No matter how she wished or bargained or cried and cursed the fates, nothing would bring her back.

That meant Avery needed to go through that pile of mail and figure out Gran's bill situation, and take care of anything outstanding. For now, she would add it to the list…once she found a blank piece of paper.

She returned the pencils and pens to the holder, closed the planner and underneath the clutter…*bingo*! She found a yellow legal pad.

As she flipped through to find a free page, a list in Gran's handwriting caught Avery's eye. *Wishlist for when Avery comes home for Christmas.*

This was the list Hazel mentioned. There were twenty-four items on the list, each one numbered.

Her heart squeezed and then thudded. In their last phone conversation, Gran had said, "I know it's early, but will you please at least give some thought to coming home for Christmas, too? I'm not giving up Thanksgiving, mind you. So this would be in addition to. I'm sure you have the vacation because all you do is work. Maybe if you give your boss adequate notice that you're planning to take off, he'll let you."

The truth of the matter was that even as much as Avery adored her gran, the thought of taking off six consecutive weeks made her break out in hives. She had gotten to where she was in her career as a photo-journalist by being available, by working the holidays and weekends that no one else wanted to work. She'd never minded being by herself. In fact, it gave her a lot of time to reflect. Until this year, Gran had always told her not to worry about her, that she always received invitations to spend Christmas with friends, but this year... This year, Gran had pushed.

Avery had the accrued vacation hours. The problem was, she didn't have the time to use them, especially when they could roll over or she could cash them out when they accumulated to a certain point.

Gran called Tinsley Cove home, but to Avery, it would never be anything other than the place she stayed after her parents died.

She scanned the list Gran had made. It contained the usual Christmas activities, such as shopping, tree decorating, cookie making. Then her gaze tracked back to one item that caught her eye: Hang mistletoe around the house/kiss someone under the mistletoe.

Avery smiled at the thought of asking Gran whom she planned on kissing under the mistletoe. In her head, she could hear Gran saying it wasn't for herself—she'd already had the love of her life in Avery's Grandpa Tom, so it was for Avery.

She squinted at the paper. The sun was setting outside, making it darker in the office, and the tears in her eyes didn't make it any easier to read Gran's writing. Avery had to pick up the paper and hold it closer to see what Gran had added in the margin.

Invite Forest McFadden over.

She dropped the list like it had scalded her and then blinked away the thought.

That wasn't going to happen.

Actually, now none of this would happen. Avery had lost her chance, thinking that she had all the time in the world. If it would bring Gran back, she might even kiss Forest McFadden under the mistletoe.

Of course, that was easy to say since it wasn't going to happen.

Her gaze tripped down the list to near the end:

Cohost the annual cookie-swap party...just like old times.

The cookie-swap party was an annual tradition that Gran had hosted for as far back as Avery could remember. When her parents were alive, on the rare occasion that they made it back to Tinsley Cove for the holidays, they would all help Gran prepare. They'd bake for days, because there could never be too many cookies, and it seemed like every family in Tinsley Cove would bring at least one platter of goodies to share.

Avery would sneak a plate up to her room and stay up there reading—mostly books about photography—while convivial party sounds buzzed below.

Gran held the party every year, with or without the help of her small family. Too bad that tradition would end, unless someone in the small beach town picked up the mantle. But that was the least of Avery's worries.

Right now, Avery needed to get a game plan in place.

She traced her fingertip over Gran's scrolling handwriting on the Christmas wish list, and wracked her brain trying to remember if she had at least told Gran that she would consider asking for vacation. She hadn't asked her boss for time off, of course, but since it was early yet, she probably hadn't given Gran a solid no. Had she? If she'd agreed to take time off would Gran still be alive? Would it have given her grandmother something to look forward to?

Tears stung the back of her eyes as she remembered when Gran had said, "I'm not getting any younger, you know."

But all the tears and regrets and what-ifs wouldn't change the situation. Avery was already planning on coming back for Thanksgiving. So Gran had had that to anticipate and she was still gone.

Avery plucked a pencil out of the holder and scribbled down the first item on her to-do list: *Tell Barry that I'm free to work Thanksgiving week.*

Her heart pinched at her new reality. The alternative to working through Thanksgiving would be to do a sort of "Friendsgiving" with her roommates and others in the city with no place to go. She'd be better off throwing herself into work since it was all she had left. She made a note to follow up on a couple of story possibilities, all the while trying to ignore the way her entire body ached from the loss at the thought.

Next, she wrote: *Plan Gran's memorial service.* They didn't have any family, but Gran had so many friends who would want to say goodbye.

But when?

Avery needed to be back in New York tomorrow so she could catch a plane to Dublin Monday afternoon to cover the assignment for the coworker who had taken over her shoot in Dubai after she'd gotten the call about Gran.

Avery wanted the celebration of her grandmother's life to be meaningful. She deserved better than a thrown together, spur-of-the-moment gathering. That meant Avery would need time to plan. She'd revisit that one once she had a better idea of when.

She started to write "talk to Forest McFadden about listing the house," but she couldn't bring herself to do it. It was too much to think about right now. Too daunting. That meant she should probably hold off on that for now, too, just as Forest had suggested.

She got up from the desk and walked to the office window. It looked out onto the side of Forest's house. His car wasn't in the driveway. Not that she should care. It had been uncomfortable seeing him after all this time. True to form, he was still gorgeous and clearly had fooled everyone into believing he was a nice guy. Gran had mentioned that he looked in on her from time to time and once a week he rolled recycle and trash bins to the curb, returning them to the garage once they were empty. Of course, his ulterior motive for being nice could've been to secure the listing if the place had gotten to be too much for Gran to handle. It had always seemed like it would be the likely scenario. That Gran would get tired of the upkeep and decide to sell the place and move into a continuing-care retirement community.

A wave of wistfulness washed over Avery. Maybe

if Gran had given up the place, she could've spent her last years enjoying herself rather than worrying about upkeep.

Avery turned away from the window and walked back to the desk. She added to her list: *Hire someone to perform house maintenance.* Then she wrote down *look up what is involved in beach house maintenance. What needs to be done for hurricane season?* Of course, they were in the already in the middle of hurricane season—it would end in November—but it would be better to have a plan in place before she left than to be caught flatfooted.

There was so much to do.

She tossed her pencil on top of the desk, picked up the legal pad and tore off the page containing her to-do list. As she placed the pad on the desk, the pages flipped back to Gran's Christmas wish list.

Her beloved Gran's death had caught her unprepared. Such a dynamic woman seemed invincible. As Avery reread Gran's list, a hurricane of emotion stormed inside her. Avery shuttered herself because there was no time for what-ifs.

New York City
Monday, October 2

Avery glanced around the conference room at the rare sight of most of her colleagues gathered in one room. Barry Orr, the publisher of *World International* magazine, had called the spur-of-the-moment meeting last night.

So many of the magazine's employees traveled that they rarely had a chance to come together like this.

Something didn't feel right, and it wasn't just the way the kind words of condolence from her colleagues threw her off balance.

Or maybe it was.

It had only been a few days since she'd lost Gran, but trying to get back to *normal* was even harder than she'd imagined. Grief snared her at the most inopportune moments. Walking to the office that morning, she'd caught a glimpse of a tall, slender woman of a certain age, who reminded her of Gran. It had nearly gutted her. The worst was when something would happen and she'd think, *I can't wait to tell Gran...*and then she'd realize there would be no more late-night phone calls like they enjoyed when Gran was still alive.

So maybe this feeling that something wasn't right stemmed from her hollow grief.

She'd read that the first year after losing someone, going through all the holidays and birthdays without them was the most difficult. Forest had been right when he'd mentioned that grief experts suggested not making any major decisions in that first year. Avery had decided to hold off listing the house until she had a better grasp of everything keeping it entailed.

One of the things she discovered was that the annual property tax bill, which was greater than ten thousand dollars, had been due on September first. Gran had not paid it before she died. There was a penalty-free grace period through the fifth of January. But Gran's bank-account balance had been less than two thousand dollars at the time she passed away. With her pension and social security, she might've been able to scrape together enough to pay the bill in January, but it would've left her with very little to live on.

Her grandmother had never asked for help. Now, Avery wondered how she had gotten by.

Barry clapped his hands. "Good morning, everyone. I appreciate you all making the time to be here today. As I'm sure you figured out by now, I have an important announcement to make. I felt strongly about doing this in person rather than over email." He looked around the room, making eye contact with each person. "I'd be remiss if I didn't acknowledge that it's somewhat of a miracle to have everyone in the same place at the same time. It warms my heart to see you all together."

The flipside to the nagging feeling that something was wrong was the hope that he would have more information about the photo editor position he'd talked about creating or say whether or not they would all get a quarterly bonus—which would go a long way toward the property taxes—but that hope faded fast after seeing the look in his eyes. There was a definite note of caution in the way he spoke. It eclipsed the hope and ignited the burning dread in the pit of Avery's stomach.

"I've worked with some of you for close to a decade." He looked directly at Avery and smiled. Only, his smile looked so sad. "So many of you have given up holidays and weekends with your families to help us make *World International* what it is today. I can't thank you enough. However, these are uncertain times. They have taken their toll on the entire news industry. I'm bereft to report that at the close of business on November twenty-third, *World International* will be closing its doors permanently."

A collective gasp sounded throughout the office.

Barry ran his hand through his hair and squeezed

his eyes shut for a moment. "If it helps, please know this hurts me as much as this must be hurting you. I'm here to help in any way I can, such as references and…" He shrugged. "I guess the good news is you all can spend the holidays with your families." He laughed, but the attempt at levity was met with stunned silence.

Avery's heart clenched. Who could think about the holidays when they were all unemployed? Wow. First, she'd lost Gran. Now, she'd lost her job.

What was she supposed to do?

She needed to figure out how she was going to make a living. She needed to find another job.

But who was hiring this close to the holidays?

"Anyhow," Barry continued, "we will publish one last edition before shutting our doors. This week, I'll meet with each of you individually to discuss severance packages and how we can wrap up any other projects that might extend beyond this issue."

After at least a half hour of tears and hugs and questions, the stunned group slowly disbanded.

"Wow, didn't see that coming," said Jesse Bridges, a photojournalist who usually covered matters in the Middle East.

"I didn't, either," Avery said. "I'm completely blindsided. Barry never gave a single clue that anything was wrong."

"What are you going to do?" Jesse asked.

Avery shrugged. "I guess I'll let this sink in and then I'll make a game plan. Let me know if you hear of a promising job possibility."

"Yeah, you, too," Jesse said.

As she started to exit the conference room, Barry said, "Avery, do you have a moment?"

"Sure."

"Great. Let's go to my office."

Barry motioned for her to follow.

Avery sat down in a chair across from his desk and she was surprised when Barry sat in the one next to her rather than behind his desk.

"So, bummer, huh?" Barry propped his elbow on the armrest and then slouched to rest his chin on his left fist. "This wasn't part of my ten-year plan."

"I figured," Avery said. "Do you mind if I ask what happened?"

Barry sighed and shrugged. "Honestly? Bad business decisions. Too much focus on the artistic side of the magazine and not enough on the bottom line. We lost advertisers during COVID. I thought we could get them back, but some of them are hurting, too. I did want to assure you that there's enough in the bank to pay you through the end of the year if you'll stay on long enough to wrap up the final issue."

"Barry—"

He held up his hand. "No arguing. It's the least I can do. The last thing I wanted was to leave everyone high and dry over the holidays. Since we won't be printing a magazine in January, I'll have just enough to pay everyone through the end of the year and call it a wrap."

While all stories involving travel had been canceled, they discussed the local projects that Avery would focus on in the final weeks—photos to accompany a story on a food-bank program in Brooklyn and a photo essay about a seventy-eight-year-old "starlet" making her leading role debut on Broadway.

"Only two stories?" Avery wondered aloud. "That's

a light load, Barry. If you need help with anything else, I'm happy to take it on."

"I may have to take you up on that," he said. "I won't be surprised if some people bail early." He shrugged. "We'll make it work. We will have more than enough content for the final issue. It will be a love letter of sorts to New York City."

Avery blinked back the tears that stung her eyes and threatened to spill onto her cheeks. One of the things she loved the most about working for the magazine was the creative freedom Barry afforded her when she worked. Her photos showcased people at their best. Her sanctuary was behind the camera.

After losing Gran, her *World International* coworkers were the closest thing to family she had left.

Now, she was losing them, too. They would all be going their separate ways. Many would have to relocate, depending on where the work took them.

"I hate it that we have to cancel the carousel project," Barry said.

"Me, too," Avery said. "That was my holiday plan. I was going to see if I could head to France early."

She was going to propose leaving the Monday of Thanksgiving week and flying to Paris, where she'd cover the "red dinner," a copycat version of the celebrated Dîner en Blanc, only this surprise pop-up event was going to be *en rouge*. Since Parisians didn't celebrate the American Thanksgiving, it seemed the perfect distraction to the gaping hole left in her life that reminded her she would never look at Thanksgiving the same way again, because she'd always spent it with Gran.

After the red dinner, she was going to spend December traveling around France shooting as many antique carousels as she could find. There were several in Paris alone.

The carousel project had been a dream assignment.

Avery sighed. So much for that. The magazine had been funding the project and Avery certainly couldn't afford to foot the bill for a month in France. Maybe that was why the publication was closing its doors.

"I know this is a difficult time for you, Avery," Barry said. "You're welcome to spend the holidays with Patricia and me and the kids."

Avery smiled, but waved him off. It was a nice offer, but if she crashed their holiday gatherings, she would definitely feel like a fifth wheel. "Thanks, Barry. I appreciate the offer, but I'll be good."

"I may have something for you to look forward to." He scrunched up his face. "Ah, I probably shouldn't say anything. It's too soon, but if I don't plant the seed, you'll probably be off for greener pastures and not looking back."

"What is it?" She quirked an eyebrow at Barry.

"Well, I happen to think you're one of the most talented photographers on staff and, of course, you've been here since we opened the doors."

"Why do I feel like you're buttering me up for something?"

"Oh, ye of little faith. No, listen, this could be good. But *could be* are the operative words. There still may be an opportunity to send you on that French carousel shoot."

Avery's eyes widened and she sat up in her seat.

"Don't get too excited yet. It wouldn't be until sometime next year, but it's not completely dead in the water.

It would be a work-for-hire situation and you're the only one I'd send on the shoot… That's all I'd better say for now, but keep the faith, okay?"

Keep the faith.

That was easier said than done, but at least it was something.

After the meeting, she stopped by her cubicle, which was really just a place to regroup as she finished one assignment and flew out for the next. There was a docking station for her laptop, a canister holding a couple of pens, an unused notepad and an unframed picture of her and Gran that Avery had tacked to her cubicle wall.

She took the photo off the wall and studied it, the heaviness in her heart was almost more than she could bear.

On top of everything else, she still had to face the monumental task of cleaning out Gran's house and figuring out what she wanted to do with it. And, of course, there was the matter of the property taxes.

Since November and December weren't the optimal months for job hunting, maybe it would be a good time to go back to Tinsley Cove and get things in order.

She could work hard and complete her assignments, and then take off for North Carolina. Spending the holidays at Mistletoe Cottage and getting things in order would be better than staying in the city alone and feeling sorry for herself.

Chapter Three

The Uber driver dropped off Avery at 2:47 a.m. She stood on the wraparound front porch of Mistletoe Cottage, with its green cedar shingles that needed to be restained, and the red lacquered front door, which needed to be touched up. The red-and-green color combo had earned it the name Mistletoe Cottage. It was a cottage because it was smaller and less beach-house chic than most of the newer homes that lined the beach, including the two houses that flanked her Gran's modest house... Avery's house now. Gran's will had clearly spelled that out.

Bess Loughlin had lived there so long that the mortgage had been paid off. Everything had transferred to Avery, Bess's only living relative.

Even though the place was free and clear, Avery still had to pay property taxes and insurance, utilities and upkeep, because one didn't just lock up a beach house and leave it standing for months on end. That brought her full circle to the question of what she was going to do with the place. She couldn't quite wrap her mind around what lay ahead.

She'd spent the past two months helping Barry wrap up the final edition of *World International* and close down the business.

He'd insisted on paying her through the end of the year. Now, she was back in Tinsley Cove with a plan to spend the month of December getting the house ready to put on the market…unless she could get the place sorted out sooner than that. It was a tempting challenge to get in there, keep her head down and get it done; that way she could get back to New York and start looking for a job.

The less time here the better because it was the last place she wanted to be.

Especially without Gran.

The cool ocean breeze blew her hair into her eyes, where it tangled with the unshed tears caught in her lashes. After pushing the strands out of her face, Avery set down the box that contained Gran's ashes. While she was here, she'd have the memorial service her grandmother deserved. Balancing her purse on her rolling bag she fished out the door key that Bess had always insisted she keep.

"Who knows, maybe someday you'll surprise me and show up out of the blue," Gran had said. "You would need a key to let yourself in just in case I was at the store or somewhere else when you arrived."

Why hadn't she surprised her when she'd had the chance? Now it was too late, she thought as she eyed the red lacquered front door.

Avery closed her eyes. In the distance, she could hear the faint roar of the waves and she imagined them rolling up on the beach behind the house. It took her back to the year she'd lived here.

She took a deep breath as she turned on her phone flashlight and fumbled with the keys, looking for the one that opened the front door.

The briny air smelled of the beach. Normally, it calmed her, because it hinted at the Thanksgiving fun in store for her and Gran, but right now, it made her feel displaced. Bess wouldn't be on the other side of the door. There would be no week of cooking and prepping more food than two women could eat in a month, much less the few days she always stayed.

At least she had managed to find room in Gran's deep freeze for all the food people had brought when she was here in September.

Other than that, it would just be an empty house with a freezer full of food. It all belonged to her now, and she didn't even want it since Bess wasn't here.

A scream seemed to be building deep down in her core. She feared it would escape at the worst moment and once she started screaming she wouldn't be able to stop.

She inserted the key in the dead bolt and the lock tumbled. She knew good and well that Bess wouldn't be inside, but in the split second it took to push open the door, a childlike wish welled up inside her and she hoped that some kind of Christmas miracle would prove that this was all a joke.

See the lengths I have to go to get you home for Christmas, girl?

Avery closed her eyes, imagining she could hear the words as clearly as if Bess had spoken them. In her mind's eye, Avery could see her grandmother standing there in her apron-covered dress and pearls. But when Avery opened her eyes and stepped over the threshold, the place was eerily still and the air was stagnant. There wasn't even the sound of the ever-present grandfather clock, because no one had been there to wind it while she was gone. It was one of the many tasks that Bess had always taken care of, and Avery had taken for granted.

All of this would be waiting for her in the morning.

Bone-tired, Avery took the urn holding Gran's ashes out of the box and set them on the fireplace mantel.

"Welcome home, Gran."

Then she dragged her suitcase upstairs to the room that Gran had kept for her after all these years and put herself to bed.

Lightning cracked the horizon. Wind howled and needles of rain punished everything within reach. Avery was drowning, caught in the undertow, drifting farther out to sea...

She startled awake, and realized the storm was a dream, because sunshine was streaming in through the window.

As she blinked at the turquoise ceiling, it took her a moment to get her bearings, but then it all came flooding back. She was in her bedroom in Mistletoe Cottage, which had remained exactly the same as when she'd lived here with Gran.

The same white wicker furniture, the same whitewashed beadboard on the walls, the same sheers embossed with delicate white starfish, and shell-and-bead fringe along the bottom.

Avery sat up and smoothed her hand over the aqua-and-white hunter's-star quilt Gran had sewn for her.

A crushing heaviness weighed down so hard on Avery that she wanted to lie back down, pull up the covers and put a pillow over her head.

Instead, she yawned and forced herself to get up and get busy. She had a lot to do if she was going to get the house ready to sell after the first of the year.

Grabbing her phone off the nightstand, she saw that it was 9:00 a.m. Six hours of sleep. No wonder she didn't feel rested, but experience with traveling had taught her that even though the first day might be tough, it was best to push through and go to bed that night at a decent hour. It was the best way to get back on a normal schedule.

As she swung her legs over the side of the bed, the sound of a motor—maybe a generator—roared to life. Then the sound of water hitting her bedroom window at a powerful force made her cry out.

"What the hell?" she screamed, but her words were swallowed by the noise.

She could see the water through the sheers. She might've thought a tsunami was hitting the house, but her bedroom was at the front and the window faced the side of the house. The ocean was in the back.

This was as if someone was blasting her house with a firehose.

After wrapping the quilt around her, she pulled back the drapes, but she couldn't see through the rush of water pounding the window.

The jeans and blouse she'd worn yesterday were lying on the chair, where she'd left them. She threw them on and bounded downstairs.

Barefoot, she followed the wraparound front porch toward the side that her bedroom window faced. Before she rounded the corner, she spied an orange machine sitting in Forest McFadden's driveway sputtering and buzzing, making the most obnoxious noise. A cord attached to it pointed in the direction of the spraying sound, where she found Forest pressure-washing Mistletoe Cottage.

"What the hell are you doing?" she yelled.

He was angled away from her, and apparently, he couldn't hear her over the noise.

Avery sprinted over to his driveway and pulled the electrical cord out of the socket.

The machine choked to a stop and Forest uttered a couple of choice words that Avery would've never guessed were in Mr. Perfect's vocabulary.

When he turned toward the pressure washer and saw her standing there, he said, "Oh, sorry." Then it seemed to register that she was holding the cord. He frowned and pointed to her hands. "What are you doing?" He shook his head. "Wait, what are you doing here? When did you arrive?"

"Never mind me," she said. "What the hell are you doing?"

"I'm power-washing your grandmother's house, *er, uh,* sorry—your house."

Power-washing. It figured. Most people would *pressure-wash.* Forest McFadden *power-washed.*

"Why are you *power-washing* Gran's house?"

He turned the nozzle and stopped the stream of water that had been trickling from the hose.

"I always did this for Bess. Once a year. The last day of November, before she put up her Christmas decorations. It was on my calendar."

Wow. She knew Forest really wasn't a saint, even though he played one on television. That meant he was working overtime to get the listing.

Avery scoffed. "Is this your version of helping a little old lady cross the street?" He frowned at her. "You probably volunteer at the soup kitchen, mentor disadvantaged kids and foster animals in your spare time, don't you?"

His face fell, but then he recomposed his features into a more neutral expression.

"Well, yes, I do some of those things. Is there something wrong with helping others?"

Okay, it was mean to say that, but once, a long time ago, he'd been mean to her, too. Still, she shouldn't have said it out loud.

Avery tried to ignore the pang of guilt that stabbed her insides and suggested that maybe if she channeled her energy into doing nice things for others, her life wouldn't be such a directionless mess.

Everything was so overwhelming that it seemed like it was all she could do to take care of herself these days.

"No, there's nothing wrong with it, but even though it was very good of you to do this for my grandmother—"

Her voice caught on the words.

"As I was saying, it was good of you to do this for Bess, but you don't have to do it for me."

"I don't mind," he said.

"Why?" she asked before she could stop herself.

Was this some sort of penance to appease his guilty conscience for what he did years ago? If so, they could just call it even and coexist. They didn't have to interact. He certainly didn't have to work it off by doing home-maintenance chores for her.

"Why? Because it needs to be done. Beachfront houses are susceptible to rot and corrosion because of the salty air. This is part of the upkeep."

Something else to add to the list.

"Look, thanks, but you don't have to do this for me. I'll hire someone."

"It's no problem. I've got everything ready to go. I'll be done in no time."

She sighed. "I got in really late last night and you woke me up."

He started to apologize, but she waved off his words. "It's okay. You had no way of knowing I was here. But I am here and I'll be working to get Mistletoe Cottage in order."

"Are you selling it?" he asked.

"I don't know," she barked.

Liar. Since she was unemployed, she could barely afford to take care of herself, let alone pay taxes and upkeep on a house she had no intention of living in. She needed to sell the place. Not only would it give her some breathing room financially while she searched for a new job, but it would also be one less thing she needed to worry about.

Of course, it also meant that she would be letting go of the last link she had to Gran. What a double-edged sword. Mistletoe Cottage meant the world to Gran, but Tinsley Cove, with all its bad memories, was the last place that Avery wanted to be.

"Whatever you decide to do, I'm still here to help you if you need anything," Forest said. "Whether or not I get the listing."

"Okay, Forest," she said. Inwardly she cringed because even she had to admit that it sounded dismissive.

As she turned to go, she saw his brow knit. He put the hand that wasn't holding the power-washing hose on his hip.

"Can I ask you one question?"

"Sure," Avery said. "Ask away."

"Have I done something to offend you?"

"You mean other than waking me up when I've only had six hours sleep?" she said.

"Yes," Forest said. "Every time I talk to you, it seems to annoy you. I was wondering if I'd done something to upset you."

Mind whirling, she turned back to face him directly. She was tempted to unload on him, but she thought better of it.

"I have no idea what you're talking about."

The sea breeze blew a strand of hair into her eyes. She pushed it back and was suddenly aware that she hadn't even brushed her hair, much less washed the sleep out of her eyes or brushed her teeth.

"I don't believe you," he said. "I don't take you for the type of person to decide you don't like someone before you even get to know them...because you don't like their face."

Oh, honey, I love your face. It's the way you treat people that's the problem.

Did the guy have amnesia?

"Well, I suppose this will come as a shock to someone like you, but in life, not everyone is going to like you."

As she turned and began walking away, he said, "I don't expect everyone to like me, but I do hope people won't dismiss me without getting to know me."

She put her hands on her hips and faced him once again. "Okay, since you asked. I know it was a long time ago and you and your high-school friends were full of yourselves. But what you did to me was mean."

He blinked, then furrowed his brow. "I'm sorry, Avery. I don't understand… Can you be more specific?"

She felt like an idiot. He didn't even remember and now it appeared that she'd been nursing a high-school grudge.

"It doesn't matter. It was a long time ago. Believe me, I've forgotten it, too."

"Wait a minute," he said. "Could there have been some sort of misunderstanding?"

Why was he being so nice?

People changed as they grew up.

"If I hurt you or upset you in any way, I need to know about it. I want to make it right. Or at least apologize."

He seemed so sincere and she hated herself for letting him draw her in. But on the other hand, if it didn't matter, why not tell him? Get it off her chest and get over it.

"You and your friends set me up. Your friend Breanna Tate told me that you had a crush on me and was too shy to ask me out. So she was helping you out."

"What?" He shook his head. If he was lying, he was a good actor. "Breanna Tate was my high-school girlfriend during sophomore and junior years. By that time, we were broken up, but I can't imagine that she'd set me up with anyone."

"Well, she did. Believe me. I was there."

"So she told you I had a crush on you?" Forest asked. "It was true. When you got to Tinsley Cove High School, you created somewhat of a stir. I'd told my friend Mike I wanted to ask you out."

What? Avery's heart pounded and her skin broke out in goose bumps, which she prayed he couldn't see.

"You had a crush on me?" she asked.

No, I had a crush on you.

She wasn't about to tip her hand, because she didn't feel that way anymore. Despite the heart palpitations and the heat that seemed to be enveloping her whole body.

"Yeah, big-time. The first time I saw you I was blown away."

"Then why did you ask me out and stand me up?"

He sputtered, "I—I didn't."

"Yes, you did. You invited me to have dinner with you at Le Marais. Actually, Breanna invited me on your behalf because you were busy with an important student-council commitment, but she insisted that you wanted to take me to dinner at Le Marais that night. It was a Friday night. You, or someone, made a reservation. I was supposed to meet you there because you were coming straight from school, which I did. I sat there for about twenty minutes and then you texted me and said you were running late and asked me to order for you, which I did. You were specific about what you wanted, and you were pretty hungry. Then you never showed up and stuck me with the bill."

Forest looked horrified. He shook his head as if it was all news to him.

"I'm so sorry that happened, but I promise you, Avery, I had no part of it. I don't want to point fingers, but Breanna and I broke up the summer before our senior year and she wasn't happy about it. She was the one who told you to meet me there?"

Avery nodded. "Pretty stupid of me to go on a date with a guy who didn't ask me out himself and then wanted me to meet him there. Breanna delivered the message Friday morning. I saw you in the hall that afternoon and you smiled, like you were going to talk to me, but then the bell rang."

"I remember that day." Forest raked a hand through his hair. "You said, 'See you later,' and I was over the moon. I was going to ask you out for the following weekend, but that next week, you wouldn't even look at me. Anytime I got close to you, you'd give me the look of death and head in the opposite direction."

"Because I was mortified that you'd stood me up. Not only that, but for the rest of the year Breanna and her buddies would crack jokes about coq au vin, which was one of the things you'd asked me to order for you."

"Oh, no," he said. "I remember the coq-au-vin jokes, but I never knew what they were about because they seemed pretty sophomoric to me. I had my sights set on bigger and better things."

She scrutinized him for a moment. Did she really believe that he heard the jokes but didn't ask what they were about? It could happen. Kids hated it if their friends discovered they weren't in the know.

"You have no idea how many random people would walk up to me in the hallway and ask if I liked coq au vin and other more colorful plays on the word, which I'm sure you can imagine."

He cringed. "I'm sorry. I wish you would've confronted me about it."

"Seriously? I was new to the school, the popular crowd had it in for me and was already making my life miserable. Do you really think I was going to pick a fight with their king?"

"King? That's a little bit over-the-top."

Avery held up her hands. "Hey, I'm just saying. When you're seventeen years old, you can only take so much coq au vin thrown in your face, even if it was figuratively. I just kept my head down for the rest of the year and set my sights on college. But they were your friends, Forest. Can you blame me for wondering how you didn't have an inkling that something had happened? You are the company you keep."

He was quiet for a moment, as if weighing his words. "I can see your point," he responded, his voice gentle. "I can only tell you what I know. I know that Tinsley Cove High was a small school. With a graduating class of seventy-five, we were all thrown together. Mike Parker was my best bud and remains so to this day. The rest of them… I haven't heard from Breanna and her group since graduation. A few of them still live in town. I'm the mayor, so I serve them, but I can't say I socialize with them. So as far as being the company I keep, I believe you have to judge a person by their current circle and not the past."

Avery's mind whirled as she filled in the missing pieces of the puzzle.

Breanna was the one who had set up the date. Maybe

she was the one who'd texted Avery as she sat waiting in the restaurant and had asked her to order.

Avery hadn't known Forest's phone number. It could've been anyone texting her.

Maybe the most telling evidence in Forest's defense was that she had never heard him tell a coq-au-vin joke. The same went for his friend Mike Parker. While it was true that she'd avoided Forest for the rest of the school year, she couldn't recall an incident of him or Mike being cruel to anyone else, and certain individuals in that group—mostly Breanna and her minions—seemed to take pride in making jokes at the expense of others.

"That's not all that happened," Avery said. "The Monday after Le Marais, Breanna cornered me at my locker and said you had asked her to apologize for standing me up, but the two of you had gotten back together. Her parting shot was that I should remember my place at Tinsley Cove High. That someone like you would never date someone like me."

"Unbelievable," Forest said. "I am so sorry."

"I thought you were in on it. You know, torture the new girl."

"No. Being unkind was never my gig."

"But you dated Breanna for two years."

"I was a teenager. I was young and stupid. She was pretty and bossy. You learn a lot about a person over two years. That's one of the reasons I broke up with her. For the record, she and I did not get back together."

"Weren't you homecoming king and queen?"

"We were, but I had no control over that. She wasn't my date. In fact, I didn't take anyone to the dance, because by that time, I was just over it. I was so ready to get out of town. But I would've asked you, if you would've let me get within ten feet of you."

Her stomach did a ridiculous twisty, bendy thing at the thought.

She was not in high school anymore. She was thirty-two years old. For that matter, so was Forest. At this point, he would have nothing to gain by lying about the prank. Not even for a potential listing if she chose to sell Mistletoe Cottage.

All the evidence pointed toward his innocence. She believed him. It was remarkable how letting go of a past wrong could set you free.

"Again, I'm so sorry that happened," Forest said. "Would you let me make it up to you?"

Avery's walls went up. "No. We're good. I'm busy getting the house in order before I leave and you have your mayoral duties. And your television show. And your real-estate business." She laughed. "I see you're still the overachiever. But I'm glad we were able to sort this out."

"Will you allow me to finish power-washing the house? It's the least I can do. It will only take an hour or so."

With all this newfound information pinging around in her head, there was no way she'd be able to go back to sleep.

Avery shrugged. "Sure, why not. Thanks."

As she walked away, she couldn't stop thinking that once upon a time, Forest McFadden had a crush on her.

But that was then and this was now.

Chapter Four

Tinsley Cove
November 30

Forest couldn't stop thinking about Avery sitting alone in Le Marais waiting for him, only to have him not show up.

For more than a decade, she thought he'd been in on the prank. *Nah*, it wasn't just a prank. It was mean-spirited and a cruel way to treat another human being.

"Forest? Does that work for you?"

Forest looked up from where he'd been sitting, staring at his hands, which were steepled on the conference-room table in the Sandcastle Real Estate office. After he'd put away the power washer, he'd showered, gotten ready and come into work for the first production meeting for season two of *Selling Sandcastle*. After a successful first season, they were due to start filming season two tomorrow.

All eyes were on him: his mom and dad, Bert and Bunny; his sister, Sophie; his brothers, Owen and Logan; Logan's fiancée, Cassie; their cousin Lucy; and Dalton Hart, the person who had asked the question that Forest hadn't heard.

In addition to being a Tinsley Cove native, Dalton owned Top Drawer Productions, the company that produced *Selling Sandcastle*, the reality television show that followed the McFadden family's luxury real-estate business.

"It was good of you to show up today, Forest," Dalton said. "Too bad your brain is somewhere else."

"Sorry, I have some things on my mind. Would you repeat the question, please?"

"I asked who wanted to see you wear a chicken suit and dance the chicken dance on stage at the tree lighting on Sunday night while we're filming. Everyone thinks it's a good idea and since you didn't protest, majority wins."

Forest frowned. "A chicken suit at the Christmas-tree lighting? That doesn't even make sense."

Everyone in the room laughed.

"Of course it doesn't, but maybe you'll pay attention from now on."

The thing was that even as absurd as the chicken suit sounded, Dalton had suggested crazier things in the past. Forest wouldn't have been surprised if Dalton had been serious.

Still, it wouldn't hurt to have his head in the game and not dwell on things that happened in the past, things he couldn't change.

He couldn't stop thinking that there had to be some way he could make it up to Avery. He hated the thought of her suffering.

Dalton shrugged. "I don't know, though—a mayor in a chicken suit dancing the iconic chicken dance. Sounds like a crowd-pleaser. I'll file that one away for later."

Forest rolled his eyes.

Forest had recently been voted in as mayor of Tinsley Cove. At thirty-two years old, he was the youngest person to have been elected to the office. It had been a close race and his opponent had zeroed in on Forest's age and lack of political experience, not to mention, the fact that he was on *Selling Sandcastle*... It seemed that people either loved reality television or hated it. Forest did his best to keep it classy and not say or do anything that would embarrass himself or his hometown. He considered the show another layer of transparency.

That was one of the many reasons he needed to keep Dalton in check and make sure he didn't push the envelope too far. Dalton Hart was the classic case of someone who would try to commandeer a mile after he was granted an inch.

They went over the call sheet for the next two days.

The family was gathering at Forest's house for a Sandcastle Real Estate lunch meeting tomorrow. It would be filmed. They usually held their meetings in the very conference room where they were sitting now, but Dalton thought a change of venue would be nice. Forest had offered his place.

After they filmed the meeting, they were scheduled to shoot Forest volunteering at the charity Christmas-tree lot. The trees had been donated by a local tree farm and proceeds from the sales would benefit underprivileged families.

On Sunday, they would film the tree lighting in Springdale Park, where he would be doing his mayoral duties—presiding over the event, giving a welcome speech and complimenting the various organizations who had made the night possible, mostly the Tinsley Cove Department of Parks and Recreation and the chamber of commerce. Everything would lead up to him giving the signal to flip the switch that illuminated the tree and signaled the start of the Christmas season. Everyone would ooh and aah, clap and cheer. He'd wish everyone a happy holiday, and it would be a wrap.

No chicken suits or embarrassing dances.

Dalton dismissed the meeting, but asked Sophie, Lucy and Cassie to hang back to discuss filming them with their friends at Sunday's tree lighting.

Forest slipped out to the sound of them talking and laughing. Everyone seemed to be excited that season two of *Selling Sandcastle* was underway.

Forest was, too, but last season it had been a challenging balancing act to juggle the real-estate business, which never stopped, even though they had the TV side hustle. This year, though, he was adding a third ball now that he was the mayor. It was a four-year term and he was in it for better or worse, even if it meant he had to play a lesser role in *Selling Sandcastle*. Thank goodness that the McFadden family was big enough that he wouldn't be missed if that had to happen.

The production company had come to the table with several ideas for filming scenes to anchor the season and set a tone. Last year, Dalton gave each cast member a chance to choose a couple of scenes they wanted to do and the people they wanted to film with.

All Forest wanted to do was bring attention to the various charities he supported and highlight what made Tinsley Cove shine. He wasn't sure what he'd do if Dalton demanded more of him. Not only was he pressed for time, but his heart also just wasn't in the show.

However, he had signed on for another season. He would take it one step at a time and fulfill his obligation.

With such a full plate, it was a blessing that Avery had wanted him to disengage from looking after Mistletoe Cottage.

"Forest, is everything okay?" his mother asked as they passed in the hallway.

"Sure, just busy."

His mother studied him, searching his face, her maternal intuition picking up on his unrest.

The show *Selling Sandcastle* had been his mother's brainchild. Barbara "Bunny" Bradshaw McFadden came up with the idea of a reality show that followed the day-to-day workings of their family business, Sandcastle Real Estate. She had been the driving force behind getting their longtime family friend, Dalton Hart, to produce it. Bunny had called in favors from her contacts in the Junior League and the chamber of commerce. She'd hired the best photographers to showcase the family's agency and the town of Tinsley Cove in its best light, all of which helped Dalton realize that his former hometown was a picture-perfect location for a reality show.

It had all paid off when everything had come together and Dalton had agreed to do the show. Then, two weeks after receiving the good news, disaster had struck. Bunny had been diagnosed with breast cancer.

Her family had rallied around her and promised her that when she got well that they would all do their best to make the show happen. Even Forest's younger brother, Logan, had uprooted his life to move back to Tinsley Cove from California. Bunny's treatment plan had worked and she remained cancer-free.

Healthy and happy, she was having the time of her life with the show and reveling in having her four kids close by. Nothing meant more to her than being surrounded by her big, boisterous family.

"Make sure you're getting enough rest." She reached out and brushed his hair off his forehead. "Aren't you just so excited that the show is underway again? Sometimes I just have to pinch myself to know I'm not dreaming. The cherry on top is that I get to do this and to work with my family. It's a dream come true. I am the luckiest woman in the world."

Forest forced a smile because he didn't want to rain on his mother's parade. It was great to see her so happy. He wished he could share her joy. Lately, with everything on his plate, he was feeling spread so thin that he was wondering how he could continue to try to be everything to everybody. If he tried to do it all—continue to be Sandcastle Real Estate's top producer, fulfill all his campaign promises and adequately serve the people, along with being a part of this television show—was he really doing justice to anyone or any of it?

Even so, he'd signed up for all of it, and he always kept his promises. Even if it was sometimes to his own detriment.

The jury was still out for next season, but he'd cross that bridge when he came to it.

"There you two are," Bert said. "Forest, did you hear that Bess Loughlin's granddaughter is back in town?"

"Actually, I hadn't heard, but I did run into her this morning," he said. "She's right next door."

Avery was right on one account. News traveled fast in this town. Had someone seen her come in last night? She'd said it was late, but she hadn't mentioned the time. Maybe someone had driven by when they'd been…talking. He'd been so wrapped up in trying to figure out why she was so angry at him, he hadn't noticed whether or not there had been traffic.

"Any idea what she has in mind for Mistletoe Cottage?" Bert asked.

Forest held up his hands as if pushing back his father's words. "Funny you asked. I broached that subject and she said she hasn't decided what she's going to do with it. She was very clear that she knows I'm in real estate and she did not want to be pressured about selling."

Bert's eyebrows lifted. "I see. I've been working with a group of investors who would love to get their hands on that property. Well, I guess you'll just have to court her until she does make up her mind."

Court her? He knew his father was talking figuratively, in a business sense. Not personal. He'd have better luck rounding up the litter of feral cats that Pru Edwards had complained about to the town council than trying to court Avery Anderson.

"Didn't you date her in high school?"

"No, I didn't, and bringing that up would not help your cause."

"What won't help the cause?" Lucy asked as she

joined the conversation. "For that matter, what cause are we talking about?"

Bert gestured between Forest and himself. "We were talking about Mistletoe Cottage. Bess Loughlin's granddaughter, Avery, is back in town. Do you know her?"

Lucy shook her head. "I don't know the granddaughter, but I knew Bess. Wow, it's been a couple of months since that sweet lady passed away. Did the granddaughter ever have a memorial service for her?"

"Not that I know of," Bert said.

"Avery lives in New York and she just got back to town to sort out Bess's estate and figure out what she's going to do with it," Forest said.

"Is she selling the place?" Lucy asked. "Are we getting the listing?"

"It's too soon to tell," Forest said.

Bert smiled. "I have no doubt Forest will turn on the charm and sweet-talk her into it."

The next day, when Avery went out onto the front porch to drink her coffee and write a grocery list, she noticed several vehicles, each emblazoned with a Top Drawer Productions logo, parked in Forest's driveway and on the street.

Avery pretended to be busy as various crew members wheeled out production equipment, including cameras, lights, microphones and large black utility boxes. Some stuff they packed away, while other equipment was switched out and rolled back inside her neighbor's house.

Apparently, they were filming again.

She'd watched a couple of *Selling Sandcastle* episodes, when she hadn't been traveling. Mostly because

Gran had been so excited about the production taking place in Tinsley Cove and always wanted to talk about the latest storyline. She'd been as giddy as a teenage girl when she got to be an extra in a scene they filmed at one of the local restaurants. She and her friends had heard a rumor that they'd be filming at the restaurant and they'd decided to treat themselves to lunch, hoping to have a front-row seat for the action. It turned out that they not only had a good seat, but they also got to be in the scene. They'd had to sign photo releases and were even paid the standard extras' fee.

Avery had been out of town when the episode had aired. Gran had assured her that she had recorded it on her DVR and made Avery promise to wait and watch it with her when Avery came for Thanksgiving.

Avery's heart gave a little squeeze as she realized that the recording had been lost when she'd canceled Gran's cable service when she'd gotten her grandmother's affairs in order in the weeks after she'd died. Now, she wished she'd kept it. It would've been worth it to see Gran alive and happy.

She'd done a quick search on her phone to see if she could find a rerun, but it appeared that the only way it was available was through a subscription to a cable or streaming service. That wasn't in the budget right now.

Her list of regrets seemed to grow longer with each passing day.

Out of the corner of her eye, Avery saw the front door to Forest's house swing open. When it registered that it wasn't another crew member, but a man and woman walking out onto the driveway, Avery watched with interest as the distinguished-looking middle-aged couple got into one of the cars and drove away. Avery recognized them as Bert and Bunny McFadden, Forest's parents.

The cast and crew filming must be disbanding for the day. A group of young men and women about Forest's age appeared in the driveway. His siblings, no doubt. And there he was, the man himself, walking out with them.

Suddenly shy, Avery sank down into the ruffled cushions, trying to make herself small and hidden. It's not that she didn't want to see him. She just didn't want to seem like an overeager fangirl.

Then again, they were reality TV stars. Who wouldn't be curious to know what was happening?

It was refreshing to know that Forest hadn't played a part in the Le Marais incident. Knowing that made her feel better about being here. Some mean kids had made her the butt of a joke, but the past was in the past. According to Forest, most of the kids involved didn't even live here anymore, and one would hope that they'd grown up and were ashamed of themselves for hurting someone that way.

Forest certainly had grown up nicely, and he seemed like a decent guy. He'd admitted he'd had a crush on her back in the day, before everything went south.

What would've happened if things had worked out? Avery gave herself a moment to ponder the what-ifs, but came back to the reality that it never would've worked out.

It came down to the fact that they were just so different.

He had his family, who were apparently comprised of a cast of thousands.

Now that Gran was gone, she was alone. Her dad

had been estranged from his family. They didn't approve of his never putting down roots. She remembered hearing her father say that his parents had accused him of going where the wind blew. He'd been offended, because if they'd taken the time and interest in what he was doing, according to him, they would've seen that his work, though unconventional, was important.

Her dad's parents—her paternal grandparents— were gone now, and Avery didn't see much of a point of trying to connect with extended family on that side. It felt too complicated. Too messy.

She'd known her parents had loved her in their own curious way. Sure, they were unconventional, but they'd certainly instilled in her a love of travel, photography and independence. What more did one need?

Especially after Gran had loved her so unselfishly and unconditionally.

The line from the Tennyson poem—"'Tis better to have loved and lost than never to have loved at all"— skipped through her head, and for some reason, her thoughts turned to Forest, which was crazy. Once upon a time, he may have had a schoolboy crush on her, but that was ages ago.

She needed to put his candid confession to rest, along with any animosity she'd felt in the past. That was the best way to offload unnecessary baggage while she was getting Mistletoe Cottage ready… But ready for what?

She still didn't know. But just like she'd made peace with her history here, she needed to make peace with what she wanted to do with the house.

After that was taken care of, she could find a new job and move on.

After all the cars were gone, Forest's garage door opened and the white BMW backed out. She could see his silhouette through the lightly tinted window, but if he saw her, he didn't stop to say hello.

After waiting for a car to pass, he steered the car onto the road and drove away.

About an hour later, Avery grabbed the grocery list she'd made to supplement the food that was in the freezer, backed Gran's green Mini Cooper out of the garage and drove to the store.

Once there, she was forced to maneuver around a tented Christmas-tree sales depot positioned in the center of the parking lot that took up several prime spaces, forcing her to park closer to the street.

She had no intention of getting a tree, as it would just get in the way of the sorting and organizing that she'd be starting soon, but as she walked by the tent, she heard Christmas music coming from inside—an instrumental version of "Silver Bells."

Gran's favorite Christmas song. It was so beautiful that it took her breath away.

Hearing it out of the blue like this made it feel as if Gran was nudging her from the beyond. Of course, it was an old standard, but it tugged at her heart.

It was starting to get chilly. Rather than standing in the parking lot, Avery wandered into the tent to listen. The place smelled like pine, hot chocolate and briny beach air. Rows of trees lined the tented space. Some were set up in stands, but most were wrapped in netting and lying on the ground waiting for someone to pick them out and take them home to decorate and make their Christmas merry and bright.

Wistfully, Avery wandered through the maze of trees,

noticing a table set up with a silver urn and sign that said, Free Hot Chocolate. She took a deep breath, savoring the comforting chocolaty goodness. Around the next bend of trees, she located the ensemble playing the tune, set up in the tent's farthest corner. A sign on the ground in front of the group indicated they were from Tinsley Cove High School's orchestra—a violin, viola, cello, bass, harp and percussionist.

The sound was so lovely it brought tears to Avery's eyes. If she had at all been inclined to get into the Christmas spirit, this would've tipped her over the edge, but really, what was the point? she wondered as a mixture of melancholy and longing tugged at her heart.

When the song was over, she blinked back tears, pulled a twenty-dollar bill out of her wallet and placed it in the tip jar that was set up next to the sign.

As she turned to go, she ran right into Forest Mc-Fadden.

"Hello, neighbor," he said.

"Hi, uh, I was just going grocery shopping." She motioned in the direction of the store.

"Did you pick out a tree? If so, I can help you with it."

"Oh, no. I just—"

"All of the proceeds benefit a local charity." He gestured to the banner hanging on the tent's wall.

Before she could stop herself, she snorted. Avery's hand flew to her mouth.

Forest flinched. "Is there a problem?"

"No. No problem. But you really do volunteer in you spare time."

Yesterday, she'd been half-kidding when she'd asked

him if his hobby was volunteering, and here she'd caught him out in the wild, doing just that.

And now, she felt like a jerk. She wasn't making fun of him. She was just bewildered that Forest really did seem to have a good heart. Over the years, she'd become pretty jaded.

She was racking her brain for something to say that wouldn't dig her in deeper when some of the film crew that she'd seen in his driveway earlier came around the corner.

"We got that, Forest. Good job." A tall guy in a suit turned to Avery and stuck out his hand. "Dalton Hart with Top Drawer Productions, and your name is?"

"I'm Avery Anderson."

"Nice to meet you, Avery," Dalton said. "How would you like to be on an episode of *Selling Sandcastle*? We're filming here tonight and you were in our shot."

Okay, so maybe Forest wasn't completely altruistic. Maybe it was fodder for reality TV. Forest had been aptly cast as the *good son*... Avery didn't know his siblings well enough to know who would be the contrasting *wild child*. Albeit, a grown-up wild child.

Forest had grown up nicely. She blinked away the thought, wondering where it had come from.

"I don't know, Dalton," Forest said. "Maybe not this. Maybe we can shoot something else?"

"You don't want to be in a scene with me?" Avery asked, firing back, even though she didn't particularly want to be on television. She wasn't dressed particularly nicely and she might have put on some mascara and lipstick if she'd known she'd be filmed.

"I have no problem filming with you," Forest said. "I just didn't want to force this on you."

She'd been joking before, but maybe he really didn't want to be seen with her.

"Why don't you pick out a tree and I'll load it onto your car." He was changing the subject. She noticed that the guy with the camera was aiming it at them.

"Well, I, um, I'm in Gran's Mini Cooper. It's not big enough to haul a tree, but since the sales benefit such a good cause…" She opened her purse and pulled out a fifty-dollar bill. "I'd love to make a donation."

She placed the bill on the table with the cash register and walked out.

Forest parked in front of Mistletoe Cottage and killed the engine. He made quick work of undoing the bungie cords that had secured the Fraser fir to the top of the BMW, then hoisted the tree onto his shoulder. It was heavy, but he made it up the steps of Mistletoe Cottage and leaned it against the side of the house before retrieving the tree stand and lights from his trunk.

He was on the top step when the porch light flickered on and the front door opened.

"What are you doing?" Avery asked.

"You left before you could get your tree."

"I don't want a tree," she said.

"You paid for it."

"The money was a donation," she said. "Please take the tree back or give it to someone who wants it."

Before he could answer, a woman's shrill voice cut through the air. "Hey, there! *Yoo-hoo, hello-o-o!* Mayor McFadden, is that you?" Both of them squinted into the dusk, toward the sidewalk.

Doris Smith was trotting up Mistletoe Cottage's driveway.

"Help me out, will you?" Forest asked in a low voice. "If I give her an opening, she'll have me cornered all night, grilling me about when the town council is going to add speed bumps on her street."

"Speed bumps?" Avery whispered. "In this town?"

"Exactly. Just let me come in, and as soon as the coast is clear, I'll leave you alone."

To Forest's relief, as Doris reached the foot of the steps, Avery whispered, "Of course."

"Mrs. Smith, how are you?" Forest asked.

"We'll, I'm not very happy, Mayor. Three cars were speeding down my street today. I'm telling you, we need to install speed bumps."

Forest gave Avery a meaningful look.

Ever so slightly, Avery raised an eyebrow in solidarity.

"Mrs. Smith, have you met Avery Anderson?"

"You must be Bess Loughlin's granddaughter." The woman extended a hand, which Avery shook as she nodded. "I'm so sorry about your grandmother. Such a loss for this community. My husband, Harry, and I have a cabin in Maine. We were away when she passed. Otherwise, I would've brought you a casserole. Are you living here now? I know the property was sitting vacant since Bess passed. We were all beginning to wonder. Lucky you to have such a gracious next-door neighbor to watch over the place while you were gone."

Forest shot her another meaningful look, but this time Avery kept her gaze trained on Doris.

"Yes, it was good of Forest to keep an eye on the place," Avery said.

"You can never be too careful these days," Doris said. "If the burglars don't get you, the caustic salt air will corrode your home. Lots of upkeep on these beach-front houses. You can't just go off and leave them. My husband and I hire a property manager to look after our place when we're away for an extended period."

"That's smart of you," Avery said. "It was nice to meet you, Mrs. Smith. Forest was just delivering my Christmas tree. We'd better get inside."

"A Christmas tree, huh?" Doris said. "I guess that means you'll be here through the holidays then. Good, good. I'll drop by with one of my chicken-and-broccoli casseroles."

The woman looked Avery up and down. "You're skin and bones. Do you cook for yourself, dear? Forest, this girl doesn't eat. You need to take her out to dinner."

Avery opened the door and backed inside. He picked up the tree and followed her. "It was nice to see you, Mrs. Smith. Have a good night."

"Right. I'm going to come by your office on Monday to talk about the speed bumps," Doris said as Forest backed farther into the foyer. "And I'll drop off that casserole tomorrow…what was your name again, dear? Bess mentioned you often, but I'm so bad with names."

"My name is Avery. Thank you, Mrs. Smith. It's nice to meet you."

Avery closed the door and turned to face Forest. "You weren't kidding, were you?"

Forest set down the bag containing the lights and the stand, but continued to hold the tree upright. "Mrs. Smith means well, but she has no concept of bound-aries."

"So that's what it's like to be the mayor of Tinsley Cove." Avery sounded amazed by the concept.

"It's a constant challenge between being accessible to everyone and setting boundaries. Now that the tree is in the house, I hope you won't ask me to haul it away," Forest said. "I might end up passing Doris on the way back to the lot. That wouldn't be a good look."

Avery smiled. "Well, I suppose the place could use some Christmas cheer."

"Ideally, the tree should soak in a bucket of water for a few hours to give it a chance to hydrate," he said. "The needles won't dry out as fast if you do that."

She shook her head and waved off the suggestion. "That sounds like way too much trouble. Especially considering that I didn't even want a tree. If we don't get this baby in the stand now, it probably won't happen at all."

Then again, if he did put the tree out to soak, he'd have a reason to see her again.

"I would come over and set up the tree up for you tomorrow."

"Thanks, but no. It's now or never."

"In that case, where would you like me to put it?" he asked.

Avery walked into the living room and turned in a small circle before pointing to the front bay window. "I guess right there would be as good a place as any. Any idea where Gran kept the ornaments?"

"I do," he said as he carefully moved an empty crystal candy dish and its doily from the round table that stood between two armchairs in front of the window. "Last year, rather than putting them back in the attic, where she'd stored them, Bess had some shelves built in the garage. I moved them out there for her."

"You really did a lot for her, didn't you?" Avery said.

Forest shrugged. "It was the right thing to do."

"Thank you for everything you did for her."

"Bess was a wonderful woman. She didn't ask for a lot. So I was always happy to help her when she did ask. Sometimes I did things without waiting for her to ask. Like the power-washing."

"To get rid of the corrosive salt buildup that Mrs. Smith was talking about?"

Forest laughed. "Exactly."

"Well, I guess I have a lot to learn when it comes to upkeep for a place like this," she said.

"Does that mean you're staying?"

Her brown eyes darkened. Forest held up his hand and waved off the question.

"No pressure. Just curious. I won't ask again."

He turned his attention to the tree, and began fitting it in the stand. "Can you help me by eyeballing it and telling me if it's sitting straight in the stand?"

As they were adjusting the tree, someone knocked on the front door.

Their gazes locked.

Avery grimaced. "Could that be Doris with my chicken-and-broccoli casserole? Something tells me she's a woman who gets things done."

"Maybe so. If you're not expecting someone." Forest shrugged, looking up at her from where he was seated on the floor tightening the bolts in the tree stand. "Nothing would surprise me."

"I'm not expecting anyone," Avery said. "Maybe if I don't answer they'll think I'm not at home."

Or if it was Doris, it would be all the fodder she'd needed to start a rumor about how she saw both of them go inside, and when she came back they were too busy to answer the door.

A slow heat ignited in his belly and he sucked in a breath, as if he could blow out the fire.

A look crossed Avery's face, and if he didn't know better, he might've thought she was thinking the same thing he'd been thinking.

"You'd better get that," Forest said.

"Yeah. I'll get that."

As she disappeared out of the living room, he got to his feet and opened the first box of lights. He heard the door open, but the only voice he heard was Avery's.

"What's this?" she asked.

Forest joined her in the foyer. She was holding a large package wrapped in Christmas paper and decorated with a large red bow.

"It looks like a Christmas present," he said.

"Looks like it."

"Who's it from?"

"I have no idea. I didn't see anyone when I answered the door, but there's a note on it."

They walked into the living room, where she set the package on the sofa and carefully pulled the note out from under the red bow.

"What in the world?"

"I have no idea." He didn't, but she was giving him the side-eye, like he was in on some kind of a joke. "Open it and see."

With one last wary glance, she carefully slid the card out of the plain white envelope, squinted at it and made a dubious face.

"What does it say?"

"It says I should open the present now." Her gaze went from him to the package. "I don't think so."

"Why not?" he asked, but her eyes were assessing

the gift as if it might be full of snakes or something else just as vile or dangerous.

"Come on," he urged. "Someone has given you a gift. How bad could it be?"

"I'm not usually in the habit of accepting gifts from anonymous donors."

"First of all, you're in Tinsley Cove. I can almost guarantee you it's some kind of a welcome package— like cookies or candy or, who knows, maybe Doris decided to get fancy and wrap her famous chicken-and-broccoli like a Christmas present."

"That would be weird," Avery said.

"Yeah, maybe, but people around here do things like that. I wish you'd let down your guard for just a minute and let people do something nice for you."

"Tinsley Cove doesn't hold a good track record for me when it comes to surprises." She held up her hands. "I know. Not everyone here gets their jollies from playing mean jokes. But I also have a hard time letting people be nice to me."

"If you won't let them do it for you, think of it as them doing something to honor Bess."

She bit down on her bottom lip. For a moment, Forest was afraid she was going to start crying. Then she picked up the package and moved it up and down, as if weighing it.

"It's heavy," she said. "That must be some casserole. What does she put in it?"

Forest lifted his eyebrows. "You're not the first person to ask that question."

Avery looked horrified. "If I have to eat it, so do you."

"I'm only joking. Mrs. Smith is a good cook."

"So you've been the recipient of one of her casseroles, too?"

"One of the perks of being the mayor."

Slowly, Avery started to peel away the wrapping paper, until she revealed a sturdy cardboard box.

Avery lifted the lid and gasped as she pulled out a solid, whitewashed wooden box. When she set it on the coffee table and stepped back from it, Forest noticed all the color had drained from her face.

"What's wrong?" he asked.

"Is this some kind of a joke?" she asked, as if he should know the answer.

"I don't know," he said. "It doesn't look very funny to me. It looks like a wooden advent calendar."

"This is not funny— What is it with people around here?" She choked on the words and the tears started flowing.

"Hey, hey, it's okay." Even though he had no idea why this was hitting her so hard, he pulled her into his arms and was surprised when she let him hold her as she sobbed on his shoulder. He wasn't sure how much time had passed. The only thing he was aware of was the scent of her shampoo—something soft and floral and slightly fruity—and the fact that she was crying, and he shouldn't be so aware of how she smelled and that she felt good in his arms.

But she did smell good.

And she felt good.

So he held her, battling the strange sensation in his chest—as if something was simultaneously tightening and unfurling at the same time, which made no sense, but neither did anything right now. The only thing he knew was that Avery Anderson was a contradiction, and never in his life had he been so content to be this confused.

Finally, she drew in one last shuddering breath and pulled away, wiping the tears that made her eyes look luminous and amber. Like honey on a warm summer day.

"I'm sorry," she said. "You must think I'm crazy."

"No. But I am concerned that this thing… It's an advent calendar, right?"

She nodded.

"I'm concerned that an advent calendar would make you cry."

She bit her bottom lip again, then stepped forward and ran her hand over the top of the wooden box. She picked it up, turned it over and pointed to a signature. Tom Loughlin.

"My grandfather made this before he died. That's his signature right there. He was a wonderful wood-turner. He made it for Gran. It was one of her favorite Christmas decorations, and—"

She blinked and frowned. Then she set down the calendar and put her hands on her hips.

"How did someone get ahold of this?" Her voice was accusing. "You said you helped Gran relocate her Christmas decorations. Did you get into them? Did you give this to someone?"

Again, Forest held up his hands. "I have not stepped foot in Mistletoe Cottage or its garage since you put Hazel Buckminster's cake cover and dish in there and asked me to give them to her."

"Did you lock the garage door?"

"I did. I may have been helping with the upkeep of the outside, but it's not my place to give anything away or lend anything out. Everything here belongs to you now. I can promise you that I don't know who had the advent calendar or how they got ahold of it. But it does look like they're giving it back to you. Is there another note?"

As Forest was looking in the box, Avery opened the door with the number *1* painted on it.

"There's a note in here," she said as she pulled it out. She read it and flinched a little.

"Is everything okay?" he asked. "What does it say?"

She cleared her throat.

"It says, 'Dear Avery, we are delighted to return your Grandmother Bess's beloved advent calendar to you. We know how much it meant to her and that it would bring you comfort, to have it.'

"'Everyone knows it was Bess's fondest wish for you to spend the month of December here in Mistletoe Cottage. We have taken it upon ourselves to fill the advent calendar with Christmas spirit. Behind each door, you will find a Christmas surprise. Please don't peek at the days ahead, as it will ruin the fun. Plus, if we may be so bold, the only way to work through your grief is to live in the moment and take one day at a time.'

"'Today's treat was open a Christmas present. See how much fun that was? Isn't it exciting to know that you have twenty-three more surprises to which you can look forward?'

"'Welcome back to Tinsley Cove—Your Secret Santas.'"

Avery stared at the note. "I don't know whether to be moved or horrified."

"It's a nice gesture," Forest said.

"That's easy for you to say because a group of Secret Santas didn't pillage your grandmother's garage and take things that don't belong to them. I find it more SantaCon NYC than *It's a Wonderful Life*."

"What's SantaCon?" Forest asked.

Avery's eyes widened. "You've never heard of Santa-Con?"

Forest shook his head.

"It's when people from all over converge on New York City for a big booze-fest. They all dress up like Santa Claus and go on a drunken pub crawl all over the city. It's like something out of a nightmare to see all these Santas stumbling around and puking on the sidewalk."

When Forest grimaced, Avery laughed.

"Yeah. See how I might draw the parallel here?" she said.

"This is nothing like that," Forest said. "Don't be so jaded. Let someone do something nice for you."

"Jaded?" she snapped. "If I'm jaded, you're gullible. I have no idea who these so-called Secret Santas are or how they got ahold of my grandmother's advent calendar. They do a ding-dong ditch to return my family heirloom and I'm supposed to be grateful?"

Forest flinched. "I don't even know what to say except I'm sorry that you have mistaken an act of kindness for something sinister. Whoever did this for you went to a lot of trouble to do something nice—something to bring you comfort—but you can only see it in a bad light. I just—"

He shook his head and shrugged. "I guess that's something you need to sort out…or not. I'll leave you to figure it out."

He bent down and plugged in the Christmas tree lights. They glowed brightly against the green branches, but there was something stark and cold about it in the void of Christmas cheer.

"Merry Christmas, Avery," he said as he turned to go.

"Wait, Forest. Why would this person or people, whoever they are, do this for me?" she said.

He turned around and his face softened.

But then she made the mistake of questioning the Secret Santas' motivation. "What's the catch? Why are they being so nice when they don't even know me?"

His face fell.

She knew she sounded prickly and ungrateful, but it was a legitimate question. She wasn't used to people doing nice things for her. She rarely let people get that close because, on the rare occasions that she had… things hadn't ended well. It was much easier, much cleaner, to keep to herself, do her job and move on.

"Maybe they just wanted to do something nice for you. Everyone who knew your grandmother loved her." He stopped and sighed, then shook his head. "I guess you'll never know if you keep pushing people away."

Chapter Five

The night before, after Forest left, Avery had turned off the Christmas tree lights and had gone to bed, hoping to sleep off the dark dread weighing her down like a force.

His words swam around her head, causing her to toss and turn like a boat that was being hurled around on the ocean.

I guess you'll never know if you keep pushing people away.

Maybe the problem wasn't so much that she pushed people away, but more that she'd never learned how to let people in.

Even the thought made her squirm.

Her reality was that she had been an only child, and

while her parents had provided everything she needed, they'd been remote and consumed with their work in zoology. They'd been more interested in studying the habits and habitats of animals in the wild than caring for their own young'un, to whom they'd gifted a Pentax K1000 single-lens reflex camera and challenged her to photograph various species related to their projects. They'd moved around a lot throughout her childhood and teenage years. After the accident, when she had to move to Tinsley Cove to live with Gran, she'd gone from the Outback and the savannas of Africa being her vast—yet solitary—backyards, to a small fishbowl where the inhabitants at first seemed to be nosy about the new girl, and then disinterested once they decided she wasn't like them.

The upside was that the year she'd spent living with Gran, she had been, as far as Avery was concerned, the most selfless and giving person in the world—she'd have to be to willingly give up her only daughter to the wild world of zoology. While Avery's social awkwardness must've been an embarrassment to Gran, she never made her feel bad. Gran had been the one person in the world around whom she could be her socially awkward self and not feel bad about it.

Now, here she was, grown up, yet feeling seventeen and awkward all over again. While she had enough social skills to navigate the world, she still preferred to keep to herself, especially in Tinsley Cove. Why get attached when she would be leaving as soon as she decided what to do with Mistletoe Cottage?

If she sold it, there would be absolutely no reason to return to this place. Especially if a greedy developer decided to level the house and squeeze two brand-new, too-big houses on the lot.

She ran her hand over the quilt. The question was, could she sell it, knowing the last connection to her Gran would be mowed down and forgotten?

The gentle light of dawn filtered in through the sheers illuminating the embroidered starfish and sea-shells, turning them a soft shade of blush. Avery sat up in bed and hugged her knees to her chest.

She'd barely slept a wink and things didn't really look better in the light of morning. Was Forest right? Did she need to get a better attitude? Did she need to stop pushing people away?

What she needed was coffee.

That was one problem she could solve right away. She threw off the bedcovers and padded downstairs.

The clock on the microwave glowed 7:00 a.m. As the coffee brewed, she pondered how Forest didn't think there was anything weird about this anonymous group of Secret Santas taking Gran's advent calendar.

Well, at least they'd given it back. What else had they taken? And, worse yet, how would she even know?

Last night, she'd made up her mind that she wasn't going to play their game.

It was definitely time to open another door...or all of them, if she wanted to. There might be a clue hidden in the advent calendar about who was doing this. She could ask them how they'd gotten ahold of this family heirloom.

While the coffee maker sputtered and dripped, Avery went into the living room and faced the advent calendar as if she was confronting the enemy. It sat there like a sentinel on the table, right where she'd left it the night before.

She pulled open the door with the number *2* painted in red and entwined with a lacquered green sprig of holly.

"All right, what do you have for me today, Santas?"

December 2
    Since you're living in Mistletoe Cottage, you must start off the season right. Kiss someone under the mistletoe before the strike of midnight.
    Your Secret Santas

"What?" She dropped the piece of paper like it was hot. "No. Just no."

And the attempted rhyme didn't make it any cuter.

Clearly, someone was playing a joke on her. Or at least trying to. She glanced around the room as if she might discover a group of miscreants huddled together laughing, just like they'd done at Tinsley Cove High School.

Avery yanked open door number three, pulled out the piece of paper and unfolded it.

Ah, ah, ah. Caught you looking ahead. You're not supposed to peek. Remember what we said?
Your Secret Santas

"Okay, this is just creepy," she murmured as she crumpled up the piece of paper and tossed it onto the table. How did they know that she'd peek? Was there a hidden camera in the house?

Just in case, she waved at each of the four corners of

the room, then pointed to the advent calendar. "You bet I peeked, and now I'm going to look inside each door."

One by one, she opened each of the other doors, bending to look inside, but they were all empty.

"And what if I hadn't peeked at tomorrow," she said to the air. "What if I'd opened door number three right on schedule? The joke would be on you all."

Actually, the joke was still on her. She was the one talking to an imaginary hidden camera and pawing through each of the tiny doors like a rat scavenging for scraps.

Only because she was looking for clues that might out her tormentors.

She made a show of dusting off her hands.

"Well, good. That's the end of that."

She could pack away the advent calendar until she figured out what she was going to do with it. Sadly, before it had been commandeered by the Tinsley Cove Evil Elf Society, it might've been something of Gran's that she would've kept. Now, it just felt tainted. Like everything else in Tinsley Cove.

Suddenly, the back of her throat burned and her eyes stung. Before she could stop it, tears crested and spilled down her cheeks.

She didn't have to stay here. She didn't have to do this now. She was free to go and then come back when she was ready to deal with the house, because she clearly wasn't in the frame of mind to sort through what was left of her beloved Gran.

She swiped away the tears and glanced around the room again, this time taking in Gran's living-room set and the curio cabinet with her collection of salt-and-pepper shakers in all shapes and forms—opera-singing pigs, twin Eiffel Towers, ceramic ears of corn. Gran had made it a mission to add to her collection whenever she went somewhere. There was the Queen Elizabeth and corgi set that Avery had picked up for her when she'd been on assignment in London. They were perched right next to the mermaids with iridescent tails and green hair.

There had to be at least one hundred sets crowded in the little cabinet.

Gran had loved these collectables. They had brought her so much joy.

Avery wondered, with a pang of guilt, what in the world she was supposed to do with them. They wouldn't fit in her tiny apartment back in New York City.

She closed her eyes and mentally put them in the same pile that she'd put the advent calendar—and what she was going to do next with her life.

She'd figure it out later.

But first, coffee.

She went back into the kitchen, blew her nose, washed her hands and poured herself a cup. After the first hot sip, she gathered the ingredients for the pumpkin muffins that she'd purchased. Whenever she was stressed out, she loved to bake. Sadly, she didn't get to do that often since she was on the road so much. But while she was here, she planned to take full advantage of the spacious kitchen in Mistletoe Cottage.

As she stirred the ingredients and scraped them into the muffin tin, she started to feel more like herself again. By the time she was taking the confections out of the oven, she had the semblance of a plan.

Forest was the mayor of Tinsley Cove. It stood to

reason that he wouldn't be in on the advent-calendar joke—if it was a joke.

If it wasn't a joke, if it was a welcome gesture just as Forest had claimed, maybe he could help her figure out who was behind it…so she could *thank* them.

She took a basket down from the top shelf of Gran's pantry, lined it with a blue-and-white-checked napkin and placed six of the muffins inside.

She carried them next door.

"Good morning," he said, looking just as pleasant as if he'd been expecting her.

"Good morning," she said, holding out the basket. "I come bearing a thank-you gift."

"A thank-you gift? For what?"

"For the tree. And the stand and lights. It's kind of an apology, too."

He cocked his head to the side.

"For being less than gracious," she said. "Having my grandmother's advent calendar turn up on my doorstep kind of freaked me out. I wasn't expecting it and I feel like I behaved badly."

"Well, if you really want to make it up to me, come in and eat a muffin with me."

Her stomach rumbled at the suggestion. She'd wanted to bring the basket over while he was still home and she hadn't eaten any of the muffins she'd put back for herself.

She smiled at him. "If you insist, how can I refuse?"

He held the door open, and, with a sweeping gesture, he motioned for her to enter.

She looked around, taking in the place—his place. It was perfect. Like something out of a magazine. Of course it was.

It was the perfect balance of casual and designed, done up in sea-blue, white and other natural tones. White beadboard wainscotting, whitewashed wood accents, with jute, rattan and linen fabrics. It was like a model beach home.

Clearly, he'd had an interior designer decorate it for him.

Gran had been giddy when he'd bought the place next door five years ago. She'd called Avery right away. Of course she had. Every time they talked during their once-a-week phone dates, Gran always had to give her the Forest McFadden update. She'd been at the height of her glory when he'd become her neighbor.

If Gran could've handpicked a man for Avery, it would've been Forest. She'd made no secret of it.

Wouldn't it be ironic, now that Gran was gone, if after all these years, Avery ended up with Forest?

She blinked away the weird thought. Because it wasn't going to happen.

To end up with someone, first, you had to be interested in him. Then the interest had to be mutual.

Strike one and strike two.

Forest was just a nice guy. A nice guy who was nice to everyone.

And she had no idea why she was even thinking of Forest McFadden and whether or not he might still be interested in her.

Maybe because it was the first time she'd been inside his house. Houses were an intimate portrait of an individual. Especially when someone lived alone and the place wasn't a blending of two lives.

And she suddenly noticed that he didn't have a Christmas tree. At least not from what she could see of the house's open-concept lower level. He'd been dog-determined that she had needed a tree. So determined that he'd taken it upon himself to deliver one, even though she thought she'd made it clear that she didn't want one.

Pretty brazen.

"So where is your Christmas tree?" she asked.

"I haven't had a chance to pick one up yet. It's only December second. There's plenty of time."

She opened her mouth to ask why he hadn't just taken the one he'd foisted upon her, but she bit her bottom lip to keep the words from slipping out. She already knew how that conversation would go. He'd tell her she'd paid for the tree. It belonged to her. Blah, blah, blah. End of story.

Besides, she'd come over here bearing pumpkin muffins to forge a peace treaty, not rehash how presumptuous it was of him to bring it to her after she'd been clear that she didn't want a Christmas tree.

As she followed him into the kitchen, she clamped both her top and bottom lip between her teeth because she was dying to ask him if he realized that even the best of intentions were impolite when a person didn't listen.

Thank goodness, those words didn't slip out. Instead, she said, "Well, you'd better not wait too long or the best trees will be gone."

He nodded and set the basket of muffins on the marble island. "Coffee?"

"I don't want to put you to any trouble."

"It's no trouble. I'm having a cup."

He nodded to the single-cup coffee maker.

"Okay, then. Yes, please."

"Pick your poison." He pointed to an assortment of coffee pods displayed in a silver holder next to the coffee maker.

She surveyed to assortment and chose a dark roast.

"A woman after my own heart," he said as he popped the pod into the coffee maker and pressed the brew button. As the machine wheezed and hissed, Avery's heart shipped a beat.

A woman after my own heart.

She knew what he meant. Not that she was after his heart. But that they liked the same kind of coffee. That much was clear, since he set the same type of coffee pod next to the machine, ready to go when hers was finished.

As he turned to take two turquoise ceramic plates off an open-concept shelf, she squirmed on her seat at the island, silently reinforcing that she wasn't after anything. Certainly, not his or anyone's heart.

Not that it mattered.

What was wrong with her? Why did he make her so jumpy? Clearly, she shouldn't have had that second cup of coffee.

"What was behind door number two?" he asked as he set the plates on the island and placed a muffin on each one.

"I beg your pardon?"

"Door number two. The advent calendar. It's December second. I'm curious to know what your Secret Santas have in store for you today."

"Nothing," she snapped.

"Nothing?" He placed knives, napkins and a butter dish on the island. "I thought they said they had a full calendar of fun planned for you."

He cocked an eyebrow at her and she felt a strange heat ignite and work its way up her neck.

She cleared her throat. "What I meant was I haven't opened it yet. I was too busy making these muffins."

Again, she wondered if he'd had a hand in this advent-calendar thing? It would answer the question of how this supposed group of Santas had gotten their hands on it.

He set a steaming mug on the island in front of her. "Let me know if you need any help fulfilling it."

What would he do if she said, "As a matter of fact, you can help me." She'd whip out a sprig of mistletoe and hold it over his head and— The thought of kissing him made her stomach somersault and sent the heat that had started on her neck blazing its way up to her cheeks.

She ducked her head and took a long sip of her coffee, scalding her mouth.

"H-hot," she spluttered, setting the mug down with a thud.

"Careful."

"Thanks."

Yeah. No. If he'd had a hand in suggesting a kiss under the mistletoe as part of the great advent-calendar welcome, there was no way he'd offer to help her complete the tasks.

So much for that theory.

"Whatever day two holds for you, I hope you'll have fun with it."

She glared at him. Since there weren't any more tasks in the calendar beyond today, for all she knew this was the end of the road.

"Come on, Avery. Think of it as something to look forward to every day."

"Something fun, huh?"

He bit off a piece of the muffin and nodded while he chewed.

"Why not?" he asked after swallowing the bite. "What do you have to lose by having fun?"

"Let's see. Somehow a group of people who identify themselves only as my Secret Santas got ahold of my grandmother's advent calendar and have taken it upon themselves to torture me with daily Christmas tasks. What's fun about that? I think it's creepy."

He gave her a disapproving look.

"I'm serious, Forest. Okay, I lied. I did look to see what was hidden behind door number two and since I'm staying in Mistletoe Cottage, they thought it would be a barrel of laughs to make today's task 'kiss someone under the mistletoe.' That is not going to happen."

His eyebrows shot up.

"I mean, what the hell am I supposed to do? Walk up and kiss the first person I see in downtown Tinsley Cove?"

He didn't answer. Because what could he say?

"After I saw that bit of nonsense, you know what I did?"

He shook his head.

"I looked ahead to see what other *welcoming gestures* they had in store for me."

"You weren't supposed to look ahead, Avery."

She snorted. "Oh, right, because that ruins the game. Well, the game was forfeited the minute they expected me to smooch a random stranger."

Forest's face was unreadable, but she thought she

detected a mixture of horror and pity. For a moment, she was back in high school, the outsider, the butt of everyone's jokes.

Only this time the joke was on them—whoever *they* were—because she refused to play in to their hands.

"Listen, I need to go. Thanks for the coffee. I'll get the basket later…or, you know what? Keep it. That will be one less thing I need to get rid of."

She stood and started to walk toward the front door.

"Avery, wait a second. May I show you something?"

She seriously considered pretending like she hadn't heard him, but against her better judgment, she turned to look at him. He motioned with his head in the direction of the living room. He stopped just in front of the other side of the archway that divided the spaces.

She stopped, too.

"What?" she asked.

He pointed upward at a small sprig of mistletoe hanging on the other side of the archway. "I just happen to have some mistletoe lying around. They tacked it up there yesterday during the shoot."

He leaned in and kissed her on the cheek.

She drew in a sharp breath. He smelled good. Like the coffee he'd been drinking and something clean and fresh…soapy and woodsy.

The smell of him made her pulse kick up, made her want to lean in closer and breathe in deeper. He didn't move away and she didn't, either. They stood there, their faces a fraction of an inch apart.

If she just tilted up her head ever so slightly… Like that—

Their gazes locked and the next thing she knew, her hands were in his hair and she was kissing him…

Even though it had started as a whisper of a kiss at first, a slow, tentative brushing of lips that made her nerve endings spark, she was now leaning in for more.

He pulled her closer and she answered by winding her arms around his neck and parting her lips, inviting him inside. Lost in time, she wasn't sure how long they stood there like that, wrapped up in each other, kissing each other so thoroughly that her head was spinning and she couldn't feel her feet where they were supposed to be touching the ground.

He tasted of pumpkin and cinnamon and spice, mixed with the coffee they'd been drinking. It was delicious. He was delicious. She would never eat pumpkin muffins again without thinking of him.

When they finally broke apart, they stood there, breathless, forehead-to-forehead.

Who knew that Forest McFadden kissed so well—

But…wait—she was the one who had initiated *this* kiss.

He'd simply given her a polite peck on the cheek— Oh, what had she done?

"There." Forest's voice was low and raspy. "Now you can cross day two off the list."

Chapter Six

The next day, Forest stood in the kitchen of a newly constructed, three-story beachfront house, allowing his clients to wander about and fall in love with the rambling 6.5-million-dollar abode.

While they were emotionally moving in, Forest's mind kept wandering to Avery, and yesterday's kiss. It had been great. Until it wasn't.

Until he'd asked her if she was free for dinner that evening and she'd mumbled an excuse that had translated to "thanks, but no thanks" before she'd left in a hurry.

He'd only meant for it to be a quick, innocent peck, allowing her to complete day two of the advent calendar, but when she'd leaned in and initiated a real kiss, it had been like lighting the fuse on a stick of dynamite.

He'd wanted to kiss Avery since the first time he'd seen her all those years ago. He'd almost go as far as admitting it had been love at first sight.

Love at first sight that had been shut down before he'd even gotten to know her. But the thing was, he felt like he knew her. He'd certainly never forgotten her. It was a strange pull that made it feel like he'd known her all his life and possibly even longer than that.

Now he worried that he'd moved too fast and had blown up everything before this second chance even had the opportunity to get started.

Because of that, he had decided the best thing to do would be to give Avery some room. It went against his grain because he wasn't the type to passively stand by. If something was broken and it was within the realm of his power to fix it, he fixed it.

It was usually that simple.

This was not simple, no matter how you looked at it.

Avery was a complex woman and she was still coming to terms with the changes in her life on top of all of the revelations of what had happened between them all those years ago.

It had been a lot.

A lot to digest.

A lot of thoughts and feelings to dust off and reframe.

A lot of old feelings that had been written off as never going to happen, but had been resuscitated and were suddenly alive and kicking.

When his clients, George and Wendy Lester, joined

him in the kitchen, Forest was grateful for the distraction. "What do you think of the house?"

"This place is great," George said.

"Exactly what we've been looking for," said Wendy. "And we've been looking for a long time."

Yes, they had. Forest had shown them plenty of places up and down the North Carolina coast that had been perfectly good, but, for one reason or another, not exactly what the couple wanted. Forest understood where they were coming from, as his mind wandered back to Avery.

He'd dated plenty of perfectly good women over the years, and he'd even gotten involved with a few, but over time, he'd realized that while they were wonderful people, something that he couldn't define was missing. They'd always parted as friends, and some had become clients or sent him Christmas cards with photos of the men they'd eventually married and their children. There was never a sense of loss or a pang that they were the ones that got away... Was that what he was feeling with Avery?

Was she the one who'd gotten away?

Was she the lid to his pot, as Hazel Buckminster had said?

"You really can't beat that view." Forest pointed to the picture window that overlooked the beach. George and Wendy walked into the family room and then huddled, deep in conversation, in front of the window.

"Let me know if you have any questions," Forest said, suddenly aware that he might have left George and Wendy a little too much to their own devices.

"Just one question," George said. "How would you like to write up an offer?"

"At your service," Forest said, putting his briefcase on the marble-topped island and taking out a form on which to write the offer.

An hour later, Forest was on his way back to the office to submit the Lesters' bid to the listing agent. His clients had gone back to their hotel and Forest had a little time to get organized for the week ahead before he had to leave for Springdale Park in downtown Tinsley Cove, where he would officiate the town's annual tree-lighting ceremony.

Rather than turning onto the road that would've taken him away from the coastline and toward the Sandcastle Real Estate office downtown, which was just over the causeway, he steered his car toward home.

After he pulled into the driveway, he walked across the lawn separating his house from Mistletoe Cottage and knocked on Avery's door.

So much for giving her some space.

When she answered, something flashed in her eyes and her cheeks flushed. She looked gorgeous in the pink sweater she was wearing with jeans that hugged her curves. He was doing his best to look her in the eyes and not look at her curves, but he knew they were there, just as sure as he knew his hands were tingling because they wanted to reach out and touch her.

But he wouldn't do it.

"Hi," he said.

"Hi." She stepped out onto the porch, pulling the door closed behind her.

"I wanted to make sure you knew that the annual Tinsley Cove Christmas tree lighting is happening tonight. In Springdale Park. Downtown."

"Oh. Okay. Thanks," she said. "That's nice of you. I didn't know about it."

"Does that mean you'll come?"

He was about to offer to pick her up, but she said, "I can't. Not tonight."

"You don't have to stay away because of me," he said.

"Because of you? What?" The color in her cheeks deepened and she shifted her weight from one foot to the other. "Why would I stay away because of you?"

"Because of yesterday."

"I don't know what you mean," she said.

"What I mean is after we kissed, you couldn't get away fast enough. I never meant to make you feel uncomfortable. I'm sorry if I did. I don't know what I was thinking."

Actually, that was a lie. He knew damn good and well what he had been thinking. He'd wanted to kiss her. He wanted to kiss her again right now. Hell, he wanted to do a lot more than that, but he never intended for something as wonderful as a kiss to push her away.

"It's my fault," she said, but she wouldn't look at him. She was studying a spot on one of the porch's floorboards in the distance.

"Believe me, as far as I'm concerned, you have absolutely nothing to worry about," he said.

"I don't?"

"No, you don't." He had to shove his hands in his pockets to keep from reaching out and tilting up her chin so that she would look at him.

"Then can we just start over?" she asked. "Pretend like it didn't happen?"

That was the last thing he wanted, but if it was the way forward—

"Or something like that," she added.

"Something like that" was better than "let's forget about it."

It could mean "let's take things slowly."

That, he could deal with.

"If you change your mind about tonight, the tree lighting is always a lot of fun. Keep it in mind."

Before she could answer, he'd turned and was headed down the stairs.

Twenty minutes later, Forest had sent the offer to the listing agent and was about to leave the office when his father appeared in the doorway of Forest's office. Dalton was standing behind him.

"There he is," Dalton said. "I've been looking for you all morning. Don't you check your texts and voice mail?"

"Did you have a showing?" Bert asked.

"I did and, even better, I just submitted an offer for the three-story new construction on Figure Eight Island, which is why I haven't had time to check texts and voice mail, Dalton."

"Fantastic," Bert said. "That's what I like to hear. Who are the clients?"

"George and Wendy Lester."

"Good job," Bert said. "You've been working with them for a while."

"I have, but I knew that it would pay off soon enough."

"I wish you would've let me know," said Dalton. "I would've had the crew follow you over there and get some footage."

Forest gave Dalton the side-eye. "Not these clients. They're pretty private people."

He turned his attention to his dad. "The offer is a little low, but there's room to negotiate. We'll see what happens."

Forest was used to taking things slowly. When he waited, his patience usually paid off.

"Any developments with Avery Anderson?" Bert asked.

Forest blinked. It took him a moment to digest that his father was talking about Mistletoe Cottage. Not about personal developments between him and Avery, but that's where his mind had gone. There was no way Bert could've known, of course, but considering how thoughts about Avery were still swimming just below the surface of his subconscious, Forest shouldn't have been surprised that his mind automatically went there.

"It's a little early yet," Forest said. "I don't know that she'll even decide what she wants to do with the house until well after the first of the year. Even that might be too soon. Why do you ask?"

"I have a client who is looking for a house just like Mistletoe Cottage."

"Avery? That's the woman I met at the tree lot the other night, right?" asked Dalton.

Forest nodded.

"Maybe we could work this Mistletoe Cottage into the season," Dalton said. "You want the property, but she doesn't want to sell. We could play it up a bit to give it some zing. You know, is she or isn't she going to sell?"

Forest frowned. "I don't think so. From what I can tell, she's not much into reality TV, and as I said she has made it clear that she won't decide what she's going to do with the place until after the holidays."

"But what if you brought her a buyer. You know, made her an offer she couldn't refuse?"

The strangest push-pull warred in Forest's chest. With property values as high as they were right at the moment, Mistletoe Cottage would fetch a nice price, which could be a win-win in that it would be a good cash-out for Avery and, of course, it would mean a nice commission for Sandcastle Real Estate if they managed to snag the listing and provide the buyer.

But if they brought her a buyer who offered the right price, it might be all the impetus she needed to sell. He wanted her to stay. He would gladly give up the commission to have her close.

If she wanted to go, Forest would understand. He'd have no choice.

After all these years, Avery was right next door. If she sold Mistletoe Cottage, she would likely go back to New York, or wherever a new job might take her.

Avery's kitchen window had a view of the opposite side of the property from where Forest lived, which was a good thing because it allowed her to wash her dishes without the fear of seeming like she was stalking him.

Instead, she could stand at the sink, wash dishes and do her best to not invade her other neighbor's privacy as she tried not to rehash every mistake she'd made when it came to Forest.

Learning the truth about what had happened in high school had been a game changer, even if she was still coming to terms with it.

The more she thought about it, the more she saw exactly how kind Forest was being to her now. He'd brought her a Christmas tree. He'd been trying to help her see the Christmas spirit that the advent calendar could bring if she'd just get out of her own head and let herself have some fun for a change.

Then he'd given her that peck on the cheek under the mistletoe. She was the one who had turned it into something heavy. Then she remembered the delicious feeling that had zinged all the way down to her toes when she'd initiated the second kiss.

Why did she have to make everything so heavy? Sometimes she was her own worst brooding enemy.

At least she owned that reality. Admitting she had a problem was one of the first steps toward fixing the problem.

Through the kitchen window, a flutter of motion caught her eye. She got a quick glimpse of her other next-door neighbor moving around her living room, making sweeping gestures with her arms as she glided past the window.

What was she doing now?

Was she dancing? If not dancing, she was having a convulsive fit.

But, hey, it looked like she was having fun.

As the woman, who appeared to be around Avery's age, turned her head from side to side, Avery caught a glimpse of something white in her ears.

Cordless headphones.

Eyes closed, the neighbor raised her arms over her head and jumped up and down, moving her lithe body to a soundless tune.

As Avery scrubbed the food off the plate that she'd used for her lunch, she admired the woman's stamina and her original dance moves, but she was really in awe of her abandon. Not only was she getting a great work-out, but she was also dancing like no one was watching.

How wonderful it must be to be so carefree. Avery needed to borrow a page from her book. If she tried, could she be that free? Not just while she was dancing, but in life in general?

Why had she said no when Forest had asked her out to dinner? And then refused the invitation to come to the tree lighting tonight?

She knew the answer to that question—it had been equal parts reflex and the assumption that he was inviting her out of obligation to cut through the awkwardness of the kiss.

Avery held a glass under the faucet and watched the warm water wash away the dish soap. That might've held true for the dinner invite immediately following the kiss, but he'd really gone the extra mile to let her know about the tree lighting.

She'd hated it when she'd thought the Secret Santa had *assumed* she'd be staying long enough to complete all the tasks. Here she was assuming she knew what Forest was thinking. Was she projecting her own issues onto others?

Speaking of the Secret Santas, it was getting close to one o'clock. What was she supposed to do about day three of the advent calendar? They'd assumed—*huh*, there was that word again—they'd guessed correctly that she would look ahead, even though they'd asked her not to. And she had. Did that mean the game was over?

But what if she hadn't looked ahead? What if she'd played by the rules and had opened door number three and found nothing there but the nasty note accusing her of peeking?

Ahh, who cares.

The phone rang, startling her out of her thoughts.

She dried her hands on a dish towel and tossed it onto the counter, noticing that sometime during her daydream her neighbor had danced out of the frame of the window. Good for her. Maybe someday Avery would gather the energy to have a dance party of her own. Even if it meant closing all the blinds. Baby steps.

As she picked up her phone, she saw her former boss's name displayed on the screen.

"Hello, Barry. How are you?"

"I'm doing great, Avery." Barry chuckled. "This call is a bit premature, but I had to share the news with someone, and since the French carousel project will be yours—if you still want it, of course—but cutting to the chase. I spoke with one of my backers and we are so close to finalizing everything. I wanted to update you so that you could pencil in the assignment for right after the first of the year. I should know something in the next couple of weeks. That's how close we are to finalizing things."

"Wow, that's great news," Avery said.

Barry made a dubious noise. "It could still fall through, but I'm choosing to think positive, which is why I'm giving you the heads-up.

"I've already started working on a preliminary list of carousel locations, which I'll send to you so you can add to it if you come across something that looks interesting. In the meantime, make sure your passport is up to date."

"You know it is, Barry."

After the call ended and Avery set down the phone, the big, wooden advent calendar, which was sitting on the kitchen counter, caught her eye.

Even though she'd found the Secret Santas and their games annoying, she had to admit she was curious about what would happen next.

She opened the calendar's door number three and peered inside. It was as empty as it had been the last time she'd checked it, which was both a relief and a disappointment. It was a relief that no one had been in the house. It was a surprising disappointment that the absence of a note might mean game-over.

As if moved by a force outside of herself, she walked to the front door. Maybe they'd left something on the porch? What could it hurt to check? She opened the door and was nearly overcome with joy and relief when she saw a red envelope with Day Three written in bold script lying on the porch floor about a foot away from the doormat.

She looked right and left as if she might discover who'd left it, but no one was around. Before she bent to pick it up, she glanced at Forest's house again to see if she could detect any signs of life, but his car was gone and the place was as quiet as if it had been abandoned.

Again, she wondered if Forest might've had a hand in it.

Smiling to herself, Avery took the envelope over to the porch swing and sat down. Pushing off with her foot, she made the swing sway back and forth. Before she could open the missive, her neighbor, the unabashed dancer, was bounding up the stairs.

"Hello, I'm your neighbor, Kaitlyn Quinn. You must be Bess's granddaughter." Kaitlyn offered a hand.

Avery slid the envelope under one of the swing cushions, then stood and accepted Kaitlyn's hand, before introducing herself.

"I saw you through the window earlier," Kaitlyn said. "I thought I'd come over and introduce myself. So, hello."

"Hello, it's nice to meet you," Avery said. "I promise I don't make a habit of staring into people's windows, but you were in my line of sight while I was doing dishes."

"I'd close my curtains if it bothered me," she said. "I keep the drapes open because it seems like a mortal sin to block out all that gorgeous sunlight. Even though that window faces north, thanks to the ones on the east, most days my living room is absolutely drenched in sunshine. But, don't worry, I don't make a habit of walking around naked. At least not in front of the windows."

"Good to know," Avery said, hoping the horror she was feeling inside wasn't telegraphing her discomfort on her face.

"Anyway, enough about that. I came over because I wanted to introduce myself and tell you how sorry I am about your grandmother. I was away on business when it happened. I just couldn't believe it. I'm sorry for your loss."

"Thank you," Avery said, nodding to the house next door. "I appreciate it. How long have you lived here?"

"I bought the house in January. So it's been almost a year."

That's right. Avery recalled Gran mentioning she had a new neighbor, but she couldn't remember the exact timeline.

With her honey-brown hair, startling blue eyes and long legs, Kaitlyn was tall, thin and model-pretty. Living so close to Forest, Avery was surprised the two of them hadn't found their way to each other.

A strange feeling slithered around Avery's insides.

Why would she be jealous of them being together? They'd make a gorgeous couple.

"Have you met your other neighbor?" Kaitlyn asked, as if reading Avery's mind. "Hottie McTottie over there sold me my house."

Okay. So maybe Kaitlyn was interested...

"I've known Forest since high school."

As soon as the words left her mouth, Avery wondered why she'd said them. She'd made it sound as if she and Forrest were besties, or even more than friends. At the very least, she made it sound as if they went way back, which they didn't. They'd spoken more in the past three days than they had over the last dozen years.

She had no right to feel territorial. Yet, for some weird reason, she did.

Kaitlyn smiled. "In addition to being hot as hell, he's a nice guy, too. He used to help your grandmother out a lot. Where do you find a guy like that these days?"

Another, different sort of pang stabbed Avery in the solar plexus. She shouldn't have been so self-absorbed when it came to Gran. She should've done more to help her. Look where she was now. She'd given everything to a job that didn't love her back.

The best she could do now was pay forward that time she should've spent with Gran. Do it for her and believe that it would somehow make her happy.

Avery's mind flashed on the list on Gran's desk and then to the Secret Santas.

She'd only completed two tasks, but it was interesting how both of them had been on Gran's list.

Her gaze tracked to the porch swing, where she

could see a corner of the red envelope sticking out. It would be interesting to see what day three held for her.

From out of the blue, it hit Avery that Kaitlyn was awfully young to own such a nice house on the beach.

"What do you do, Kaitlyn?"

"I am a recently retired fashion model and aspiring fashion designer," she said. "I'm thirty, so I'm aging out. You know how that goes. It's best to leave the party before they show you the door."

She'd heard that before. One of her former coworkers, Ben, lived with a woman who modeled. He laughed about how she was constantly moaning that she was an old woman and would be washed up once she hit her thirtieth birthday. She was only twenty-six. But when Ben had pointed out that thirty was four years away, she'd said that being on the downward grade of twenty-five meant it was a quick glide to colliding with the big 3-0.

Avery had always been grateful to have time on her side. Each year that she'd invested in her career had honed her photographer's eye and her skills, making her better at her art.

"What type of fashions do you design?" Avery asked.

"I just collaborated with a designer in LA who specializes in ready-to-wear. It was a great crash course, but I'd like to do something a little quirkier. I'll show you some of my designs sometime. What do you do with yourself when you're not washing dishes and staring out the window in Tinsley Cove?"

"I'm a photojournalist, but I was recently laid off from my job at *World International* magazine. I'm here sorting out Gran's house and trying to figure out what to do next."

"How lucky are you to have grown up in a town like this. What a wonderful place to land. I love it here. So much so that out of every place in the world I could've gone, I bought a house here."

"Oh, no, I didn't grow up here."

"Oh… I thought you said you and Forest went to school together. Did you mean college?"

Avery shook her head. "I moved here in my senior year of high school."

She started to add that she couldn't get away fast enough, but stopped herself. Clearly, Kaitlyn loved the place. There was no need for Avery to bash it.

"If you don't mind me asking, what do you love about this town? It's always nice to try and see it through someone else's eyes."

Kaitlyn nodded. "First of all, what's more gorgeous than this?" Arms stretched wide, she made an all-encompassing sweeping gesture. "I feel like I'm waking up in paradise every morning. Plus, the people here are so nice and welcoming. It just immediately felt like home after living out of a suitcase for so much of the past decade. Now, my design studio is in my house, even though I have an apartment in New York, too. You know, I've got to be close to the action. Listen, I have to run now, but maybe next week you can come over and see the collection I'm creating. Who knows, maybe when it's complete, I can hire you to photograph it?"

"That would be amazing," Avery said. "Let's talk about it sometime."

"All right, it's a plan," Kaitlyn said. "Are you going to the tree lighting tonight in Springdale Park?"

Apparently, Forest was right. The entire town did turn out for the festivities. She couldn't remember why she hadn't gone to the tree lighting the year she'd lived with Gran, because surely her grandmother had gone. Something like that was right up Gran's alley. Avery probably had begged off, saying she had homework or was in the middle of a good book. Gran never pushed her.

It was after the Le Marais incident, so no doubt, Avery had stayed away, hiding at home rather than going with her grandmother.

Avery shook her head. "No, I'm totally swamped. I have so much to do."

Her excuse sounded lame. It was one thing to be a homebody like Kaitlyn, who was creating a fashion collection, but it was quite another to sit home and sort through the possessions of the only person who'd ever really loved her.

But it was the tree lighting in the park. With the whole town. It felt like a lot. Like too much. Like something she needed to ease into rather than cannonballing right into it.

"Let's do something another time, okay?" she said. "And I'm definitely in for seeing your studio next week."

"Perfect," said Kaitlyn. "Just come on over whenever. And if you change your mind about going tonight, just give me a holler. It will be so pretty with all the decorations. Maybe you could even bring your camera?"

Avery smiled but shook her head. "Have fun."

After Kaitlyn left, Avery pulled the red envelope out from under the swing cushion and opened it.

Day Three
   Star light, star bright,
   The first lights will shine tonight.
   Go to the tree lighting in Springdale Park tonight.
   It's guaranteed to be a beautiful sight.
   Your Secret Santas

Chapter Seven

Tinsley Cove
Sunday, December 3

"Welcome to Tinsley Cove's annual Christmas-tree lighting," Forest said into the microphone. The crowd, which stretched to the edges of Springdale Park, responded with cheers and whistles, and the Christmas music that had been playing over the park's PA system faded. So many people had turned out tonight that it seemed that most of the town was here for this annual tradition. Of course, it didn't hurt that they were filming the event for the show *Selling Sandcastle*. Whenever word of them filming got out, it guaranteed a good turnout.

Before continuing, Forest glanced at his producer, Dalton Hart, who gave him the thumbs-up that everything was in order and he was good to carry on.

"As mayor of Tinsley Cove, can I tell you how happy I am to see so many of you here tonight? Give yourselves a round of applause for coming out."

As Forest clapped and others joined in, he scanned the crowd, taking in the faces of the people gathered for the festivities. Many were wearing Christmas sweaters—ugly and otherwise. Some had on Santa hats and others donned flashing necklaces made out of multicolored Christmas lights. People stood in groups, laughing and talking and sipping steaming cups of hot holiday cider, sold by Bean and Press's mobile coffeeshop.

He hoped that Avery might change her mind and show up, but so far there was no sign of her. There was still a chance, but it was all the more important that he focused on the positive: there was a large crowd and it was heartening that this quaint annual tradition was still a favorite of the locals.

"This is a great way to kick off the holiday season," he said. "It's a tradition that goes back as far as I can remember. When I was a kid I used to look forward to it, and I never dreamed that one day I would be standing up here as your mayor. That reminds me, I want to thank everyone who voted for me. And to those who didn't, I promise you I will work extra hard to earn your trust because I am here to serve all of the residents of Tinsley Cove. Each and every one of you."

Jordy Griffin, who was the head of parks and recreation, gave Forest the sign that the tree was ready to go.

"Without further ado, let's get to it. Will you help me count down?"

Avery rode to the tree lighting with Kaitlyn, who was proudly sporting an ugly Christmas sweater depicting a cat tangled up in tinsel garland. The cat was knitted into the sweater's pattern, but the tinsel was the real deal, shiny and gaudy, sewn on to give the garment a three-dimensional look. It was from Kaitlyn's line of novelty clothing.

When Avery had commented on it before they left, Kaitlyn had disappeared into her bedroom, emerging with another sweater, this one showing a corgi wearing a Santa hat and juggling Christmas ornaments.

"Here, you can wear this one," she'd said to Avery.

In a similar fashion to the one Kaitlyn wore, this one was decked out with real ornaments dangling off the sweater.

"Oh, that's okay," Avery had said. "This looks like it would need to be dry-cleaned after I wore it and I don't want to take a chance of messing it up."

"The ornaments detach, and it's machine-washable," Kaitlyn had replied. "It'll be a fun way to get into the Christmas spirit. Plus, you'll be doing me a huge favor since you'll be like a walking billboard for my business."

What was the harm? Avery had figured if one of the future advent tasks challenged her to wear an ugly Christmas sweater—and she wouldn't put it past her Secret Santas to include that task—she'd be one step ahead of the game. If nothing else, it was fun to be in solidarity with her new friend and help her out.

After reading the note for day three, Avery had gone next door and told Kaitlyn she'd changed her mind and said she would love to go with her to the tree lighting if the invitation still stood.

Kaitlyn had been delighted.

"That's fantastic," she'd said. "I'm meeting my friends

Cassie, Sophie and Lucy. I'll introduce you…if you don't know them already. Cassie is engaged to Forest's brother Logan. Sophie is Logan and Forest's sister, and Lucy is their cousin."

For an instant, Avery thought about backing out because she'd thought it would just be Kaitlyn and her. She had no idea that a contingency of Forest's relatives was part of the bargain, but Kaitlyn said, "I'm so glad you changed your mind. I found the more I opened up to the town, and the more people I met, the more the town seemed to embrace me back."

Kaitlyn was right, Avery justified. Plus, it would be nice to be out in the company of women…even if the degree of separation from Forest was razor-thin.

This night wasn't about him, though she supposed it wouldn't be such a bad thing if she happened to run into him.

They arrived at the park and had just enough time to grab a cup of hot cider when they heard Forest's voice addressing the crowd over the sound system.

"I told Sophie I'd meet them by the stage." Kaitlyn glanced around, looking for her friends. "We should probably make our way over there."

By the time she and Kaitlyn got to the area close to the stage, Forest and the crowd were counting down to the tree lighting.

The two of them joined in on the *five, four, three, two, one.*

As the tree lit up and the crowd cheered and clapped, Avery sensed Forest's gaze on her.

When she turned toward him, he smiled and raised a hand in greeting and then mouthed the words *I'll be right there.*

Avery nodded, as a sudden rush of anticipations spiraled in her stomach that he'd seemed glad to see her.

"Well, well, well, there's our hot neighbor now, front and center," Kaitlyn said. "He seemed to have picked you out of the crowd right away while I remain invisible. Could someone have a crush?"

"He's just being neighborly," Avery said as her body reacted to the memory of his lips on hers. "I think he is angling for the listing on my house if I decide to sell."

"Somehow, I think that's not all he wants," Kaitlyn said. "Are you interested?"

Am I interested? That's a loaded question.

Before she could answer, Forest returned to the microphone and Avery pretended to listen with interest.

"Thank you all for coming tonight. On behalf of the city of Tinsley Cove, I wish you and yours a very happy holiday season."

Before he left the stage, he turned to her and held up a finger, which Avery understood to mean he'd be right there. Her stomach somersaulted.

"I don't know, Avery," Kaitlyn said. "I'm getting a vibe."

"I have no idea what you're talking about," Avery said as she tried not to squirm.

Kaitlyn arched a knowing eyebrow. "Don't think I didn't notice how you artfully ignored my question a moment ago. I'll form my own conclusion and guess that you are interested."

For some reason, Avery couldn't bring herself to protest, especially when once again, she sensed Forest's presence before she turned and saw him walking toward her. A strange, but vaguely familiar feeling—something she hadn't felt in ages—buzzed through her.

Was she interested in him?

Then he smiled and it hit her. That feeling was attraction.

Something she hadn't allowed herself to feel for a very long time, because she'd been too busy, too focused on work. She'd had tunnel vision when it came to getting promoted to photo editor. She'd been determined not to let anything or anyone distract her.

But there was no denying what she was feeling, and it was very much alive and kicking open the compartment in her heart where she'd buried it, deep down, all those years ago.

Oh, no. This couldn't be good.

Could it?

She tried to round up the feeling and stuff it back down where it belonged, where she could lock it away and carry on as usual.

To no avail.

Every nerve ending in Avery's body vibrated and she surrendered to the possibility that maybe she should just go with it, especially when Forest said, "I'm glad you decided to come after all."

Avery half hoped he would lean in and kiss her on the cheek, like he had yesterday, and was strangely disappointed when he didn't. But after their conversation about the kiss earlier this afternoon, it might've been heavy-handed on his part if he had.

Clearly, he was keeping a respectable distance, and that might've had something to do with the fact that he was acting in an official capacity at the tree lighting. He was the mayor. He had to be concerned with the possible impropriety of public displays of affection.

She not only understood, but she also appreciated his discretion.

He hadn't run in the opposite direction. In fact, he'd seemed glad to see her.

That gave immense pleasure to the traitorous part of her heart that had unleashed the attraction.

"Oh, hey, Forest." Kaitlyn put a hand on his arm. "I'm the one who convinced Avery to come tonight. You can thank me later."

Hmm... What exactly did she have in mind when she wanted him to thank her later? If Kaitlyn thought she had dibs on Forest, Avery wouldn't get in the way.

"Hi, Kaitlyn," he said. "I'll thank you now because I'm glad you convinced her."

Oh.

Really?

He was glad? And he wasn't shy about saying so.

Well, okay.

Avery smiled as a warm feeling unfurled inside her.

Kaitlyn eyed Avery and raised an eyebrow. While she wasn't exactly shooting daggers at Avery, she didn't look resigned, either. More like a woman who smelled a challenge and was there for it.

Not wanting to get in the middle of anything, Avery mentally retreated back to her original stance of reining in the weird feelings that had been jumping out unbidden since she'd kissed Forest.

She had to admit, he looked nice in the green sweater he was wearing over the white button-down. It brought out his green eyes. Forest seemed a bit too conservative for someone as worldly as Kaitlyn, who probably was as at home in a couture evening gown as she was in her cat-fighting-with-tinsel sweater.

He was more Ralph Lauren while she was more Betsey Johnson.

While Ralph Lauren was a household name, the reason Avery knew of Betsey Johnson was that she'd photographed her for a story *World International* ran in celebration of the designer's eightieth birthday.

But even if Forest and Kaitlyn resided at polar ends of the spectrum, opposites did attract, and they would make a gorgeous couple.

"There you are," said a woman who appeared to be about Avery's age. With her dark curly hair and blue eyes, Avery thought she looked vaguely familiar, and she wondered if she was someone she'd gone to high school with back in the day. But when Forest pulled her in for a hug, the resemblance was clear—same nose, same eye shape, and despite the different color, same dimple that winked from her left cheek when she smiled.

"Avery, I want you to meet my sister, Sophie. Soph, this is my new neighbor, Avery Anderson."

A blonde and another brunette walked up and hugged Forest, too. "And this is my soon-to-be sister-in-law, Cassie Houston," he said. "She's engaged to my brother Logan."

Avery congratulated her.

"And this is my cousin Lucy."

After Avery exchanged pleasantries with the women, Kaitlyn said, "We met at a yoga class at Bar None Fitness Studio. You should join us sometime."

"Thanks," Avery said, even though she was sure if she tried to do a backbend or any of the challenging poses that were in the yoga repertoire, she'd probably end up with her leg stuck behind her head and not be able to get unstuck.

The guy Avery had met at the Christmas-tree tent in the grocery store parking lot the other night walked up and slapped Forest on the back.

"Hey, Forest and ladies," he said. "Good job on the tree-lighting introduction. We got it all. So as soon as Gary gets some B-roll footage, we'll call it a wrap for tonight. Let's hope everything goes that easily this season."

Suddenly, it hit Avery why Kaitlyn's friends looked vaguely familiar. She'd seen them on the television show *Selling Sandcastle*. Once, when Avery had been between assignments, she'd caught an episode when Cassie—the blonde—had reunited with her father. It had seemed a bit fraught, as if they might never work it out, but Gran had been happy to inform Avery that she had learned during the finale that father and daughter had mended things and they were working on their relationship.

"Since we're done here," said Dalton, "how about if we all head over to Harry's on Main and get a bite to eat?"

Kaitlyn and her friends were all in, but Forest hung back.

"Did you want to go with them?" he asked.

Avery shrugged, trying to ignore the strange pull in her stomach induced by Forest's question. "Why? Do you have a better offer?"

He answered her with a smile and that dimple winked at her. A thought arose unbidden, that that dimple just might be able to convince her to go anywhere.

"I have something to show Avery. We will catch up with you a bit later."

"Be home early," Kaitlyn called. "You know nothing good happens after midnight. I'll be waiting up."

They started walking and once they were out of earshot of their friends, Avery said to Forest, "I think she might be interested in you."

"She who?" Forest asked.

"Kaitlyn."

"Kaitlyn?" Forest did a double take that suggested he'd never considered it.

"Yes, Kaitlyn. Who else would I be talking about? Certainly not your sister, your cousin or your brother's fiancée."

"Good, because that would be weird," he said.

"Yes, it would be very weird," Avery said.

"There were a lot of people in the park," he said. "I thought you might've been talking about any one of them."

"So back to Kaitlyn, who is not related to you. Have you ever considered asking her out or, better question, have you two dated in the past?"

"Who wants to know?" he said.

Avery stopped walking and looked up at him. "I want to know, Forest. Because after you came by today, I started thinking about things."

"What kind of things?" he asked.

She raised an eyebrow at him, debating how much to say. "But then I met Kaitlyn and she seems nice and I think I can be friends with her."

"I thought so," he said. "You're wearing one of her sweaters, aren't you? She presented a pitch to Dalton to showcase her clothing line on the show."

Avery glanced down. Even though she couldn't fathom how she could've forgotten that she was wearing the, er, unique garment, she'd been so wrapped up in everything else going on around her that it had momentarily slipped her mind.

"Kaitlyn designed this sweater and it's adorable," she said as they walked past the lit Christmas tree and through the crowd. "Don't tell me you don't like corgis in Santa hats."

"Would it be a deal breaker if I didn't?" he asked.

"An absolute deal breaker." She stopped on the sidewalk.

He turned to face her. "For the record, I love all dogs. Especially when they're wearing Santa hats. Also, for the record, Kaitlyn is a wonderful woman, but she's not my type. I wish her well in love and life, but I have never dated her. Nor do I have any intention to do so because I'm interested in someone else."

Avery's heart hammered in her chest. She drew in a deep breath, trying to calm it, and mentally replayed what he'd just said to make sure that she'd heard him right.

"Well, okay then," she said.

"'Is that the response you were hoping for?"

All she could do was nod.

He reached out and took her hands in his, and for a moment she thought he was going to kiss her again. She decided it would be okay if he did. No, it wasn't just okay. She wanted him to kiss her.

"What I wanted to show you is over here." He held her hand as they continued down the sidewalk. Every so often people would nod at him or greet him with a "Merry Christmas, Mayor," but no one waylaid him and no one seemed to think there was anything un-usual about their mayor, whom Hazel Buckminster had taken great delight in pointing out was the most eligible bachelor in Tinsley Cove, was holding hands with someone who was a stranger to most of the locals.

"Today is day three of the advent calendar," he said. "What did your Secret Santas have in store for you?"

"A corny little poem inviting me to tonight's tree lighting. Are you sure you're not in on this Secret Santas production?"

He feigned shock and offense. "Me? Whatever makes you think I would be involved in something like that?"

"Because the card with today's task arrived shortly after you left."

"So I wasn't convincing enough to persuade you to come. It took a brigade of Secret Santas to do the trick."

"Actually, the Secret Santas were the third nudge. Kaitlyn came over before I could open the advent card and asked me to come tonight. If it makes you feel any better, I turned her down, too."

He put his hand over his heart and nodded.

"By the time I opened the card from the Secret Santas, I'd been worn down. So I figured why not."

Forest stopped in front of Le Marais restaurant.

"Here we are," he said.

"What is this?"

"It's a do-over," Forest said. "If you'll allow me. It seems that I owe you a long overdue evening at Le Marais. Would you have dinner with me tonight?"

Avery glanced down at the sweater with its dan-gling ornaments.

"This is a nice restaurant," she said. "I'm not dressed appropriately."

It wasn't really the sweater that was making her hesitate. It was all those memories of being the odd girl, the outsider, the one who didn't belong, that were flooding back, making her wish she'd stayed home tonight rather than venturing out.

Then Forest lifted her hand to his lips and kissed her fingers softly.

"Who cares what people think. You are beautiful, Avery, no matter what you're wearing."

She glanced in the window and could see that the small dining room looked different than she remembered it. It used to be a collection of tables with ladder-back chairs and white tablecloths, each with a single red rose in a clear glass bud vase positioned next to a votive candle in a clear glass holder. The place appeared to have been remodeled over the past decade, giving it a fresh, new look that resembled a wine cave.

Who didn't need a fresh start? It would be her own fault if she let this one pass by.

"I would love to have dinner with you, Forest."

Chapter Eight

Louis Garnier, the owner of Le Marais, seated Forest and Avery at a quiet table for two in a snug corner in the back of the restaurant that was shielded by a floor-to-ceiling wine rack.

"Is this table satisfactory, monsieur?" Louis pulled out the chair for Avery and helped her with her napkin after she scooted up to the table.

Forest looked at Avery, who nodded.

"It's perfect, Louis," said Forest. "Thank you."

While he didn't mind who saw him having dinner with Avery, Forest welcomed the privacy. Since they were tucked away in a private corner, there was less of a chance he would be approached with questions about the new water meters that were due to be installed in the northeast quadrant of the city beginning next month. And no one could inquire about paving, or speed bumps, or a host of zoning questions that usually came up anytime he was spotted out in the wild—at dinner, in the grocery store, at the dentist's office. You name it, and people seemed to think he was free game.

"Wonderful," said Louis as he handed them each a menu. "William will bring you some bread and a wine list."

"Attentive service," Avery said after Louis walked away.

Forest watched her glance around. "Sometimes it pays to be the mayor. Other times, people take it as a standing invitation to join you or interrupt your dinner. That's why I'm glad he seated us back here. I don't want you to get the wrong idea that we're hiding back here."

"It hadn't even crossed my mind," Avery said. "Then again, I'm all about cozy corners and private tables."

"Are you?" Forest asked.

Avery nodded. "I guess that's why I'm more comfortable behind the camera than in front of it."

"Speaking of," Forest said. "I'm surprised you didn't bring your camera to the tree lighting tonight."

Avery offered a one-shoulder shrug. "I haven't taken it out of its case since I got here."

"That's surprising. I remember you used to always have a camera with you in high school."

"You remember that?"

"I do."

"I didn't even remember that, but I guess it's true. I've always loved to take photos. It was like stopping time. If I captured something, like a person smiling or laughing, or even staring somberly into the camera, I'm capturing them in that decisive moment, in that specific moment in time. All the things—the emotions or environs or circumstances that led to that moment—will probably never be exactly the same because that moment is gone, except for it being captured in the shot."

"I never really thought of photos like that. It gives an entirely new meaning to them. I'll never look at them the same way again."

Avery nodded. "We are all evolving and changing from one second to the next. The person you are today is ever so slightly different from the person you were yesterday. Those small changes add up over time. That's why I'm fascinated by the long-term projects I've seen some photographers do, where they take a photo of a person—maybe a son or a daughter—every day for years. When you're around someone every day, you don't notice the subtle changes, but if you compare the photos, day to day, month to month, year to year, the change is astounding."

Her hand was resting on the table and he reached out and covered it with his. "I'm glad you believe that people are capable of change."

He half expected her to pull away, but she didn't. So he slid his hand under hers and laced his fingers through it. Her hand felt good in his, like it belonged there.

"Everyone changes physically," she said. "It's inevitable. But it's up to the individual whether or not they change and grow on the inside."

"You mean not making the same mistakes over and over again?"

She nodded. "So you know, I believed what you said about not being part of the big Le Marais joke. You didn't have to bring me here to make up for it."

"I brought you here because I wanted to have dinner

with you," he said. "I'm glad you believe me. Maybe part of me did want to make it up to you because I think what they did to you was horrible."

William appeared, looking sheepish. "Hi, folks. I don't mean to interrupt, but I wanted to leave this basket of bread and ask if I can bring you a bottle of wine."

"No problem, William," Forest said. "Avery, would you care for some wine?"

"That sounds delicious."

They decided on red and Forest ordered a bottle of Châteauneuf-du-Pape before William left them alone.

As soon as their server walked away, Forest continued. "As I was saying, I hope that by bringing you here tonight we can start over. Even though I feel like I've known you for a long time, I realize this is new." He gestured between them. "If we can put the past behind us, I promise you I will never lie to you. You may not like what I have to say sometimes, but I promise you it will be the truth."

She was looking at their joined hands and he could see the wheels in her mind turning.

"What are you thinking about?" he asked. "I'm starting to recognize that look and it usually means there's a lot going on up there."

Her gaze met his and he smiled at her.

"I'm just wondering how many hearts you've broken with that brutal honesty you were just talking about. More than that, why are you still single? Although, it just dawned on me this second—you're thirty-two years old. Maybe you have been married and I don't know about it."

"I've never been married. The truth is, I've been so wrapped up in my career I haven't had time. I got my undergrad from the University of North Carolina, then I went to law school. After that my dad really wanted me to join the family business. So I did."

"If you went to law school, why are you selling houses?"

He smiled. "Luxury real estate is…lucrative. But I still look over contracts. So I'm also in-house counsel."

"You're busy."

He nodded. "It hasn't left me much time for a serious relationship."

"What's the longest relationship you've ever had?"

"Six to nine months seems to run the course."

Avery's eyes widened.

"That's usually when the where-is-this-relationship-going portion of the program starts and I haven't had the answers they were looking for. Don't get me wrong, I've dated some wonderful women. I just haven't met the right one."

Until now. He stopped before he said too much. He didn't want to scare her, but sitting here with her, holding her hand, he had the strangest sensation that none of the other women had ever measured up because they weren't her.

If he said that to her, she would get up and run out of this place faster than a cork out of a champagne bottle. First, she would probably say "you don't really know me." In a way, she was right, but in another way, on a different realm, he knew a different type of connection with her than he'd ever known with any of the women with whom he'd spent months.

"So you're a serial monogamist?" she asked.

"Is that what it's called?" he asked. "I've always looked at it as waiting for the right one to come along."

Luckily, in the pregnant pause that followed, William returned with their wine. After it had been tasted and poured, and they'd made a toast, Forest asked, "What about you? Have you ever been married?"

A *Mona Lisa* smile curved up the edges of Avery's lips. "Nope. I got close once, but he said I was too much of a workaholic and gave me the ultimatum of him or the magazine." She shrugged, then sipped her wine.

"You chose the magazine," Forest said.

"I had worked hard to build my career. Jobs like the one I held with *World International* didn't come along very often."

"What do you mean by that? It sounds like you're talking about it in the past tense."

She shrugged and then nodded.

"The magazine has closed down. And look at me now. It's going to take a while to find another job like that." She ran a finger around the rim of her wineglass, watching her finger as she traced the edge. "I guess the joke's on me because here I am in a similar situation that I feared I'd be in if I gave up everything to get married. Only I have more experience and, luckily, I received a small severance package when I was laid off." She looked up at him again. "Life is so uncertain, I always wanted to be able to make my own way in the world. You know, not depend on anyone but me."

He remembered that she'd come to Tinsley Cove to live with Bess after her parents had been killed in a car accident. It seemed like losing them when she was still a minor had done a number on her.

"What about your grandmother? It seemed like you could depend on her."

She shook her head and the look on her face made

him realize she probably thought he was insinuating that she could live off her grandmother.

"Gran was wonderful, but she was careful with her money. She'd raised her daughter. She'd done her duty. No one counted on my parents dying. My dad had made some bad business decisions, believing that he could somehow monetize the study of animals, but we were living from grant to grant. Those sources dried up, and not only did my parents leave behind a mountain of debt when they passed away, but they had no savings or life insurance. Gran took me in and never made me feel like I was a burden, but I know I was a financial strain that year I lived with her. I vowed that I would always make my own way in the world. That's one of the reasons I was so desperate to get out of Tinsley Cove. In addition to not feeling like I fit in, I knew there was no opportunity for me here."

Every sense in Forest's body went on high alert. The unspoken part was that now more than ever, there was nothing keeping her in Tinsley Cove. As soon as she found a job, she would be out of there.

Forest sipped his wine and weighed his words. "Sometimes you have to create your own opportunity."

"Thank you, Yoda. I'll keep that in mind."

She touched her glass to his.

"I'm serious," he said. "Think about what you really want to do with the next phase of your life and what it would take to make it work. If you did set up your own business you'd never be at risk of being laid off again."

Her face softened, as if she was thinking about it.

"What's more is…if you stayed in Tinsley Cove, you wouldn't have to sell Mistletoe Cottage."

She flinched and opened her mouth, as if she was going to object, but Forest beat her to it.

"I told you I'd always be honest. In that vein, I'm not ashamed to let you know I want you to stay."

"Why? So you can have a nine-month relationship with me and then we can go our separate ways?"

"Don't write me off just yet."

I have a sneaking suspicion that you're the reason my relationships have had an expiration date.

Tinsley Cove
Monday, December 4

She'd be an idiot to believe that someone like Forest McFadden had been pining for her all these years. He barely knew her, but the first time she saw him, she'd felt something she'd never felt for anyone. After all that had happened and all the intervening years, she'd written it off as a first love, or better yet, a schoolgirl crush.

Yet here they were again—some sort of powerful magic was drawing them to each other. They'd both confessed that there hadn't been another love that had stolen their hearts after all these years.

Now, she was wondering if it was similar to her favorite movie, *Serendipity*, only with a twist. Had fate brought the two of them back together because now they were ready for each other?

A day ago, Avery would've thought that was the most ridiculous notion. But last night after dinner, he'd driven her home and walked her to the door of Mistletoe Cottage, where he had kissed her so soundly it had made the rest of the world disappear.

It was nothing like the debacle under the mistletoe, when she'd kissed him and freaked out and ran.

Last night, he'd pulled her into his arms. He didn't even have to ask if it was okay because there was an electricity pulsing between them that spoke for both of them. He'd covered her mouth with his, and for a moment it had been as if there was no past or present or worries of the future. It was just them. His hands in her hair, on her back, around her waist, pulling her closer. Without saying a word, he made her believe that she was not only the most beautiful woman in the world, but that she could also manifest everything she ever wanted in the world if she just fell in love with him.

This morning, she could still feel his lips on hers. They tingled with promises that seemed so...promising.

The best part was—or maybe it was the worst— after the two of them had come up for air, he'd made sure she'd gotten inside without pressuring her to take things faster than she was ready.

She knew he'd been turned on—she could feel the evidence of his attraction when he'd pulled her in close. But he'd said he'd see her tomorrow, which was today, and he'd left her with her entire body aching for him and a promise that good things were worth the wait.

She rolled over on her back and threw her arm over her forehead as she stared at the ceiling, wanting him even more this morning, if that was possible. Maybe she was fooling herself, but these were not the let's-get-this-party-started actions of a man with a ticking relationship clock. This was a man who was willing to take things slowly, and not do anything that would jeopardize this budding... What exactly was it that was budding between them?

A relationship?

Maybe it was too soon to tell, but he'd distinctly said that he'd see her tomorrow, and it felt like her pulse was beating in time with a love song—one she didn't know the words to yet, but a beautiful song she knew they'd both be singing soon.

The ring of the doorbell brought her out of her thoughts. Was that him now?

It was Monday, but his schedule was flexible.

She sat up, smoothed her hair and ran into the bathroom, where she splashed water on her face to remove last night's sleep and ran a quick toothbrush over her teeth to tame the morning breath.

She grabbed a robe and went downstairs.

When she answered the door, no one was there, but a green envelope was lying on the porch two feet in front of her.

She picked it up and opened it.

Day 4
O Christmas tree,
O Christmas tree.
How your beauty moves me.
You attended the tree lighting last night.
Now, you need one of your own to decorate.
It's only right.
Your Secret Santas

She already had a tree, but beyond the lights that Forest had strung for her, she hadn't decorated it. Come to think of it, he didn't have a tree of his own yet...as far as she knew.

It would be fun if they could go get him a tree and help each other decorate.

His car was in the driveway, which meant he was home.

Avery went back inside, then showered and dressed quickly before grabbing the card and going next door.

Forest answered the door barefoot and dressed in a pair of low-slung jeans and a white T-shirt. His hair was wet and he looked like he was fresh out of the shower.

"Hello." He smiled, and after he closed the door behind them, he pulled Avery into his arms and kissed her until she saw stars.

"Good morning," she said, still in his arms and looking up at him.

"Yes, it is a good morning when it starts like this."

He covered her mouth with his again and she opened her lips, inviting him in, losing herself again. He tasted like toothpaste and coffee and something delicious that she was already craving.

It was heavenly. He was heavenly, and she never wanted this to end.

A moment later, when he pulled away and she was able to reclaim her senses, she held up the green envelope.

"I came over to say thank you for last night," she said. "I had a really nice time."

"Yeah?" he said. "So did I."

It really did feel like some sort of universal wrong had been made right in that despite Breanna Tate's hateful efforts to do irreparable damage, they had found their way back to each other.

"Also, I wanted to let you know that the band of Secret Santas have struck again," she said. "You didn't happen to see anyone lurking around my porch this morning, did you?"

"I was too busy dreaming about you," he said.

Her cheeks heated and she considered asking him to give her a play-by-play of the dream, but she wasn't sure if she would have as much willpower to resist re-enacting that dream…if it was anything like the dream she'd had of him last night.

"What does it say?" he asked.

"Day four—buy a Christmas tree."

"You already have one," he said.

"I do, and because of that, I'm almost ready to cross you off the list of potential elves because you know I already have a Christmas tree."

He reached out and she handed him the note. Then she explained, "But you don't have one. I was thinking, in keeping with the spirit of things, and since you were so wonderful to make sure that I had a tree, I wanted to return the favor and go with you to get one for your house. I thought we could decorate them together. What do you think?"

He looked at her for a long moment and she was afraid that maybe she'd read him wrong, that he might decline. He'd been volunteering at the charity-tree lot. He was perfectly capable of getting his own tree if he wanted one—maybe that's why he hadn't already.

"If not, no worries," she said. "There was nothing in the rules that said a task couldn't be retroactive. I have a tree. With beautiful lights. All it needs is some decorating. I'm sure Gran's are out in the garage. Unless the Secret Santas absconded with those, too, when they took the advent calendar."

He laughed.

"Why would the Secret Santas take your decorations?" he asked.

"For the same reason they would take the advent calendar?"

He furrowed his brow.

"Okay, okay, I know what you're going to say," she said. "They gave back the advent calendar. They took it so they could start this game, which, I must admit, is turning out to be fun. Even though, now that you reminded me of how this got started, it does make me want to put you back on the elf suspect list."

He put his arms around her again. "If you need to interrogate me further, I'm free for lunch."

She slid her arms around his waist. "I think I do."

He pulled her close and she slid her hands underneath his shirt and up his bare back, reveling at the brand-new feel of her hands on his skin. He dusted her lips with a feather-light kiss.

"I need to go into the office for a meeting," he said. "We always have a staff meeting on Monday mornings, but I'm free after that. I'll come back around noon and pick you up. We can go get some lunch and then go get that tree. After that, I'm at your mercy."

Chapter Nine

Tinsley Cove
Monday, December 4

After grabbing a quick lunch from Pascal's Deli, Forest and Avery picked out a tree and brought it back to his place, where Forest parked it in a bucket of water on the back deck so it could hydrate before he brought it inside.

"We can set it up after it soaks up some water," Forest said. "In the meantime, we can start decorating your tree. You look cold. Let's get you inside."

The wind blowing in off the water had turned chilly. Even though Avery was wearing jeans and a red-and-white Nordic-patterned sweater, she rubbed her hands on her forearms to stave off the chill. "I'll bet the temperature has dropped ten degrees since this morning.

I didn't realize it got this cold in Tinsley Cove in early December."

"It usually doesn't," Forest said. "In fact, there have been years when I've been swimming at this time of year, but sometimes it will surprise you."

He put his arm around her as they walked across the lawn toward Mistletoe Cottage.

"Were you able to find the ornaments?" Forest asked as they climbed the porch steps.

Avery shook her head and a shadow washed over her pretty face.

"What's going on?" he asked as they stopped at the front door.

"It seems so weird going through all of Gran's stuff. I'm having a hard time with that and I just realized why. Everything is exactly how she left it. It's as if she will be right back. I mean, I know she won't be back. I understand that, but it feels like once I start moving things around that's one less thing I have of her, one more part of her that's gone."

She shook her head and unlocked the door. "That's why I haven't made much progress in sorting through her things. I'm finding it all a bit overwhelming."

As he followed her into the living room, she made a sweeping with her hand. "See what I mean?"

She was right. The living room and what he could see of the other areas looked the same as they had a few nights ago, when he'd brought the Christmas tree.

"Would you rather buy some new ornaments for the tree?" he asked.

"No, that wouldn't make any sense at all," she said. "I just need to dig down deep and find my courage. I keep reminding myself that Gran loved Christmas, and she would've already had the entire house decorated by now."

Forest nodded. "Yes, she would've. I think she'd love the idea of you going all out and decorating like she used to. Do you want me to show you where I think her decorations would be?"

Avery took a deep breath and nodded. "Yes, let's do this."

The decorations were on a shelf in the garage, right where Forest had thought they'd be. As he took down each bin, he and Avery separated them into two groups: inside and outside.

"I used to love helping her put up the outside decorations," said Forest as they carried the tree decorations inside.

"You were so good to her, Forest." Avery set down a large plastic bin of ornaments on the floor near the Christmas tree. "I can't even begin to tell you how much I appreciate it. You don't know what I'd give for a do-over to set aside some time to spend Christmas with her. If I've learned anything, it's that you might think you have all the time in the world, that there's always tomorrow, then one day you wake up and realize that time doesn't wait for anyone. You have to seize the moment when you can and not wait until tomorrow."

He nodded as he plugged in the tree's lights. "I'm realizing that, too."

He wanted to remind her that same principle applied to love, too. As far as he was concerned, he'd lost her once and he wasn't going to let her slip away again, but she was opening up about her grandmother. It didn't seem right to shift the subject to them, to where they stood, when she was coming to terms with the task of sorting through Bess's belongings.

He opened a small box, found a plastic baggie filled with ornament hooks and set them on the coffee table. "These will come in handy."

Clearly, it wasn't the time to ask her what she was doing for the rest of her life. Although, it did dawned on him that after hearing her talk last night about how important it was for her to have a career so she could make her own way in the world, the key to making her want to stay was to find her a job locally. That would come, but first things first.

"Have you ever thought of going through and photographing each room in the house, capturing it exactly as Bess left it?"

Her face lit up.

"You're pretty amazing," she finally said. "As obvious as it seems, no, I hadn't thought about it. In fact, since losing my job, I haven't really been able to pick up the camera to capture much of anything."

Avery shrugged. "On one hand, it's my livelihood and the only thing I have left in the world, but on the other hand, I allowed it to dominate my life, costing me precious time with Gran."

Hearing her say her job was all she had left landed like a punch to the gut, but this wasn't about him.

"Don't beat yourself up over the past," he said. "Learn from it. The best medicine is to move forward."

"Says he who always seems to know the right thing to do." Avery smiled. "What's the biggest mistake you've ever made?"

Not finding out why you stopped talking to me all those years ago.

He shrugged. "I think I must have that condition where your mind blocks mistakes and embarrassing moments, because I can't think of any off the top of my head."

Avery's face fell and she turned her attention to hanging a delicate angel that was made out of blown glass. "Or maybe it's because you really are perfect."

"That's not fair," he said. "No one is perfect."

"I'm serious." As she turned to face him, the white twinkle lights illuminated the angel she'd just hung. "In high school you always had a reputation for being effortlessly…" She narrowed her eyes and moved her hand in a circle as she searched for a word. "The only word I can think of is perfect. Effortlessly perfect."

He started to protest, but she held up a hand.

"Let's see, you were the homecoming king, student body president and class valedictorian."

It hit him that for someone who claimed to not like him back in the day, she seemed to have memorized his precollege résumé.

"Now, you not only have a law degree, but you're the mayor of Tinsley Cove, you have a fabulous house, you work in high-end real estate and you're one of the stars of a television show. I mean, maybe you lead a charmed life, but that's not giving you the credit you deserve. A charmed life makes it sound like everything happens by happy accidents. I know you've worked hard for everything. It's just that from the outside looking in, you make it seem pretty darned effortless."

All this talk of perfection was hitting a sore spot.

People could tick off a laundry list of his so-called accomplishments, but no one seemed to realize that the only woman he'd ever loved remained just out of his reach. Didn't someone notable say that all the ac-complishments in the world didn't matter if a person didn't have someone special to share it with.

He knew he was truly blessed to have such a great family, but it was different than sharing his life with the love of his life.

"I'm changing the subject," Avery said as she threaded a wire hanger through a loop at the top of a toy-soldier ornament. "When I mentioned your television show a second ago, it reminded me of Gran telling me that she'd had a chance to be an extra in one of the episodes last year. I think it was one where the cast was having lunch at one of the local restaurants. Does that ring a bell?"

"It might've been when we filmed at Le Marais, ac-tually. I'm pretty sure it was the only time we filmed at a restaurant. It can be difficult to keep the set quiet when we shoot in a public place."

"I'm not sure if there's anything you can do, but I didn't get a chance to see the episode. She'd recorded it on her DVR and we were going to watch it when I was home for Thanksgiving—" Avery's voice cracked. "But I lost the recording when I canceled her cable. I didn't even think about it until it was too late."

"Let me talk to Dalton or one of his production as-sistants and I'll see if I can get you a copy."

Her face brightened. "Are you serious? I could buy it."

He waved her away. "It's no trouble at all." He held up a finger and smiled. "But I did just think of a way that you can repay me. The Sandcastle Real Estate Christ-mas party is Saturday night. Will you come with me?"

Tinsley Cove
Saturday, December 9

After a whirlwind week of cleaning, organizing and anticipating her date with Forest, the day arrived. Now, under an inky sky salted with stars, Avery took in the gorgeous landscape as Forest turned into a long driveway lined by neat rows of Italian cypress trees. She noted that the large wrought-iron gates through which they'd entered, and when closed probably hinted at seclusion and privacy, had been flung wide open, allowing tonight's guests easy access to Bert and Bunny McFadden's stately home. A few feet ahead, Avery spied an ornate, lighted fountain in the center of the circular driveway. It stood tall and proud, like a sentry guarding the sprawling Mediterranean mansion.

"Wow," Avery said as Forest steered the car under the porte cochere. "This is your parents' place? It looks like a resort. It's beautiful."

"It is."

"Did you grow up here?" She knew that many of the popular crowd who had shunned her in high school came from money, but for some reason she'd never pictured something quite this fancy. While Mistletoe Cottage was on the beach, the descriptor *cottage* was key. It was as homey as this place was elegant. It suddenly hit her that if she sold the house, there was a good chance that the buyer would level it and put in a beachfront McMansion.

"My parents built this place a few years after I went off to college. That's when the real-estate market started booming and my folks broke away and started their own agency."

"Where did you grow up?" Avery asked, suddenly aware she wasn't sure. After the Le Marais incident, she'd kept her head down for the rest of the year and did her best to learn as little as possible about her nemesis. Because what was the point? They were entitled children of privilege and she wasn't about to feed their egos with curiosity.

"We had a place over on the beach near Turtle Mound, about five miles from where we live."

So they hadn't grown up right next door to each other, but they'd only been separated by a stretch of beach. Back in the day, she hadn't gone down to the water much because her fair skin burned and that was a likely place that she'd run into the group that seemed to delight in making her miserable. Instead, she stayed safely behind her camera, building her portfolio, which would be her ticket out of Tinsley Cove.

Two valets opened their car doors. While one was helping Avery out, Forest was accepting a ticket and tipping the one who then slid behind the wheel and drove the white BMW away.

Avery smoothed the skirt of her winter white dress with the asymmetrical neckline. After Forest had invited her to the party, she'd realized she had nothing to wear, so she'd gone shopping.

Earlier this afternoon, when she was getting ready, she had a moment when she worried that she might be overdressed, but it was either the new dress or jeans. By that time, she'd already cut the tags off the garment, so she couldn't exchange it for something else even if she'd had time. So she'd finished her hair and makeup, which included a new lipstick in a deep cranberry-red, slid on the silver slingback heels the saleswoman had paired with the dress and hoped for the best.

The look on Forest's face when Avery had answered the door had been all the reassurance she'd needed. He'd been away since Tuesday on business. This was the first chance that they'd had to see each other since he'd gotten back.

Despite his encouraging words, as Avery held on to Forest's arm as they walked toward the front door, her stomach did a flip that made her pause.

"I'm a little nervous," she whispered.

"Don't be.

He was right. She shouldn't be nervous. She wasn't there to impress anyone. She was there because Forest had invited her. She'd never met Bert and Bunny Mc-Fadden, though she was about to tonight. From what she'd seen of them from afar and on a couple of episodes of *Selling Sandcastle*, they seemed like lovely, warm people. It was just…this house, and all these people, she didn't know.

They stepped through the home's front door, which, like the gates at the entrance to the property, stood open. A couple of cater waiters were stationed there to welcome guests with cocktails.

"Good evening, would you like to try a Sandcastle Snowstorm?" asked the guy closest to Avery. "It's tequila, cranberry juice and a splash of cava, and flavored with a holiday spiced simple syrup."

The tray of drinks looked beautiful and so festive. The concoctions were decorated with a sprig of rosemary, a cinnamon stick, a round of orange, and a cluster of candied cranberries. It almost looked too pretty to drink. Forest took two from the tray and handed her one.

"Thank you," he said to the server before touching his drink to Avery's, then they moved from the foyer into the living room, which was teeming with people.

More cater waiters were passing trays of hors d'oeuvres and a string quartet stationed in the corner played festive holiday music that seemed just right. It didn't overpower the convivial sounds of talking and laughter, but instead seemed to weave through the room and make the party all the merrier.

The ensemble made her think of the high-school group she'd seen in the Christmas-tree tent. She'd still been trying to come to terms with the turn their relationship seemed to be taking. Little did she know that night, when she'd run into him in the tent, that not only would she be out with him at a party, but the party would also be at his parents' home, and she'd be rubbing elbows with the type of people who once seemed like an impenetrable set.

An older woman with a stylish gray bob wearing a beautiful silver-beaded top over a long, black velvet skirt stopped Forest with a hand on his arm. "Merry Christmas, Mayor."

"Merry Christmas to you, Margaret," he said. "I'd like to introduce you to Avery Anderson. She's Bess Loughlin's granddaughter."

"Avery, it is so nice to meet you, darling," she said. "I just adored your grandmother. I'm so sorry for your loss. If you don't mind me saying so, it's a loss for the entire community."

"Thank you," Avery said.

As Margaret and Forest talked about the turnout for

the tree lighting, Avery thought about what a contrast she was to her grandmother. Gran was loved by the entire town just for being herself. She wasn't wealthy, but she'd been rich in good spirit, and generous and giving of her time.

Avery's personality tended to be more introverted than Gran used to be, and if Avery owned up to it, she'd also let a bad experience push her so far into her shell that it felt nearly impossible to crawl out. Well, a bad experience with a group of mean girls as she was dealing with the loss of her parents had wounded her. Then she'd taken a job that by nature was solitary and transient, and she'd never really learned how to let people in.

Even now, after people had been nothing but kind to her, her first instinct was to shut them out, to run so they couldn't get close enough to hurt her—because in her life, people hurt her one way or another, and out of self-preservation she'd learned it was best to shut them out before they could hurt her.

But then there was Forest. This guy had never given up on her, even after she'd spent most of her adult life thinking the worst of him and dodging him when she came to be with Gran at Thanksgiving. He had opened her eyes and shown her all she'd been missing out on.

"Well, it was lovely to meet you, Avery," said Margaret. "I hope to see you again. In the meantime, I'll let the two of you enjoy the party. Forest, your parents do know how to throw a soiree. They've outdone themselves this year. Try the crab puffs. They are delicious."

"On that recommendation, maybe we should track some down before they're gone," Forest said.

"There you are." Bert cuffed his son on the back.

"And you must be Avery. I've wanted to meet you. I was hoping Forest would bring you tonight."

Well, this is unexpected and more than a little thrilling, to receive such a warm welcome from Mr. McFadden.

They exchanged pleasantries, and then Bert and Forest talked about a house on Figure Eight Island for which Forest had successfully scheduled the closing. It was shoptalk and Avery half listened, catching words such as *all-cash deal*, *inspection* and *escrow*. Mostly, she watched as beautifully dressed women mingled with handsome men, and she thought about how this was a different side to Tinsley Cove than she was familiar with. She wondered if the McFadden's television show had raised the profile, or if this was just a world to which she'd never been privy.

"Avery, have you decided whether or not you're keeping your grandmother's house?"

Bert's question snapped Avery's attention back to the present.

"There's never been a better time to sell a piece of property like Mistletoe Cottage."

"I'm considering it, but I have some questions," Avery said.

Forest's eyes widened. "Really? I happen to know someone who might be able to answer those questions for you. I haven't wanted to hound you about it. But while we're on the subject, ask away."

"Forest had mentioned a couple of times that it's a good market to sell. I know this might sound crazy, but I'm hoping to sell it to someone—a family, maybe— who would be interested in living in it as is. I mean, with minimal improvements. I know they'd want to make the place their own. I'm worried that a developer might get a hold of it and tear it down."

Forest and Bert exchanged a look. The back of her throat burned with the words she didn't want to say, but she knew she needed to. She took a deep breath and swallowed before continuing. "I'm wondering if there's a way to ensure that if I did agree to sell that the buyer can't tear it down?"

"Mistletoe Cottage is sitting on a prime piece of land. The reality is the property is worth more as a buildable lot than…" Bert hesitated. "Please forgive me for my brutal honesty. I hope you won't take it personally, but the land is worth more than the small, outdated cottage."

His words stung. That was Gran's house. He was talking like it was an eyesore. She felt childish and a little petulant at the punch they packed. Still, she forced herself to check her emotion.

"So you're saying there's nothing I can do to preserve the place should I decide I want to sell?"

As she glanced from Bert to Forest, imploring him to reassure her, the *Selling Sandcastle* producer, Dalton Hart, joined them.

Forest said, "It is possible to write stipulations into a contract, such as it can't be torn down or the facade can't be altered too drastically for a certain number of years, but that will reduce the amount of money you can ask."

"Are you talking about that beachfront property?" said Dalton. "I understand that you're sitting on a gold mine, lucky lady. Sounds like a good time to sell. You could pocket a nice chunk of change. *Cha-ching. Cha-ching.* And if you'd like the sale to be on *Selling Sandcastle*, I can definitely make that happen."

Avery's jaw fell open, but she didn't know what to say. She shook her head.

Thank goodness, Forest stepped in. "Dalton, let's not. Okay?"

"I'm just offering. Don't get your back up. Okay?"

"Avery has not made any decisions on whether or not she wants to sell and we're not going to pressure her."

"Absolutely," said Bert. "Avery, I apologize. We didn't mean to make you feel uncomfortable. I just wanted you to know we're here for you should you need anything—whether it has to do with real estate or anything else. If you will excuse me, there's someone Dalton and I need to say hello to. I hope to see you again soon, Avery."

"It was nice to meet you, Mr. McFadden."

"Please, call me Bert."

"Thank you for having me tonight, Bert. It's a lovely party."

After they were out of earshot, Forest said, "I'm sorry about that. I did not mean for that to turn into a pressure pitch. I know my dad didn't, either. When it comes to the show, sometimes Dalton gets a bit over-zealous. I hope you'll excuse him. He didn't mean any harm."

"I understand," said Avery. "I was hoping for the best of both worlds. That there was a way I could sell yet still preserve Mistletoe Cottage, because it feels like it's all I have left of Gran. Now selling doesn't exactly feel like it would be the best of any world."

Forest shrugged. "I'll level with you. Despite all the real-estate shoptalk, I'm pulling for you to stay. Have you had a chance to figure out what it would take? I know you'd have to leave New York, but why not?"

Avery's head swam. He'd just said he wanted her to stay. She wanted to ask him why. Why did he want her to stay? But that felt too needy. "First of all, I need a job. I have to support myself. There's no mortgage, but there are property taxes, utilities, upkeep and the small matter of feeding myself."

"What if you got a job that allowed you to stay locally?" Forest asked.

"That certainly would help, but I can't say that I'm confident that jobs that I'm interested in are plentiful in North Carolina."

"What are your parameters? For a job?"

"I'd like for it to involve photography. A salary comparable to what I was making before would be nice."

"I don't know what you were making, but factor in that the cost of living in North Carolina will be considerably less than living in Manhattan."

"Good point. Although, I traveled a lot and had a per diem. So it might balance out."

"Give me a couple of days and I'll see what I can come up with."

Was he really offering to help find her a job? The burning question was…what would it mean for the two of them if she stayed?

"In the meantime, I'm behind five days on your Secret Santa advent-calendar adventure," he said. "What have the Secret Santas dished up for you since I've been gone?"

"Who has a Secret Santa?" Avery turned to see Kaitlyn, who was joined by Lucy and Sophie.

In heels, Kaitlyn stood well over six feet tall, making her tower over Avery, Lucy and Sophie, and putting her at eye level with Forest. In the sleek red dress that was cut up to her hip, she looked every bit the glamorous fashion model.

"It's true, I seem to have attracted a Secret Santa and if I take the notes this, er, Santa leaves literally, I might even have a whole team of them."

The women laughed. "What do you mean?"

Avery narrowed her eyes at Kaitlyn. "It's not you, is it?"

Kaitlyn shook her head. "Me? Hardly, I was in Los Angeles until yesterday trying to work through some things with a potential business partner. So it wasn't me. Although, I wish I would've thought of it because being someone's Secret Santa and bringing them joy sounds like a lot of fun."

"What have they brought you?" Sophie asked.

"Well, they're not actually giving me gifts. Not the material kind, anyway. It's more like Christmas themed challenges and tasks."

It dawned on Avery that the Santa collective might be Kaitlyn, Lucy, Sophie and Cassie, whom Avery had just spotted across the room with a good-looking guy who looked a lot like Forest, only a more casual version. That had to be his younger brother, Logan, who was engaged to Cassie. The four of them could've easily delivered the envelopes while Avery was gone.

However, since Kaitlyn had admitted to having a thing for Forest the day she and Avery met, it was hard to believe she'd facilitate Avery kissing someone under the mistletoe since Forest was the closest likely recipient of said kiss.

Even if Kaitlyn didn't have anything to do with it, that didn't mean that Cassie, Sophie and Lucy didn't. For that matter, the Santa, or Santas, could be anyone in this room. So many people had loved Bess that it didn't seem farfetched that they'd do this for Avery as a way to honor Bess.

"I'm eager to hear this, too," Forest said. "What have the last five days held?"

The new friends listened with interest as Avery said, "Tuesday's task was listen to Christmas music. Check. That was easy and I enjoyed it. Wednesday, I had to hang up Christmas stockings. Thursday, I had to hang a wreath on the door, but I'd already done that on Monday when Forest helped me with the rest of the decorations."

That declaration garnered some raised eyebrows from the women. Avery saw Kaitlyn flinch and blink.

"It sounds as if the two of you are hanging out a lot," she said. First, her gaze searched Avery's face, as if looking for clues about the relationship. Then she looked at Forest. For a moment, Avery was paralyzed. Then she braced herself for—for what? She wasn't quite sure. Kaitlyn seemed like she had too much class to cause a scene over a guy at the Sandcastle Real Estate Christmas party, but it seemed like she might have a thing for Forest and she seemed like the kind of woman who was used to getting what she wanted.

Avery's gaze tracked to people parting to allow something bulky and shiny to move through the arched doorway from the foyer into living room. It was one of the cameras they used to film *Selling Sandcastle*. She felt the blood drain to her feet and her flight sensation kick in.

Please tell me this is not a staged scene where two women fight over Forest.

It felt like the makings for a setup.

Then again, the camera was a little late to capture the so-called drama.

As Avery turned to Forest to hear his answer, it felt like it was becoming more of a moment of truth. If Forest had been stringing her and Kaitlyn along, or if he'd shown interest in her before Avery arrived—over a week ago—now was the time for it all to come out.

Her stomach dipped because she realized that she didn't want to learn he was a player. But better to know now than to get even more invested…if that was possible.

"Yes, we have been spending time together and I hope we will spend a lot more time together," he said.

This time all of the blood in Avery's body rushed to her cheeks. As Kaitlyn turned to her, Avery took a long sip of her drink, hoping to give her flaming face a chance to cool off.

"Then I guess that means I shouldn't ask you to the Poinsettia Ball," Kaitlyn said.

Forest looked from Kaitlyn to Avery, then back at Kaitlyn. The look on his face suggested that he was the one who wanted to run.

Then Kaitlyn said, "Just kidding. But the look on your face was priceless."

Avery was beginning to realize that Kaitlyn got a charge out of putting people on the spot. Not in a mean-spirited way, but in a manner that wasn't entirely comfortable. She could see that this conversation might be headed in an uncomfortable direction.

In an effort to redirect, Avery asked, "Did I mention that yesterday's task was to make paper snowflakes? Ironically, today's was to attend a Christmas party, which makes me think that my Secret Santas might be in this room, since this party was conveniently happening tonight."

As the others made sounds of surprise, Avery caught the look of disappointment in Kaitlyn's eyes, even though she was making a valiant effort to breeze over the exchange like it hadn't meant anything to her. Avery knew that look because she knew what it was like to have your soul crushed and have to pretend like you were fine.

As a man in a red plaid suit engaged Forest in conversation, Kaitlyn said, "I need another drink. If you all will excuse me."

"I do, too," Avery said. "Mind if I come with?"

"Sure, come on," Kaitlyn said. "Anyone else?"

Lucy and Sophie shook their heads. "We'll catch up with you in a minute."

Linking her arm through Avery's, they made their way through the crowd to the bar. As they were waiting in line, Avery took a deep breath and went for it.

"Kaitlyn, I've only been here a little over a week and if there was something budding between you and Forest, I don't want to get in the middle of it. I can bow out. Because—"

She was about to say "because friendship. Or at least the promise of friendship. The whole ovaries before brovaries thing." It had been so long since she'd had girlfriends—real friends to hang out with, it felt important to not encroach on what Kaitlyn might consider her territory.

But Kaitlyn said, "Honey, I have done everything short of tap-dance naked in front of that man to get him to notice me and he has never looked at me the way he looks at you. So you are not coming between anything except me and a situation that is never going to happen, but I appreciate you being concerned. Despite him, I think you and I are going to be good friends. You know what? The girls and I are having a little holiday get-together next weekend. We are meeting at my house for drinks and a white-elephant gift exchange and then we're going out to the Rusty Anchor to sing some Christmas karaoke. Why don't you join us?"

"Oh, that's very sweet of you. Thank you, but—"

"But nothing. I want you to come. In fact, if you want to make it up to me for stealing my crush, you'll go out and buy some kind of a cheesy gift that no one would want to get stuck with and brush up on your best 'Santa Baby' belting skills, and be at my place next Saturday at six o'clock."

It had been such a long time since Avery had even had girlfriends. Her parents had moved around a lot throughout her childhood and teenage years. Then, after the accident, when she had moved to Tinsley Cove, she'd cloaked herself in the attitude that it wasn't worth it to get close to people because they either left you or hurt you, one way or another. Gran was the only person she could count on and now she was gone, too.

Avery understood that death was a fact of life. Now that she was really and truly alone in this world—and even her job had failed her—she also realized that relationships were a two-way street. That if she invested in the right people, she didn't have to walk through this world alone.

Maybe it was time to rethink her I-am-an-island rule.

Later, they drove home, past the cheerful houses adorned with vibrant lights and festive decorations—

an inflatable Santa on a surfboard on a rooftop, animated deer raising and lowering their heads and a faux snowman stationed next to a larger-than-life snow globe that was raining snowflakes on an idyllic park scene. It seemed as if warmth emanated from most of the windows.

He glanced over at Avery, who was staring out the passenger-side window, and wished that she could see Tinsley Cove through his eyes, that this place could feel like home to her, too.

"The lights are pretty, huh?"

She smiled at him. "It's nice how everyone goes all out for the holidays with all their lights and decorations. New York has fabulous windows, but here... It's different. It's homier. In New York, the decorations are first-class, but here...it feels more accessible."

He reached out and took her hand and they rode in silence until they turned into his driveway.

"I had a good time tonight," Avery said as they sat in the car listening to the motor's pings and sighs. "It was nice to meet your parents. They're wonderful."

"Thanks," he said. "I think so. They've been a good example for my siblings and me. Showing us if you work hard and set your mind to something, you can achieve it. Speaking of, would you go to the ball with me?"

Avery gave him the side-eye.

"What is that face for?" he asked.

"It's for the *speaking of* that preceded your invitation. You said, 'If you work hard and set your mind to something you can achieve it.' Then you said, 'Speaking of.' Then you asked me to the ball."

"I suppose the working-hard part doesn't apply, but

the 'setting your mind to something' does. I've set my mind to taking you to the Poinsettia Ball. By the way, I like how you listen."

She laughed. "Don't try to change the subject by complimenting my listening skills. That was a great try, but I'm on to you."

He opened his mouth to protest or say something—anything except how hard he'd fallen for her—but she pressed her fingers to his lips. "No, in all seriousness, I'd love to go to the ball with you, but what exactly is the Poinsettia Ball?"

"It's a charity event—actually, this year is the fifth anniversary of the ball's inception. It raises money for kids and families in need at the holidays," said Forest. "It's a lot of fun, if you like to get dressed up and eat good food and drink good wine. In addition to the price of the tickets, each person brings an unwrapped toy that will be donated to a child in need. Traditionally, the ticket price provides holiday meals for families and the toys provide a nice Christmas morning for kids who might not get something otherwise."

"That sounds nice," Avery said, laying her head back on the headrest and glancing at him. She looked so sexy, it was all he could do to keep from leaning in and kissing her. Hell, it was all he could do to keep from covering her body with hers and taking her right then and there.

"I suppose the next thing you're going to tell me is that you're one of the founders of the Poinsettia Ball."

She smiled, and the full moon caught the mischief sparkling in her eyes.

"Would that be a bad thing?" he asked.

She sat up. "Oh, my gosh, of course you did. Of

course you're one of the founders. Really, I was teasing when I asked, but now that I think about it, something like that has Forest McFadden's fingerprints all over it. And it's a really great thing."

He shrugged, not quite sure what to say.

She reached out and slowly traced a finger over his jawline.

"You really are a good man, Forest."

He took her hand and brought her finger to his lips. He kissed it and then gently nipped at the tip of it. Avery sucked in a breath, then drew her bottom lip between her teeth, releasing it on the exhale.

He leaned over and kissed her deeply, as if both of their last breaths were dependent on their joining. His body was craving a lot more than a kiss.

He didn't want to push her or rush things. He wanted her to want it as much as he did.

A moment later, he said, "One of the things about being the mayor—actually, one of the things about living in a town like this—is the trees seem to have eyes. Would you like to come inside?"

Tilting her head back, she pierced him with a provocative smile that hinted at all sorts of promises he hoped she would keep.

Chapter Ten

Tinsley Cove
Saturday, December 9

Once inside Forest's house, with the door closed between them and the outside world, Avery wasn't surprised when Forest pulled her into his arms. Nor was she surprised when she didn't want to push him away.

On the contrary, as his mouth closed over hers, she wanted to pull him closer.

All night—actually, longer than that...since she'd arrived in Tinsley Cove—she'd felt a change coming on. A need to be close to Forest, to let him in, despite the warning that sounded in her head, something inside her had shifted.

Her heart was winning. Her heart wanted her to trust him, because she wanted...him. She didn't know where this was going, but one thing she'd realized since reuniting with Forest was that the future wasn't a given, that you had to seize every opportunity.

Now, as he kissed her, she understood what that meant. She was finally letting go of the doubts and fears and walls that she'd erected around her heart. All the uncertainty was drifting away like loose sand in the pull of high tide. This was what it felt like to yearn for a man. To want him, to be consumed with need for him, with little thought for tomorrow. But what was tomorrow? All she had, all that was real, was right now.

A warning voice whispered in the back of her head, telling her to be cautious, to guard her heart, to run. But it couldn't compete with the need for him that was growing inside her, making her feel things in places that she thought were dead. That voice was growing ever fainter, until her need drowned it out.

There was nothing but him and his mouth on hers, his hands on her body and an all-consuming desire that was driving them to a place that felt like destiny.

She slipped her hands under his jacket and explored his muscled back, working her way around to his flat stomach. She pushed off his coat, letting it fall to the floor so she could touch his biceps and his shoulders... loving the way he felt, from the vee of his waist all the way up to the shadowed ruggedness of his face.

He kissed her again and when he finally eased away from her, he rested his forehead on hers.

"Are you okay?" he asked.

"*Mmm...* I've never been better."

"Can you stay?" he asked.

The question should've been sobering, it should've righted her thoughts and squared up her world, which felt as though it had been tipped on its axis. But it did

none of those things. Stunned by the clarity of her feelings, she reached out and cupped his face in her hands.

"Yes," she whispered. To prove this, she moved closer
and wrapped her arms tightly around him. She kissed
him, opening her mouth to invite his tongue inside,
and he accepted the invitation. As he walked her back
against the door, she heard his guttural groan over the
rush of blood in her ears, and the sound of his desire set
her further adrift in the ocean of need.

She needed him.

"I've wanted this for so long," he said. "Every time
I'm near you all I can think of is how much I want to
hold you and never let go."

His words took away her breath.

"I love how we're on the same wavelength, because
I want you, too."

"Yeah?"

Before she could answer him, he scooped her up in
his arms and again he covered her lips with his, only
this time, as he carried her up the stairs, his kiss had
changed from tender to passionate.

All she could think of was how the sensual joining of their mouths foretold what was to come. The
thought of Forest's body joining with hers sent heat
radiating from the most private parts of her. White-
hot desire coursed through her, heating her skin and
causing her heart to beat a fierce staccato that sounded
like…*finally, finally, finally.*

The axis of Forest's priorities and plans had shifted.
With Avery back in Tinsley Cove, everything seemed
different.

He couldn't remember ever wanting a woman the way

he wanted Avery. Raw desire shot through him, feeding the fire deep in his loins that had been burning like a low-grade fever since that day he first saw her standing on the front porch of Mistletoe Cottage.

After they'd leveled with each other and sorted out the misunderstanding, it hadn't taken long to untangle the complicated knot of feelings swirling through him. Though he was still trying to understand what he would do about those feelings, he knew one thing for certain—this wasn't just his body needing a release.

This was something that felt a lot like love.

Or at least what he'd imagined it would feel like.

He'd never been in love before—he'd certainly never felt like this—and he was marveling at the realization that this was what it felt like. The soul-driving desire and need, the protectiveness of her, the vulnerability that stemmed from opening himself to someone this way.

He needed to not think about that right now.

He needed to stop thinking. Period. All he wanted was to feel the exquisite pleasure of having her body next to his.

He eased her down onto the bed and made quick work of unzipping her dress. The bodice gave way, leaving her in her lacy, flesh-tone strapless bra. The sight of her sent a racking shudder through his body and he drew in a deep breath to steady himself. As he eased her back on the bed, he made quick work of sweeping away the garment, leaving her in her bra and tiny panties.

He wanted to do away with those, too. He wanted to pull her into his arms and bury himself inside her, but he needed to slow down.

They had all night… The rest of their lives.

She was worth the wait.

The room was softly lit by a slant of moonlight shining off the ocean and in through the bedroom window. His gaze drifted down the length of her stretched out on his bed. She looked like she belonged there, like she was the missing piece. With his eyes, he worshipped her compact, curvy body. She was everything he'd thought she would be hidden under the clothes. In fact, she was even more beautiful. Much, much more beautiful, he realized as he lowered himself onto the bed next to her, barely brushing against her.

Still, the contact was combustible.

Closing the scant distance between them, he pulled her into his arms and claimed her lips. She responded by moving her hips so that they were square to his, which shook up all the want and longing that had been bottling up.

He helped her out of her bra and dipped his head in reverence, his lips finding her neck. He trailed kisses until his mouth closed over a nipple. She gasped.

The sound of her pleasure fed his want. He pulled away, only to roll her onto her back so he could stretch out on top of her. Even through his clothes and her panties, he could feel how perfectly their bodies joined together.

"Are you sure about this?"

She nodded, then kissed him on the mouth.

He slid off her panties.

While his hands explored the hills and valleys of her curves and the firm length of her muscled legs, his lips and tongue made love to her breasts.

Soon, she was impatiently pulling at his clothes, unbuttoning his shirt and tugging it off. He pulled back and put just enough space between them that she could unbuckle his belt and unzip his fly. Together, they got rid of his pants and freed him of his boxers.

She reached out and brushed her fingertips over him. His body shuddered. He inhaled a sharp breath into his lungs, and his head fell back slightly.

She stroked him as if she was learning every inch of him, committing it to memory, and driving him crazy in the process. He didn't let her linger for long. He couldn't take it.

He settled into the cradle of her hips and entered her with a tender push.

Every nerve ending exploded, intensifying the way the heat that radiated from her body seeped into his, how the two of them were fused so closely together that it seemed that they were joined, body and soul.

As she followed his lead in a slow, rocking rhythm that gradually intensified, soon their bodies carried them over the edge.

She curled into him and he pulled her close. As they lay together, breathless, sweaty and spent, three words raced around his head, dipping into his heart, trying to find their way to his mouth.

Ah, man... Don't do that. Not yet. It will spoil every-thing.

It would scare her away.

Not only that, but if he was smart, he'd also take a step back and make sure he wasn't caught up in the moment.

He was sure that wasn't the case, but he'd never told a woman he loved her. He'd never even been tempted.

Don't say things you don't mean. He needed to be one-hundred-percent sure.

But he knew he meant it.

He was in love with Avery. Always had been.

Even so, talking the talk and walking the walk were two very different things. He needed to make sure he could give her everything she needed.

Tinsley Cove
Saturday, December 16

When Avery arrived at Kaitlyn's house for their girls' night out, Kaitlyn handed her a cosmopolitan and a pointed question as Sophie, Lucy and Cassie closed ranks.

"So what's happening with you and Hottie McTottie next door?"

Avery should've been prepared for this because it was bound to come up.

"Are you blushing?" Kaitlyn asked. "Whoa, this looks good."

"This is my brother you're talking about," Sophie said, holding up a hand. "I don't want to know."

"He's my cousin," said Lucy.

"He's my future brother-in-law," said Cassie. "So, no relation yet. Which means, there is no harm in me hearing all the sordid details. Spill it, Avery."

Avery sipped her drink, trying to buy time and hoping against hope that her entire face wasn't the same shade as her drink.

"Did you sleep with him?" Kaitlyn demanded.

Avery snorted into her drink and then choked when the vodka went down the wrong pipe.

The truth was, they'd spent every night together for the past week. In fact, Avery was surprised that Kaitlyn hadn't caught one of them doing the early morning walk of shame, even if it was only next door.

Then again, maybe she had and this was her sly way of making Avery confess without Kaitlyn outing herself as the neighborhood busybody. Which brought Avery full circle. Just because Kaitlyn was asking a question—and a rather nosy one at that—didn't mean that Avery had to answer.

However, since four pair of eyes were waiting for her to answer, she figured she'd better say something.

"He's a great guy. We are enjoying each other's company."

Kaitlyn's eyes widened. "Is that what you're calling it? Okay, whatever."

"I do have to say that he seems happier than I've seen him in a long time," said Sophie. "It's good to see him smile."

It dawned on Avery how little she knew about Forest's past relationships. She'd wondered when they'd first started talking, but this past week, he'd made her feel as if she was the center of his universe—in and out of the bedroom. Ghosts of girlfriends past had been the furthest thing from Avery's mind.

Now she was curious.

It would be a great time to ask questions, but was it a good idea?

As if reading her mind, Sophie volunteered, "You know, Avery, it's been a long time since Forest has brought a woman home."

"Well, I don't know if I'd call a Christmas party bringing me home. Sure, technically, the party was at your house—"

"And he did introduce you to the folks. Bert and

Bunny had only good things to say about you, by the way."

They did?

The thought warmed Avery from the inside out, but then again, she hadn't talked to them much. Just a passing introduction to his mother, where Avery had told her that the party was lovely. Then there was the awkward exchange about Mistletoe Cottage with his father.

She blinked away the uncomfortable feeling.

"They're so nice," Avery said. "It was great to meet them. Even if it was in passing."

"Just wait," said Cassie. "I'm sure Bunny will invite you to one of the famous McFadden family dinners soon enough."

The thought both thrilled and terrified Avery, because she wasn't used to so much closeness. The sheer size of the McFadden family was a little daunting, too. Though that could work in her favor. The bigger the crowd, the less she'd have to say to keep up with everyone.

"Let's take our drinks into the living room," Kaitlyn said as she donned potholders and took a crock of baked brie out of the oven. "Lucy, would you grab that basket of crackers and someone else can take in the tray of crudités."

Avery picked up the vegetables and followed her friends into the living room, which had been decorated within an inch of its life. Where Kaitlyn's and Forest's houses were more modern, having been built in the past five years, Mistletoe Cottage was one of the few older houses on the beachfront.

Kaitlyn's living room had tall ceilings and a wall of windows that lined the back wall, which looked

over the ocean and provided the perfect backdrop for
the large Christmas tree that was the centerpiece of
the room.

The mantel of the gas fireplace was draped with
garland and gilded magnolia blossoms. A herd of min-
iature golden deer had been interspersed throughout
the garland, making it look like the tiny animals were
grazing.

After everyone was settled on the sofa and chairs
that held funky holiday pillows, no doubt part of Kaitlyn's novelty home line, she said, "Before we get to the
silly gifts, I have something special for each of you. I
want you to open it first."

Kaitlyn pulled four identically sized, but festively
wrapped, packages out from under the tree. She looked
at the tags and passed them out accordingly.

"Wait until everyone has a present before you open
yours," Kaitlyn said. "Because even though they're
different, they're kind of the same."

After Kaitlyn gave the okay, they tore into their
packages to discover gorgeous blouses designed by
their hostess. While the cat-and-dog ugly Christmas
sweaters had been fun and kitschy, the blouses were
feminine, elegant and thoughtfully designed with each
friend's personality in mind.

The pink floral print that Avery received was what
Kaitlyn called a convertible blouse.

"That thin line of smocking around the top allows
you to wear it on or off the shoulders," she said proudly.
"So when you want to heat things up with Mr. Man,
you can show him a sexy slice of shoulder."

Avery's mind tripped back to the nights that they'd
been spending together this week, where clothing was

the last thing that had been on their minds. She forced away the image of being skin-on-skin with Forest and waking up early just to watch him sleep...and to test herself to see if that old familiar panic was lurking on the periphery.

It wasn't. At least, not yet.

Sometimes Avery felt as if she was hiding out in Tinsley Cove because this wasn't real life. Surely, real life would catch up with her sooner or later...wouldn't it?

A little voice deep inside that she almost didn't recognize said, *I hope not. Maybe for once I could be happy.*

Speaking of happy, Avery was happy she'd picked up a hostess gift of a cheese board and knife set in addition to the questionable photorealistic throw blanket that looked like a tortilla and was supposed to make the recipient resemble a human burrito when they rolled up in it.

It was totally unappetizing. It looked like it should smell like a burrito smelled, which was fine if it was, in fact, an actual burrito, but was wholly unpleasant if it was associated with a person wrapped in a blanket.

And why had she picked that out?

At least Kaitlyn's hostess gift made sense. She liked to entertain and the cheeseboard would be perfect. Now, if Avery could get through the white-elephant portion of the evening without getting stuck with the burrito banket. *Hmm...* Could she get stuck with her own gift? She wasn't quite sure of white elephant rules and didn't want to whip out her phone and look it up.

"Update us on the Secret Santas," said Lucy. "Any idea who they are?"

"Not a clue," Avery said. "But they've been delivering their notes right on schedule.

"Interestingly enough, one of the tasks this week was to sing Christmas karaoke. I figured that since that was on the schedule for tonight, I could get away with doing two tasks in one day."

Avery narrowed her eyes at her friends. "I found it quite interesting that you all were among the few who knew I was doing Christmas karaoke tonight. Would the real Secret Santa please stand up?"

Sophie snorted. "Honey, in addition to the tree lighting and your grandma's cookie-swap party, Christmas karaoke is one of the holiday standards around here."

Avery's heart squeezed at the mention of Gran's cookie-swap party.

"Have you given any thought about carrying on her tradition?" Lucy asked. "It was always a lot of fun."

She had given exactly zero thought to the cookie swap because, true to her nature, it seemed like the more she avoided thinking about the fact that Gran was gone, the easier it was for her to get by—to not think about what a failure of a granddaughter she'd been, about not having a job, about what she was going to do about the house that she would soon not be able to afford if she didn't get said job.

She may have thought she'd been loosening up and letting people in, but maybe this was all just an excuse to not face the hard questions in her life that were unanswered right now. Sort of a reverse of how she used to run away from life's hard parts. Now it was as if she was sheltering in place—avoiding the pain, but going nowhere.

Later, when they finally arrived at the Rusty Anchor, which was located on the Intracoastal Waterway, it was a full house and the party was at full throttle.

The bar's rough-hewn edges had aged to a glorious patina that gave the impression that the place could've been as old as the beach itself, but in December, the place was transformed into what could be best described as holiday beach-dive decor. An aluminum Christmas tree was decked out with pink-flamingo ornaments wearing Santa hats. Avery fit right in wearing the hot pink Santa hat with a tiara sewn on it—it was the white-elephant gift she'd ended up receiving. Kaitlyn had scored the burrito blanket and seemed elated.

On second thought, Avery wasn't surprised she'd liked it, given her neighbor's appreciation of tacky kitsch. The burrito had found its perfect home.

This was what it was like to have friends. At times, it still seemed like a shoe was going to drop. Like they would realize she was a piece of work, she was too much work and wasn't worth loving. But no matter how tempted she was to push them away, she wouldn't allow herself to do it.

The quintet was taking their turn on stage doing their best *Mean Girls* impression with an eardrum-splitting rendition of "Jingle Bell Rock," when Avery spied Forest standing in the back of the bar, holding a beer and drinking in their performance. For the briefest moment, she wanted to melt into the craggy wooden floorboards, but then she saw the look on his face.

She recalled what Kaitlyn had said last week at the McFadden's cocktail party that "he has never looked at me the way he looks at you."

Rather than shrinking away, she held his gaze like she never wanted to let him go and put all of herself into the song.

Forest and Logan met them at the table. Logan

dipped Cassie into a kiss that had her friends hooting and whistling. Avery was glad that Forest was being conservative.

"Get a room, y'all," Kaitlyn called. "What are you guys here doing crashing our girls' night, anyway?"

"I'm here to buy the next round," Forest said.

"In that case, what took you so long to get here?" Cassie said. "Besides, the sign-up list to sing is so long that I doubt we'll get another chance to sing before last call."

After they ordered the drinks, Cassie, Logan and Sophie were deep in conversation about the couple's wedding, which would happen next summer, and Lucy and Kaitlyn were flirting with the guys at the next table. Forest leaned in and said to Avery, "I'm also here because I have something for you. I guess it could've waited until you got home, but I wasn't sure what time that would be and I have to go into the office early." He shrugged. "I couldn't wait to give it to you."

He pulled a tiny computer flash drive out of his jacket pocket and handed it to her.

"What's this?" she asked.

"It's the episode of *Selling Sandcastle* that your Gran was in."

Chapter Eleven

Tinsley Cove
Saturday, December 16

Avery rode home with Forest, knowing the simple action of leaving with him would answer her friends' burning questions about the nature of their relationship. The best part was she wouldn't have to say a word.

No, the best part was that she was going home with a kind, caring, thoughtful man who was not only breaking down her walls, but was also winning her heart.

The realization both delighted her and scared her to death. She knew she was taking a risk letting herself be this vulnerable to him. She was opening herself up to a potential world of hurt, because everyone she'd ever loved or trusted had either let her down, or left her. Whether their leaving had been their choice or not, it had always been untimely and unexpected, and each time it happened, they took a little piece of her with them.

After losing Gran, she believed she might not have anything left of herself to give to someone. But now that she and Forest had settled the score of the past, it was as if her heart had regenerated and grown almost whole again. Now, here she was slowly edging closer to letting herself fall again.

After he parked in his driveway, he walked around and opened her car door.

How could she not fall for him? Every day, Forest was proving himself to be kinder, gentler and more caring than the day before.

Did he have any idea how deeply it touched her that he'd followed through on getting her the copy of Gran's appearance on the show?

"Forest, I really appreciate you getting me the episode. It means so much to me."

She'd mentioned it once. She didn't even have to remind him or... Well, her mind had no expectations, he had far exceeded the hope that might've been buried deep in her heart.

"If you need some time alone to watch the video, I understand," he said as they stood in his driveway facing each other. "I can go."

She considered it for a moment. It would be a deeply private moment. She had no idea how she would react when she saw Gran looking so happy and so...alive, except that she knew she would cry. That was a given, because she was already tearing up just thinking about it.

Could he handle her emotions? Even more, did she want to share that most intimate, vulnerable part of herself with him?

She took hold of both of his hands and gave them a squeeze. "I'd love it if you would watch it with me." She hesitated. "But I would like to watch it at Gran's house. She has a computer and it seems important to watch it there."

He nodded. "I'm sure Mistletoe Cottage will always feel like Gran's house to you, but it's okay for you to claim it as your own. I'll bet Bess would want it that way."

She knew he meant well, but it gave her pause. It seemed like an odd thing to say and she couldn't help but wonder if he thought she needed to accept the place as her own before she could make peace with selling it.

As they started walking toward Mistletoe Cottage, she had all but decided to put it out of her mind, but with each step she took toward the house, it nagged at her, irritated her like a pebble in her shoe.

"Why is that important?" she asked as they reached the porch.

He shot her a confused grin. "Why is what important?"

"Calling Mistletoe Cottage my house and not Gran's house? She and my grandfather bought and worked so hard to pay for this place. The only reason it's come into my possession is because neither of them is here anymore to look after it."

Forest held up his hands. "I didn't mean to upset you. I was just trying to say it's okay for you to call it your own."

He seemed sincere and she was a little embarrassed to have let her emotions jump to the wrong conclusion.

"I know it is," she said. "It's just such a strange position to be in. This place meant the world to Gran and sometimes it feels like I have no right to it. She and Grandpa Tom bought the house in the late 1960s after they were married. It had been Gran's dream to live at the beach and my grandpa made sure her dream had come true. Gran used to love to tell the story of how buying this place meant that she had to work outside the home for them to afford it, which was different for that time and this town, where most of the moms stayed home with their kids."

It was true, but Gran had always said she didn't mind a single day that she worked at the Tinsley Cove Library. She retired in 2010.

Avery shrugged. "That's why it feels so important to do right by this place, but I'm sort of caught between a rock and a hard place. I'm unemployed, which means I can't afford it. If I get a job, it will likely mean I'll have to live out of town. I don't know that I can keep two places, but I don't feel right selling it after my grandparents worked so hard for it."

Forest pulled her into his arms and held her for the longest time.

"I think I'm going to wait to watch the video when I'm fresh," she said. "It's just a lot. A lot to process. A lot to figure out. I'm not just talking about simply watching the recording of Gran. Christmas is nine days away and I'd promised myself I'd have things figured out by the end of the month...or at least I'd have the house sorted out and I haven't even started. I think I need some time tonight to clear my head. Can I see you tomorrow?"

He nodded. "Of course. I have a showing in the morning, but I should be home by noon."

A tear slipped out of her eye and rolled down her cheek. As she reached up to swipe it away, he pulled her close.

"I know it's overwhelming, but it's going to be okay. You have to believe that. Get a good night's sleep and things will look a lot better tomorrow morning."

She buried her face in his chest and took sanctuary in his strong arms, trying to absorb his confidence.

Tinsley Cove
Sunday, December 17

Forest arrived at the Sandcastle Real Estate office well before the clients were scheduled to show up. He had picked up bagels and fruit salad, and put on coffee to brew.

He was in the process of reviewing the order in which he'd take the clients to view the houses when his cell phone rang.

"Good morning," Forest said to his father.

"Good morning to you," said Bert. "Is this a good time?"

"It's a perfect time. What's up?"

"I have some good news on the photography job you asked me about, but it may come with a little catch."

"What is the catch?"

Why did even the simplest thing have to come with a catch?

He rubbed his tired eyes. He hadn't slept well last night after leaving Avery as upset as she was. It had been her choice for them to sleep solo and, of course, he'd honored that. It was just that even though it had been a short time that they'd been together, he was getting used to her beautiful face being the first thing he saw when he opened his eyes in the morning.

"Dalton said there's money in the budget to make

another person a cast member. He likes Avery's spunk and the chemistry between the two of you. There's that and so that she'll have a purpose on the show beyond arm candy, he wants us to use her talents to photograph real estate listings for Sandcastle Real Estate as we have listings come available. At least for this season. Before we offer it to her, I wanted to check in with you to hear your thoughts?"

Forest blew out a breath as his mind raced through the pros and cons of Dalton's offer.

"So…you said it's a temporary position?"

"Yes, she would be an independent contractor doing work for us and we'd pay her as we would pay any other photographer we might hire. Dalton would offer her a standard contract to be a cast member for one season on the show with the possibility of being renewed next season, but he'll cross that bridge when we get there. That's Dalton's way of giving himself an out, if for some reason she doesn't fit in, but he likes her energy and the two of you together, and he saw her with Lucy, Cassie and Sophie at the party. And who's the tall woman?"

"That's Kaitlyn. I sold her the house on the other side of Mistletoe Cottage. Why?"

"Dalton mentioned getting her in more scenes, but he doesn't want to bring her on permanently. I think he believes she might be a good catalyst for drama."

Forest groaned. "I don't know."

"What? Do you not want Avery to be on the show?"

"It's not that. I'm…" He spun his pen on the desk as he weighed his words. "She's a photojournalist. She's traveled all over the world. Would it be insulting to ask her to photograph real estate listings?"

Bert was quiet for a few beats. "You said she needed a job."

"Yes, I did." Forest drummed his fingers on the desk. "I'm also realizing I'm not sure how much longer I want to be on the show myself. I'm not cut out for manufactured drama and that seems to be the life-blood of reality television."

"It is what it is," said Bert. "I do it because it makes your mother happy and I suppose I don't really mind it. But you're not having fun, are you?"

"Originally, I agreed to do this for the same reason you did. To make mom happy. To give her something to look forward to while she was so sick. She's better now and I'm thinking it's time I moved on."

"Are you thinking of quitting midseason?"

"No. I'll honor my commitment and finish out the season."

Of course he would. He'd spent his entire life living up to the expectations of others. For a fleeting moment, he pondered what it would be like to do something crazy. To put his finger on a map, grab Avery and take off with only the clothes on their backs. The reality was he wasn't capable of being that spontaneous.

"I guess it's decent money for the work," he said. "Avery needs something now. I'll run it by her and let her decide?"

Tinsley Cove
Sunday, December 17

The next morning when Avery woke up, the first thing she did was reach out to find Forest, but when she opened her eyes, she realized she was alone in her bed in Mistletoe Cottage.

It was the first time that they'd slept apart since they'd made love. It was also the first time that she'd slept in her bed at Gran's house since her relationship with Forest had changed. She was thirty-two years old, but Gran had been old-fashioned. It didn't just feel as if having Forest in her bed would be disrespectful to her grandmother, it also felt as if she would lose her sanctuary if she invited Forest up here.

However, she realized Forest was right. Last night, it felt like the weight of the world had been on her shoulders, but this morning, she somehow felt lighter, if not a little bit foolish for the tsunami of emotions that had crested and spilled out after he'd been nothing but wonderful to her.

She felt like she knew him well enough to believe that his comment about her accepting Mistletoe Cottage as her own wasn't part of a scheme to butter her up to sell, but he was just trying to help her take ownership so it would be easier to figure out what she was going to do. However, last night, everything had felt so overwhelming that she'd felt as if she was drowning.

He was right. It was time she took ownership and stopped making excuses and avoiding what she needed to do and get to it. She padded down to the kitchen and put the coffee on. As it brewed, she opened the front door to see if Forest's car was in the driveway where he'd left it last night.

It wasn't there. She went to the porch railing and looked left toward Kaitlyn's house to see if there was any sign of life, but it appeared dark, and quiet.

"And what time did you get home, naughty girl?"

Avery whispered to her friend's buttoned-up house. She smiled as she thought about taking a pot of coffee over and knocking on the door to see how Kaitlyn's night had ended, but she turned back toward her front door and smiled when she spied the green envelope propped up against the house.

The daily missives had become a comforting part of her daily routine.

She picked it up and took it in the house, then opened the envelope.

Day 17
> Everyone loves a party,
> Everyone loves good cheer,
> It's time for you to invite your friends
> To gather from far and near.
> Today, send out invitations to Bess Loughlin's annual cookie-swap party, always held on the fourth Friday of December...unless Christmas falls on or before that date; if it does, bump it up to the third Friday. This year the party will be on December 22. She would be proud of you for carrying on the tradition. You'll find her email invitation list on her computer.
> Your Secret Santas

A lump formed in Avery's throat. Gran's cookie party was coming up faster than she'd like to admit. She hadn't realized Gran had sent out invitations in the past. That made it difficult, because once the invitations went out—and the Secret Santa Brigade had mandated that they be sent out today—there was no turning back.

She stood in the living room holding the note, listening to the ticking of the grandfather clock, which was now *her* grandfather clock, sitting in…*her* house, where all those people would gather and eat all those cookies.

For a heart-twisting moment, Avery contemplated throwing this party without Gran and she wanted to run as far away from this place as she could. Until finally a voice broke through the twisting and squirming and asked, *Why not? Why not do it?*

Maybe the best tribute to Gran would be to host one final cookie-swap party. It could be a combination memorial and holiday party, which would be so Gran, who never wanted a sad, stodgy, weepy funeral. That was the main reason Avery still hadn't held a funeral or memorial.

She walked over to the fireplace and stopped in front of the silver urn.

"Is that what you'd like, Gran?"

The ticking of the clock was all that answered her.

"I wish I knew what to do," she said aloud. "I wish I knew what you wanted me to do because I just want to do right by you, Gran."

December 22…

Avery counted on her fingers—that was five days away.

She glanced at the card from the Secret Santas again. They'd said that Gran's invitation list was on her computer.

That was interesting

If whoever sent today's Secret Santa card knew that much, it meant that they were close to Gran, and that their name/names would probably be on that list.

Maybe it would be a good way to find out who they

were. Avery fought a pang of guilt. If she was thinking of this party being a memorial—or at least a tribute— to Gran, she shouldn't have an ulterior motive of catching the Santas.

She glanced at her grandmother's urn.

"Or should I, Gran? Somehow, I think you might get a kick out of me outing them."

Avery went into the kitchen and poured herself a cup of coffee, then took it with her into the office. She stood just inside the doorway, looking around. First, her gaze landed on the computer. Then he eyes bounced around, taking in everything as Gran had left it. Of all the rooms in the house, this was the place where Avery felt closest to Gran. The walls were lined with floor-to-ceiling shelves that housed her beloved books. She had so many that some were stacked on the floor near her reading chair, which was positioned by the window. Out of all the rooms in the house, this was the least "beachy." With its dark wooden furniture and threadbare, deep red oriental rug, the office looked more like something out of an English manor house—smaller, of course, but Avery felt Gran's soul in here.

While she felt Gran's presence in here more than any other room in the house, this was the room that she'd had the most difficult time spending time in. With every object she touched or moved, she felt like it diminished Gran's presence that much more.

Still, Avery knew she couldn't put it off indefinitely. It was time to get busy. She remembered what Forest had said, and before she did anything else, she went upstairs and took her camera out of its bag. It was the first time she'd held it since she'd arrived in Tinsley Cove after losing her job.

It felt familiar in her hands, therapeutic, like a touchstone grounding her to who she was, what she needed to do to heal.

It was time to start the healing process.

Starting with the office, she photographed every room in the house. Some of the rooms, such as the living room and kitchen, showed signs that Avery had lived in them, but others, like the office, Gran's bedroom and bath, were exactly as she had left them. These were the spaces that Avery focused on.

By the time she was finished and was ready to look back at the digital photos, she realized that somewhere along the way she'd set down her coffee with only taking a couple of sips.

That's what photography did for her. It transported her out of herself, out of her own head, and helped her see the world and others through a different lens... She smiled and rolled her eyes at the unintentional metaphor, but it was true.

Some people might think that photographing her environment kept her one step removed from the world, but it was the opposite—it put her as in touch with it as she could get.

After she flipped through the photos and was satisfied that she'd captured everything, she went into Gran's office, sat down at the desk and turned on her computer.

As she waited for it to boot up, she began to tidy up Gran's desk. If she was having this party in five days, she'd need to get the place into shape, in addition to sending out the invites and making dozens of cookies. With five days and counting before the cookie swap, she didn't have a moment to spare.

As she picked up the legal pad, she remembered Gran's Christmas wish list, which was tucked inside. Avery flipped pages until she got to it.

Avery read the items aloud until she got to today's instruction to send out invitations to the cookie swap.

Somehow, the Secret Santas had gotten hold of Gran's wish list and had been sending it to her day by day for the advent-calendar challenges.

The Secret Santas were having her complete Gran's Christmas wish list, but how had they gotten ahold of it? The only way someone could've gotten the list was if they'd been in the house.

Initially, the thought creeped out Avery, but she took a few deep breaths and put it into perspective. It was highly likely that Gran had given one of her friends a spare key in case she locked herself out.

The one thing that kept the Secret Santas from being too sinister was that each note had been delivered to her front door. The Santa perps hadn't gone in the house since she'd been here... At least not as far as Avery knew.

She glanced around and suppressed a shiver.

But how did they know that she would look ahead on day two?

Lucky guess? Or maybe Gran had told them enough about her that they would expect it from her.

"Who are you?" Avery called out.

A knock at the front door made her yelp and set her heart into a frantic staccato.

"It was just a knock," she whispered to herself. "On the front door. It's not as if someone was inside the house."

Even so, to make herself feel less vulnerable, she

grabbed the brass letter opener out of the pen caddy on Gran's desk and made her way to the living room, where she stealthily peeked out the front window.

Forest was standing on the front porch.

As relief flooded through her, she realized that she was still wearing her pajamas. She'd been so busy with the photographs and mentally planning the invite to the cookie swap that she hadn't bothered to get dressed.

Even so, she opened the front door and flung herself into his arms.

"Well, hello," he said. "I'm happy to see you, too."

After he came inside, they went into the kitchen, where she put on a fresh pot of coffee and she caught him up on the morning's happenings.

"I can change the locks for you, if it would make you feel better," he offered.

"Thank you, it would."

While Avery prepared an omelet for them to eat for lunch, Forest scrolled through the photos Avery had shot earlier that morning.

"These are good," he said. "They're not just good documentary shots, they're really atmospheric. They're like art."

Avery beamed at him. "Thanks, it felt good to have a camera in my hands again. I'd sort of taken a hiatus even though I hadn't realized it until this morning."

Forest gave her a long knowing look.

"What?" she asked as she served up their lunch.

"I have an early Christmas present for you." He smiled.

"Forest, I haven't even had a chance to go Christmas shopping yet. I was going to give you your gift on Christmas Eve or Christmas Day."

"It's not really that kind of a present. Although, now that you mention it, let's plan on Christmas Day. Don't forget, the Poinsettia Ball is on Christmas Eve."

"That's right. I need to get a dress."

She added that to her mental to-do list.

"What I have for you today is a job offer."

Her mouth fell open.

He held up a hand. "Before you get too excited, it's temporary, which might be a good thing because it's not as exciting as traveling the world, like you're used to, but it will give you an income for now and allow you to pay the property taxes on Mistletoe Cottage."

"Don't leave me hanging," she said. "What is it?"

"Dalton Hart, remember him? He's the executive producer of *Selling Sandcastle*."

She nodded.

"He would like to bring you on board as a cast member this season. Ostensibly, you'd be a freelancer, photographing Sandcastle Real Estate's listings. We'd pay you for that, and you'd also be an official cast member, which comes with a decent salary for the work required."

Avery's face fell.

"No?" Forest asked. "Doesn't sound like something you'd like to do?"

She set down her fork and pressed her palms to her face. "I'm sorry, Forest. I must seem so ungrateful and I don't mean to. I'm just surprised. That was the last thing I expected. But thank you. I'm not saying no. I need to digest it."

"I completely understand. I'll be honest with you, being on a television show like this can be stressful. Dalton loves to pull things out of left field because he says drama is the lifeblood of reality TV. One of us is usually the unwitting target of the manufactured drama."

Avery scrunched up her face. "I'll be perfectly honest, that takes me back to a certain mean-spirited joke that was pulled on me in high school."

Forest winced. "I can see how it might."

"I don't know if I'm up for that. It feels like 'fool me once, shame on you, fool me twice, shame on me.' Like I'd be inviting in drama."

He shrugged. "Dalton might take it easy on you since you're new. This time you'd be in control. You'd know that some time it was bound to happen and you could play it cool or at least gauge your reaction. You're good at that, you know."

She smiled even though she didn't feel like it. Someone saying she played it cool wasn't exactly a compliment.

"There's another intangible to consider," Forest said. "Even if you're only on the show one season, it might open doors for you for your photography. You'll get to come up with at least a couple of scenes that you want to shoot. Maybe you could plan a scene around showing your photos."

His face brightened.

"In fact, you know the children's charity that is benefitting from the Christmas tree sales? What if you set up a photography how-to demo for their after-school program? Dalton's assistants could set it up for you and get clearances to shoot. The nice thing about that is that you'd be doing something for the kids and the community, and there's zero chance that Dalton will try to squeeze a dramatic moment out of it. I've found that he understands that there's a certain amount of give-and-take in this show and he usually finds an opportunity to give back quietly in ways like this."

Avery blinked. "It sounds wonderful, but where would I get the cameras for the kids to use?"

As the words left her mouth, she came up with an idea. "I've got it. I could have them make pinhole cameras. It's the bare-bones basics of photography. Oh, my gosh, I'd love to do that, but I'd need access to a darkroom to develop their prints."

It sounded like fun and a way to help a worthy cause. Once upon a time, she'd been a lonely child whose parents moved around so much that she didn't have much to call her own…no friends, no childhood home, not even the unconditional love of her parents, who were always too busy with more important things than the issues of a child.

It should've made her independent and self-sufficient, but instead, it made her feel awkward and isolated. As an adult, sometimes she still found it easier to be by herself… until she'd reconnected with Forest.

Because of him, she wondered if just maybe she could do this. Especially if she made enough from being on the show to pay off the property tax debt. It would buy her some time to figure out what to do with Mistletoe Cottage. Maybe she could weather a little bit of drama if she knew she'd come out better on the other side.

"Any idea what it pays?"

He reached in his pocket and pulled out a business card. "Give Dalton a call. He will talk to you about salary—and make sure you negotiate it. Work in photo supplies and a darkroom and things like that."

"I have a digital camera," she said. "I haven't been inside a darkroom in ages, but I would need one to develop the children's photos."

"Maybe it's time to think about getting back to what originally made you fall in love with photography," Forest said. "Make Dalton and the show pay for it. Don't forget, he came to you."

"He must have something up his sleeve," she mused.

Even so, Avery's mood brightened at the thought of being financially sound again. She'd never worked with kids before, but the after-school initiative seemed like such a worthy program. Photography had saved her. It was something she'd been able to call her own. It allowed her to express herself and even if it was a subjective artform, it had taught her to stand firm for what she liked and valued. Taking photographs took her out of her own head and that had capturing the world the ways she saw it always soothed her soul. She'd love to inspire kids who might need an outlet. Not only that, but it would be nice to get back into the darkroom. She could virtually smell the vinegary odor of the stop bath. Because of digital camera technology and her travel schedule, she hadn't been in a darkroom since college. It might be nice to get back to her roots.

Her heart was pounding and not necessarily in a good way. Moving here, even temporarily, made her feel anxious. She'd have to give up her apartment in the city. It wouldn't make financial sense to pay for a place she wasn't using, even if she was only staying in Tinsley Cove temporarily.

Her gaze found Forest's and held it for a moment. Relocating to Tinsley Cove would also mean being closer to him.

She had to remember everything she'd ever loved in her life—except for photography—had been temporary.

How tempting it was to believe this might be a chance to change that—to face her demons and finally heal. Or would it end up just being a painful reminder of everything she'd already lost?

She'd have to give it a lot of thought.

After they finished their omelets, Avery plugged the flash drive into the computer and uploaded the show. Sitting side by side, she and Forest watched the episode with Gran.

"Oh." Avery's hand fluttered to her mouth the moment Gran appeared on the screen. "Look at her. She looks so alive. And so happy."

She reached out to touch Gran, but the monitor was cold and hard.

She wished she could talk to her grandmother right now. If she could, she'd say, "Look! I'm here for Christmas, just like you wanted. Thanks to your crazy friends, I'm doing all the things you wanted us to do together. I keep trying to feel that you're with me in spirit, but maybe I don't deserve that since I put you off when you were actually here..."

Tears clouded Avery's eyes blurring Gran's image. As she blinked to clear her vision, she drew in a deep gulping breath, which ended up sounding like a shuddering sob.

Forest put an arm around her and planted a tender kiss on her temple. "I know this is hard for you, but I'm here."

Avery tilted her head until it rested on Forest's. "It's crazy, but I keep thinking how happy Gran would be if she knew I'd had an offer to become a cast member of the show that she loved so much. She'd be beside herself. I know I haven't even heard Dalton's offer yet, but knowing how happy Gran would be makes it very tempting to say yes. To be able to help those kids and pay off this year's property taxes—those are the cherries on top."

She decided she would call Dalton tomorrow and see what he had in mind. In the meantime, she had to find Gran's cookie-swap invitation list and get out those invites today.

Chapter Twelve

Dalton had made Avery an offer she couldn't refuse. Because of it, Forest felt as if Christmas had come early. She'd be staying at least through the middle of January.

His secret mission was to figure out something that would make her stay longer.

He'd changed the locks on Mistletoe Cottage after the revelation that one or more of the Secret Santas had gotten hold of Bess's Christmas wish list. He even offered to put up security cameras if it would make Avery feel better…and if she really wanted to know the identity of her faithful elves. She had declined, saying that she was sure it was a group of her grandmother's friends who were honoring Bess by seeing that her wish list was fulfilled.

"The least I can do is play along," Avery had said. "And since I found Gran's list, I'm on to their game. I feel like I'm one step ahead of them since I know what comes next."

"Doesn't that spoil the surprise?" Forest asked.

Avery shook her head. "No, I think it's more fun to anticipate what's next."

It was fun. He and Avery were following along, looking forward to the next tasks and getting into the holiday spirit of it all. Since creating and emailing out the cookie-swap invitation on the weekend, they'd been tasked with writing a letter to Santa and delivering it to him in Springdale Park, where he was holding court and listening to children's requests for gifts.

They'd written the letter together and acknowledged that they'd both faced some challenges over the years, but since they'd run into each other again, they were both well on their way to becoming better people.

They were both hopeful that the best was yet to come.

Forest couldn't remember when he'd ever been this happy. With Avery on board as a cast member for *Selling Sandcastle*, the show felt like less of a burden. Less of doing it to make others happy and more like something he was doing for himself.

The real-estate business was notoriously slow around the holidays. Forest had asked his dad and brothers to take the few appointments he'd had on the books. City hall was closed until December 26 and there wouldn't be another commission meeting until the end of January. The city manager had basically told him to get lost and enjoy the holidays.

"I'm sure I speak for the citizens of Tinsley Cove

when I say that we all appreciate how you treat your position as mayor like a full-time job, but don't lose sight of the fact that it is a volunteer position. You're good at what you do, but we don't want you to burn out before you get started."

For the first time since Forest could remember, he was taking a few days off.

The only things he had to do before the end of the year were filming a couple of scenes for the show in addition to the scene he and Avery had filmed together that morning at her house.

With the cookie-swap party two days away, Forest and Avery had turned Mistletoe Cottage's kitchen into a baking workshop. Following a virtual cookie-swap instruction manual Gran had left on her computer in the same folder as the e-invitation list, they had a roadmap that included a list of the cookies Gran always baked, recipes and party setup instructions. They had everything they needed to prepare for the party.

Before they'd started filming, Forest had pulled Dalton aside.

"Go easy on Avery today. I don't want to scare her away before she has a chance to get started."

Dalton pulled a face and looked a little affronted.

"Of course. Of course. I mean what could happen in the safety of Mistletoe Cottage's kitchen?" He gestured around the place. "I figured this would be a gentle initiation for her. Unless you're planning to pull something out of the blue? Tell me you are."

"Why would I do that?" Forest asked.

"Well, now that you mention it, I've been meaning to talk to you," Dalton said. "You're playing it a little low-key these days, Forest. You know, the good mayor, the good son. Now, the good boyfriend."

A warmth spiraled through him at the thought of others seeing them as a couple. It had happened so naturally. It was nice to not have to make any big declarations or grandiose announcements.

They were just being themselves around each other and that's what made them so good together.

"And?" Forest asked. "That's exactly who I am. Logan is the loner. Owen is the wild card. I'm the good son. Those are your descriptions of us, Dalton. What you've used in publicity. Why would you want to change that now?"

"I believe I called you 'the heir, the spare and the dare,' but let's not squabble over the details. I'm not asking you to change, Forest. Even so, that doesn't preclude you from spicing things up once in a while. You know, making things interesting for once."

Dalton tilted his head to the side and snored to underscore exactly how bored he was with Forest.

And this, ladies and gentlemen, is precisely why I probably won't make it past the second season.

Dalton Hart had the attention span of a squirrel. Sure, he knew who Forest was—they'd known each other since childhood. Now he wanted him to change. To pretend to be someone he wasn't. Forest had enough on his plate trying to be everything to everybody else. The last thing he needed was to try to mold himself into something unrecognizable just to please a television producer.

"Give it a think," Dalton said. "If you can't come up with anything, I can help. Like…what about a romantic on-screen proposal at the Poinsettia Ball? *Huh? Huh?*"

Dalton elbowed him. "That would get people talking and we could tease it out in the preseason publicity."

"Are you crazy?" Forest asked. "This might be scripted reality, but proposing marriage shouldn't be used like a prop."

Dalton held up his hands. "Okay. Okay. No sweat. So you're not *that* serious about her. I get it. But we've gotta do something here. Forest, I can hardly stay awake, man. Making cookies in granny's kitchen is sweet, but it's not exactly riveting. Today is a freebie, but you've gotta give me something I can work with in the future. In the *very near* future. Got it?"

He didn't owe the guy anything. It was clear that he needed to talk to his parents and let them know that he would probably need to disengage from the show. He had no problem being in the background, but this tightening of the screws every season wasn't working for him.

Knowing Avery, she was bound to feel the same way after enduring a season with Dalton. If she discovered she liked it, he wouldn't make her choose. He could cheer her on from the sidelines.

"Are you ready to make five dozen of ten different kinds of cookies?" Avery asked after she'd entered the kitchen. She looked gorgeous in that red sweater she was wearing. It had to be a little warm with all the lights and the oven cranked up to 350 degrees. Even so, it looked so soft, it was all Forest could do to keep from reaching out and pulling her close.

However, he didn't know how she would feel about affection on camera. How had they not talked about it?

Instead of thinking about how her curves would

feel in that sweater, he said, "I'm ready, and don't forget, we have to decorate the gingerbread house, too."

The gingerbread house was actually tomorrow's Secret Santa task, but since they were in baking mode, they thought they might as well check that off the list. Since the footage would air at a later date, the Santas would have no clue when they'd made it.

The filming was fun and playful, showing them with flour on their faces and dabbing frosting on each other's noses. It also was perfectly clear that they were smitten with each other. Going public with their relationship felt like the best Christmas present to himself.

For a moment, Dalton's idea of proposing didn't feel like such a bad idea. What would she do if he dropped down on one knee, took her hand and slid a LifeSavers gummy on her ring finger as a placeholder?

She'd probably kick him. Something like that was a private matter, reserved for the two of them. So an on-film proposal was off the table, but it had been fun thinking about.

Proposing to her, spending the rest of their lives together, felt right.

As he stared at her across the top of a gingerbread house, three words kept popping into his brain, begging to slide off his tongue and out into the open, but when it came right down to it, that, too, was private and called for the right moment.

But it helped that he knew the feelings were as real as the diamond that he would someday put on her finger, if she would have him.

In the meantime, first things first. He took her hand across the table, dipped her finger in the royal icing and brought it to his lips.

"And that's a wrap!" Dalton called.

As the crew was packing up, he said, "Good work today, guys. Next up for the two of you, Avery and Forest, I'd like to film at the cookie swap. Because, you know, cookies. Who wouldn't want to film it?"

He laughed at himself. Avery and Forest chuckled, too. The day had gone well. Dalton had kept his promise to keep things light. What could it hurt to film the party? It would be a good chance to showcase the Tinsley Cove community's camaraderie.

As Dalton's production assistant flipped through the sheets on her clipboard and started scribbling furiously, Forest asked Avery, "Are you okay with that? You mentioned making it a memorial for Bess."

"I'll say a few words about Gran at one point in the evening, but I believe she would want us to keep it light for the most part—true to the cookie swaps she's hosted in the past. So, sure. I'm in."

"We're in," Forest said.

"Good. Good," Dalton said. "Did you have fun today, Avery?"

"I did. In fact, sometimes I even forgot the cameras were here."

"Isn't it great when you get lost in your art?" he said.

Art?

Forest wanted to snort, but he managed to contain himself. This show was hardly art...or least to him, it wasn't. Then again, one man's trash was another man's treasure. So who was he to judge? Especially if this show made his parents happy and Avery had fun.

"Do you have any idea when we're going to film the scene with me teaching the children how to make a pin hole camera?" she asked.

"My assistant, Zoe, is working on it," Dalton said. "It'll be after the first of the year, when everyone is back from vacation. The rec center was on board with the idea. We will let you know as soon as we've nailed down a date. In the meantime, you're going to be plenty busy filming the cookie swap and the Poinsettia Ball. I guarantee you we're all going to have a lot of fun."

Tinsley Cove
Friday, December 22

On the day of the cookie-swap party, as the camera crews began setting up at Mistletoe Cottage and afternoon gave way to evening, butterflies swarmed and flew in formation in Avery's stomach.

As the crew figured out the best camera angles, the first guests arrived—Hazel Buckminster and Doris Smith.

"Hello, honey," said Hazel. "This is wonderful. I know Bess would've been thrilled that you're carrying on her tradition. Absolutely thrilled. As you'll soon see, this is a party that the entire town looks forward to. The fourth Friday in December. Since it's always been a standing date, it's the first soiree on everyone's calendar."

"Hazel, I've been wondering," said Avery. "What happens if the fourth Friday falls on or after Christmas Eve or Christmas?"

"Oh, sweetie, in that case, everyone knows that it shifts up to the third Friday. We can't have Christmas without the cookie-swap cookies."

Avery nodded. "Of course."

"That tells me you're planning for future parties and I love it," said Doris.

"Well, we'll have to see about that," Avery said. "I'm so glad you're here early. I should've called you, but I had so much to do getting ready for tonight. Since so many people RSVPed yes for the cookie party, I thought tonight would be a great chance to celebrate Gran's life. Kind of an impromptu memorial, though she wouldn't have wanted anything formal and stuffy, but she loved this cookie party and—"

The words got stuck in Avery's throat. So she shrugged rather than trying to choke them out.

Hazel held up a piece of paper, which had been on top of the tray of cookies she's brought and smiled triumphantly. "Doris and I must've been picking up on your vibes, sweetheart, because we thought the same thing. We prepared some nice things to say about Bess as we kick off the party."

Doris set her cookie tray on the coffee table. "Bess would be so proud of you." She opened her arms wide and pulled Avery into a hug. While Avery was in Doris's embrace, head turned to the side, she got a good view of the note Hazel was holding. The handwriting looked eerily familiar. There was something about the way the letters slanted and looped... Avery had seen it before.

As Doris released her, something dawned on Avery. She said, "Hazel, may I see your notes for a moment?"

"Sure, honey," Hazel said, handing it over without hesitation.

Paper in hand, Avery glanced at it and then back at the women. "If you'll excuse me, I will be right back."

She went into Gran's office and picked up a couple of the Secret Santa notes and compared the writing on them to Hazel's writing on the paper she'd brought this evening.

It was a match.

"I thought so," Avery said out loud. "You sneaky little Santas, you. Now, I know who you are."

Armed with the Santa missives and Hazel's note, Avery marched into the dining room where the two were rearranging the array of platters on the table.

"I know your secret... Santas." She held up a Santa card in one hand and Hazel's notes in the other.

The women seemed unfazed by Avery's discovery.

When Hazel said, "Yes, well good for you. Please set my notes about Bess over there on the buffet. I'm guessing you'll want to wait until a good crowd has gathered before we make our remarks."

Avery blinked at them. Were they really going to brush it off like it was no big deal? They'd been found out. She'd found them out.

"Well, yes, I want as many people as possible here when we honor her, but don't you have anything to say for yourselves about your sneaky Santa escapades?"

Hazel's eyes flashed. "I beg your pardon?" She sounded indignant and for a moment, Avery was afraid she was going to deny that they were her Secret Santas.

Before Avery could say anything else, Doris held up a finger. "I'll tell you what I used to tell my children when it came to Santa Claus. I told them, Santa is all about the spirit of the season. He's not only about gifts and material things. He—or she—represents digging down deep and getting past the cynicism and commercialism and finding the best in the season. Just think how much better life would be if we found the magic in every day and lived in the moment rather than putting off important things as if we had all the time in the world."

Hazel nodded, but her demeanor had softened.

"Honey, I was with Bess two days before she passed. She showed me the wish list she'd drafted of things she wanted the two of you to do when you came home for Christmas."

Avery had to bite her tongue to keep from saying, *but this isn't home.*

She had never had a home…except for the year that Gran had taken her in. And that's where everything got muddy. How could she feel so at home with a person, but like a fish out of water in a town?

Then she had to swallow hard as the grief of losing Gran, losing her mornings, swept over her, like it was going to pull her out to sea.

"Doris thought it would both honor Bess and help you if we provided a little anonymous and fun encouragement for you to complete your Gran's Christmas wish list."

Avery opened her mouth, but she had no words.

Leave it to her to turn something so nice into something so…ugly.

After a lingering pointed look at Avery, Doris turned to Hazel. "I think it would be best to group the sugar cookies together, don't you?"

The two women set about rearranging the table while Avery stood there trying to digest the upbraiding she'd just received.

Even though Doris had delivered the words with a smile and a twinkle in her eye, they landed like a punch to Avery's gut.

Doris was right. Avery had lived her life—or more

like had put off living—like she had all the time in the world. Now, no matter how many envelopes she opened or items she crossed off Gran's Christmas wish list, it was too late. Gran was gone.

That old familiar feeling of wanting to run away, wanting to be by herself gripped her. If she was alone, no one could hurt her.

However, Forest had just entered the room, the house would soon be full of people and the *Selling Sandcastle* production crew would film the entire thing.

She would just have to get through it.

Ostensibly, this shoot would be easier than the cookie-baking session they'd filmed a couple of days ago because there were so many other people to focus on—they would be looking at this through a wide angle lens, rather than the zoom lens that had been focused on her and Forest.

Actually, she had no idea what kind of lenses the film crew used, but there was so much more to focus on at the party, which took the pressure off her. Then again, more people meant more chances for drama to erupt, but if it happened, surely, it wouldn't be focused on her and she could find some out of the way place to hide. That was one of the benefits of the party being at Gran's, er, *her* house. She took a deep breath. Mistletoe Cottage was *her* house.

The thought rolled around her brain like a marble as Forest arrived and all the people started filing in with trays of cookies.

A half hour later, the house was filled with people and the convivial sounds of laughter and conversation. Forest's parents were there, and so were his brothers, sister, cousin, Cassie and Kaitlyn, along with dozens of faces she recognized from back in the fall, when it seemed like the entire town was delivering casseroles. Tonight, they all had cookies.

So many cookies and so many people.

And, of course, the film crew, but Avery reasoned that if Gran had been happy to be an extra in an episode, she would've been delighted to have a scene dedicated to remembering her.

However, Avery wasn't so sure about being the center of attention. Her heart hammered and she fought the urge to disappear—to go anywhere but here. Somewhere calmer, quieter, out of the spotlight...but she couldn't. She had to stay. She owed this to Gran.

She took a deep breath and tried to calm her nerves, and said, "Welcome, everyone. I'm so happy you could be here. I'd like to dedicate tonight to my grandmother, Bess Loughlin."

The entire room broke out into applause. People clapped and cheered and whistled. Their adoration of Gran was so moving, it rendered Avery verklempt. So she let them show their appreciation until they naturally quieted down.

"You all are making me cry," Avery said. "But I know Bess loved each and every one of you and would appreciate this so much. I'm not very good at public speaking, especially when it comes to talking about someone who was my whole world—"

Her voice caught and she was afraid if she tried to force out more words she would fall apart in front of everyone. All it took was one look at Forest and he was at her side.

"Not only were Bess and I neighbors, but she was like a surrogate grandmother to me."

As others stepped forward to share their fondest memories of Bess, Avery felt as if she was observing everything from afar. Some people might have thought it a strange sensation, but Avery was used to the feeling of being alone in the middle of a crowd, especially when Forest had to step away at Dalton's beckoning. At first, Forest balked and discreetly tried to put him off, but Avery whispered, "It's fine. It seems important."

Hazel was the last to speak and after she read her prepared remarks, she seemed to take pride in concluding the memorial and signaling that party should resume.

"That was beautiful, Hazel," Avery said. "I know Gran would've appreciated it."

She was just about to reopen the Secret Santa discussion, but with gratitude this time, confessing some of the stunts were fun, when she was interrupted by Forest who was approaching her with the film crew and two guys dressed in business suits.

"Avery, there you are," Forest said. "Excuse me, Hazel, but I need to introduce Avery to these gentlemen."

A muscle in his jaw ticked and there was a certain gleam of triumph in his eyes that made her want to ask what was going on?

"Certainly, hon." Hazel took ahold of Forest's arm. "It sure is nice to see you and Avery getting along so well. I told you you'd make a cute couple, didn't I? I called it."

Avery's cheeks warmed and she made a mental note to ask Forest if he wanted to be the pot or the lid, but then she remembered that the cameras were on them.

"Carl Harlow and Perry Hines, this is Avery Anderson—"

He was interrupted by a crash, and someone called

out, "We've got some broken glass over here. Can someone help?"

Avery was just about to seize the moment to get away from the cameras, but Forest beat her to the punch. "I'll get it. I believe these two gentlemen want to make you an offer you can't refuse."

What? What kind of an offer?

She locked gazes with Forest, who smiled and said, "I'll be back in a minute."

As one of the men made nice about the cookie party—she wasn't sure if it was Harlow or Hines, because the blood rushing in her ears made it hard to hear—she had the sinking feeling that she knew where this was going.

There were two cameras, one trained on Avery, and another one pointing at the men. Dalton had told her that rule number one was never to look directly at the camera—it was of vital importance that they pretend it wasn't there to allow the viewer the illusion of intimacy, that they were eavesdropping on the conversations.

As Avery played along, she felt the gazes of those standing near on her, watching, smiling and happy to have a front-row seat to witness her being turned into the butt of golden boy Forest McFadden's drama.

"We've had a chance to look around the grounds and this property is exactly what our development company has been looking for," said Harlow…or maybe it was Hines—neither had bothered to put on a nametag. "We are prepared to make you a very handsome offer."

But Avery ignored rule number one of reality TV, looked right at the camera and said, "Forest McFadden, you set me up."

As she looked at the faces staring at her with greedy

eyes and prurient interest, the walls began to close in on her and her body vibrated with panic.

She had to get out of there.

Chapter Thirteen

Forest had never seen such rage in a person's eyes.

One minute he had been sweeping up the shards of the wineglasses that Ann Wright had accidentally knocked off the table when she'd reached for another one of Miriam Winston's snickerdoodle cookies. And the next minute, Avery had been giving him the look of death as she'd said, "How dare you do that to me," and then stormed out of the place.

After he'd disposed of the glass, he'd planned on bringing her a glass of cava to celebrate what he thought was good news. If he had, she probably would've thrown it at him. And with good reason.

They'd both been duped by Dalton Hart.

Forest had let Avery go so she could cool off. She'd

stayed away until after the last guest was gone. He was about to lock up her house and go out looking for her, when he heard footsteps on the stairs.

She startled, looking just as surprised to see him as he was to see her.

"Why are you still here?" she asked.

"Because I want to talk to you, to set things straight," he said, then went and sat on the sofa.

"It's pretty clear what you and Dalton were up to," she said. "Get me on camera, put me on the spot with an offer I can't refuse and you think I'll cave and you can pocket a nice commission for selling the place. How much is six percent of a million and a half? It's ninety thousand dollars. I trusted you, Forest."

"Dalton introduced Harlow and Hines to me as gallery owners. He said they were a fan of your work after seeing it in *World International* and they wanted to talk to you about showing some of your photographs in their Atlanta gallery. Dalton lied, but I didn't know it, and at that moment I didn't vet Harlow and Hines, which I now know isn't a real gallery. So the joke is on both of us."

She blinked a few times, as if she was trying to digest what he was saying.

"And by the way, neither Sandcastle Real Estate nor I had a signed listing for Mistletoe Cottage, nor did we bring the supposed buyer so you wouldn't have owed us a cent of commission."

She opened her mouth as if to speak, but no words came out. She clamped her lips shut, then opened them again in the shape of an *O.*

"So, um, okay. Wow."

She walked over and sat down next to him on the sofa.

"So both of us really were duped by Dalton."

Forest nodded.

"Is that how things work on shows like this? Does the producer manufacture drama and randomly throw it at you like this?"

Forest gave a one-shoulder shrug. "Sometimes. He gives us the opportunity to bring the goods and if we don't, he has been known to throw us a few curveballs. Has Cassie told you about the stunt that Dalton pulled on her last season?"

Avery's brown eyes went wide. "What happened?"

"He managed to find her estranged father and spring him on her during filming."

"Wow. And she came back for season two?"

"In the grand scheme of things, I guess Dalton did her a favor because they ended up mending their rift and they're working on their relationship."

Avery shifted in her seat. "Sounds messy, airing your dirty laundry on national television. I'm not cut out for it. I don't think I'm going to be able to do this."

"Are you talking about the show or us?" he asked.

She stared down at her hands, then drew in a deep breath.

"Tonight, after I left the party, I heard from my former boss at *World International* magazine, Barry Orr. When he closed the magazine, he told me that there might get funding for a special project where a photographer went to France and tracked down and photographed old carousels—they're kind of a thing in France. He wants to write a book about it. He had applied for a grant and he texted me tonight with the good news that the grant was approved and the project is a go. He wants me to do the photographs."

"That's great," Forest said. "Congratulations to him, but that's a one-time assignment, right? You're coming back, aren't you?"

She chipped at the red polish on her fingernail with her thumb.

"I don't know, Forest," she said. "This project will take several weeks."

"But you'll be back, right? You can't let someone like Dalton Hart run you out of town and ruin things for us."

As soon as the words left his mouth it dawned on him how the stunt Dalton had pulled tonight almost paralleled what had happened to them a decade ago. The only difference was, this time he wasn't going to let her walk away. He'd lost her once. The first time, he hadn't fully realized that he loved her, but this time was different. They were older and wiser, and now he knew that what he felt was real.

"The contract stated that I had to be in three scenes and I've fulfilled my obligation." She shrugged, but she wouldn't look at him.

"I don't want to lose you, Avery. I love you."

He knew he shouldn't do it, but he reached for her, anyway. If she would just let him hold her, he knew he could make things right.

She shrugged away and looked up at him with the saddest eyes that were shimmering with unshed tears and shook her head.

"I—I just don't see how it would work, Forest. I care about you so much, but we're just… We're just too different. We come from different backgrounds and want different things. It's just not going to work."

Tinsley Cove
Sunday, December 24

Avery did one more turn in front of the full-length mirror. The sleeveless, V-neck red satin gown Kaitlyn had designed for her was perfect. The subtle ruching at the side nipped in her waist and showed off her curves in the best possible way. The slit on the left side ran to midthigh. Not only did it show off just the right amount of leg, but it also allowed the bottom of the gown to flare out in a graceful trumpet-style when she walked.

She'd almost bowed out of going to the Poinsettia Ball with Forest, but when it came down to it she'd promised him… promised herself… this one last night.

Yesterday, the day after the cookie party, the Secret Santa task, which was presented in its usual form with no mention of Hazel and Doris, had delivered right on schedule. The mission had been to look at Christmas lights, and Avery had done just that. She'd put on her coat to protect herself from the biting beach wind and had taken a long walk by herself, looking at the festive lights and decorations that illuminated the entire town, and replaying Forest's declaration over and over in her head.

I don't want to lose you, Avery. I love you.

She had desperately wanted to confess her feelings, too, but she couldn't.

She couldn't bring herself to say those four sacred words: *I love you, too.*

She did love him, but in her experience, that's always where the story took a tragic, twisty U-turn. When she loved someone, she lost them.

She knew that on some level, she'd loved Forest

since the moment she'd first seen him, but she'd done fine by herself, hadn't she?

Wasn't she better off by herself?

The perverse thing was that after losing Gran, Avery could've easily answered that question. Yes, she'd done fine on her own. She preferred it that way, but after spending time with Forest, it didn't seem so cut-and-dried.

Last night, as she'd walked, she'd thought about her choices, pondering whether she should stay in Tinsley Cove or go.

Of course, she was going to take the assignment in France. If she couldn't have the photo-editor position, the extended time in France was second best.

The carousel job was temporary. She had no idea what she would do after it was finished, but temporary had always been her way of life. Clearly, she got itchy when anything tried to tie her down.

But still…there was Forest. She knew he'd had nothing to do with Dalton's setup. Forest had been as unwitting a participant as she had, and she'd played right into Dalton's hands, delivering the drama he'd wanted.

She hoped that the time away would help her figure it out, give her time to sort out her head…and her heart.

Common sense told her that loving Forest didn't mean he would die, even though the love-equaled-loss equation had become a natural reflex. On a subconscious level, she feared it. It was like a muscle memory.

If she was honest with herself, it masked something else. A deeper personal flaw.

Could she really stay in one place—especially a place as small and sometimes smothering as Tinsley Cove—for an extended period of time…like forever?

Forest's family was all here. They were the pillars of the community.

After the cookie swap, when the two of them had sorted out what had really happened and who was behind the Carl Harlow and Perry Hines offer for Mistletoe Cottage, Avery knew it was no more Forest's fault than it was her own for walking into that situation with her guard down.

That's when she realized that her anxiety wasn't directed at Forest, it was more about whether she could really be content in Tinsley Cove. Because she'd have to be if she let herself love him.

She sighed. She already loved him.

Right now, it felt as if she had it contained and she needed to get away from here before these feelings, which were way bigger than she, clawed their way out of the proverbial bag where she'd stowed them.

She would take this assignment in France and while she was gone she would try to sort out what to do with Mistletoe Cottage—and her life—afterward.

Because she knew she was leaving, she had all but resigned herself to skipping the Poinsettia Ball. She had called Forest and told him she wasn't going. Then she had received the final missive from the Secret Santas.

December 24
Merry Christmas Eve, Avery!
> Your Gran would be proud of the way you've completed her wish list day after day.
> Christmas is the most magical time of all,
> Tonight have fun at the Poinsettia Ball.
> With this final note, we will bid you adieu,

With love and best wishes from all of us to you.
Love,
Your Secret Santas

How could she go and leave just one task—the very last one—undone? The thought made her itchy. She had purchased the children's toy she would donate. Of course, she could send it with her friends, but Kaitlyn had worked so hard creating this perfect, perfect gown and she was depending on Avery to show it off and tell everyone who asked that it was a Kaitlyn Quinn design.

Kaitlyn had also made gowns for Sophie, Lucy and Cassie, but it seemed ungrateful for Avery to say *Never mind. My plans have changed. I don't need the gown that you've spent countless hours sewing when you could've been doing other things.*

Kaitlyn had become a friend. And friends supported friends.

She'd called Forest to tell him she'd changed her mind, that if he still had her ticket, she would love to spend one more evening with him.

Tonight, as she got ready, she felt like Cinderella going to the ball. Everything would change tomorrow. She'd say goodbye to Forest, board a plane and return to New York City, where she would prepare for her trip to France.

Tonight, however, she would have one last night with her very own Prince Charming before the clock struck midnight and everything reverted back to the way it was before she'd returned to Mistletoe Cottage.

A small voice that she was desperately trying to ignore told her things could never go back to the way things were. Nothing would ever be the same because she was a different person.

When the knock sounded at the door, and Avery opened it to see Forest standing there in his black tux with black shirt and black tie, the look on his face was priceless.

"You look stunning." He took her hand and gave her a twirl.

"You don't look so bad yourself," she said. In fact, he looked practically edible, but she blinked away the thought. He hadn't kissed her...because Forest was a good guy. Even though she was desperate to taste his lips one last time, she didn't want to send him mixed signals.

"This is for you." He handed her a single red rose that she didn't realize he'd been carrying.

She brought it to her nose and inhaled its sweet perfume.

"Thank you. It's beautiful."

She hadn't gone to her high-school prom, but this was what she'd imagined it might have been like to get all dressed up and have Forest come to the door to claim her as his date.

For a moment, she questioned whether she was doing the right thing accepting the job that Barry had for her, when this gorgeous, kind, thoughtful man was standing right here in front of her looking as smitten as she felt.

She stopped herself right there. Tonight she would live in the moment. Tomorrow, she would get on that plane and go toward her future.

Or at least get far enough away from this place—from Forest—that she could figure out what to do next.

After they were settled in the car, she said, "Kaitlyn

said it wasn't a problem to look after the house. That way it won't be as big a burden on you."

Really, looking after the place didn't entail much. She didn't have any house plants. She'd arranged for a local company to take care of the lawn and for the utility costs to be deducted out of her checking account.

All that was left was to lock it up. Forest and Kaitlyn would be there in case of an emergency.

"She goes out of town a lot," Forest said. "I really don't mind."

"Thank you. I really appreciate it, but if you need a backup, Kaitlyn is prepared to step up."

Of course, she still needed to work out matters with Dalton. She had signed a contract and had already cashed the check and paid off the property taxes. The contract stipulated that she participate in at least three scenes. She had the cookie-baking scene, the cookie swap and a segment she'd done between the two, where she went with Forest to a property and shot photos. They would be shooting tonight, of course, which should make four. She wasn't sure if the Christmas-tree-lot footage would count, but she could argue that it should—especially when it was combined with the footage at the tree lighting…even if she had only been in the background.

It wasn't as if she was running out on the contract. She would tell him tonight that she was leaving in the morning.

"I have to talk to Dalton tonight to let him know I'm leaving," she said.

Forest nodded.

"I can't help but feel that he owes us for the way he set us up, manipulating us into an on-camera fight that was so bogus and such a misrepresentation," Avery said. "Did you ever want to expose him and the show?"

Of course, the contract contained a nondisclosure clause, as if not talking about the absurdity made it real. However, it might be fun to contemplate doing an exposé of the show's manufactured drama, the last thing she needed was to get embroiled in a lawsuit now that she was finally flush.

With the taxes for Mistletoe Cottage paid in full for a year, she would have enough time to come up with a game plan after she returned from France.

"That's one of the reasons this will probably be my last season on the show. I'm done," Forest said.

He's done.

A strange little voice sounded in her heart—*Forest, please don't be done with me, too.*

But she knew she couldn't have it both ways. Even if they were parting on good terms—as friends—that meant that he was free to see other people. Avery's mind raced to Kaitlyn and the big crush she had on him.

The next time she came back, if there was a next time, would the two of them be a couple? An irrational pull of jealousy tugged at Avery's heart.

She had no right to expect Forest to wait for her. Kaitlyn adored him and Forest deserved a woman who loved him completely, without reservation, and wanted to be where he wanted to be.

They really were perfect with each other.

Except they weren't.

"You'd be okay with the show going on and not being a part of it?"

He nodded. "I'd be more than okay. I'd be elated."

"Maybe tonight, we should go out with a bang? Do something to give Dalton a dose of his own medicine."

Forest slowed to a stop at a red light and turned to look at her. His face softened. "Did you have something in mind?"

"Not right off the top of my head, but since they'll be filming tonight, maybe we can think of something?"

They arrived at the rambling Seaside Hotel, a three-story resort that resembled a majestic mansion, sprawling and proud, like a whitewashed treasure chest that had washed upon the beach.

As Forest maneuvered the car through the parking lot toward the porte cochere, the place seemed to go on forever, spanning as far as her eyes could see.

A week ago, Forest had suggested they stay at the hotel after the ball, but he hadn't mentioned it again when she'd called him back and said she would like to go after all.

It was just as well. A car was scheduled to pick her up at Mistletoe Cottage early tomorrow morning. It would be easier to say good-night when he dropped her off and make a clean break.

The ballroom was decorated to look like a winter wonderland, with flocked Christmas trees decorated in silver and gold with twinkle lights. Tables covered with white tablecloths were adorned with centerpieces composed of red and white poinsettias, and candles in mercury glass holders. It was such a beautiful, festive scene.

After they had enjoyed a glass of champagne and talked to a few people, the band started playing "The Way You Look Tonight."

"Will you dance with me?" Forest asked.

"I'd love to," said Avery.

He pulled her into his arms and they swayed together on the dance floor. As she rested her head on his chest, she wanted to memorize everything about that moment. The way he looked. The delicious way he smelled. His strong arms around her, and the way their bodies fit together so perfectly.

She smiled to herself. Like a lid and a pot.

"I had an idea," he said.

"About what?"

"How we could call Dalton's bluff."

She pulled back a little to look at him. "Do tell."

"I don't believe that Carl Harlow and Perry Hines are real investors," Forest said. "I've been in this business long enough to be able to spot a phony when I see one. I think after hearing you talk to my dad and me about Mistletoe Cottage at the company Christmas party, Dalton came up with this cockamamie idea, because he knew it was the one thing that would cause maximum drama and send you into a tailspin. What if you'd called his bluff and told me on camera that you were willing to sell? I don't believe they have the money to buy the place."

She stiffened. "But I still don't know if that's what I want to do. What if they are real developers? I'm not ready to commit to that. Now that I've bought myself some time, I don't have to decide."

"I don't think they're sincere. Dalton lied to me about them being gallery owners. I'd bet that he's lying about them being real-estate developers, too. I tried to do some research on them and nothing came up under their names individually or as a company. I would wager that they're not who they say they are."

"Oh, yeah, what would you wager?" she asked.

"Something big. Something to the tune of if I'm right than you'll promise me that you'll come back to Tinsley Cove."

The music stopped and she took a step back. "Forest, I can't promise you that."

"Even if you can't promise me that, your reluctance to selling the house tells me that there's a possibility that you're going to keep it."

"Why do I get the feeling that you're not talking about the house but you're talking about you and me?"

"Okay," he said. "What if I am?"

The music started again. This time the band played a fast song and people flooded the dance floor.

"I don't know what you want me to say, Forest."

"If you can take a wait-and-see approach with the house, I'd love it if you give us the same leeway. It doesn't have to be an all-or-nothing situation, Avery. I think—no, I *know* that you and I have something good, something rare and I don't want to lose you. Just promise me you'll consider it."

It was too much.

Too much pressure when she needed time and space to sort it out.

She nodded. "Will you please excuse me? I need to find the ladies' room."

Instead, she fled to the lobby and called a car to take her home.

Chapter Fourteen

New York City
Monday, December 25

Avery caught a flight to JFK International Airport at the crack of dawn. One of the benefits of flying on Christmas morning was that the plane was nearly empty. It was better to be in the city alone than alone in Tinsley Cove with the ghosts of all she couldn't change.

The night before, after she'd gotten back to Mistletoe Cottage, she'd felt bad about leaving Forest at the ball. After she'd changed out of her dress, she'd written a note of apology and taped it to his door. Then she'd spent the rest of the night preparing to leave.

By the time she took a car from the airport to her apartment in the city, it was almost noon.

The apartment was empty as her roommate, Val, was spending Christmas upstate with her boyfriend's family, but even the city seemed strangely quiet...or maybe it wasn't really quiet as much as it seemed different. She'd been gone not quite a month, but somehow, even her apartment didn't feel like home anymore.

Even though she used to travel a lot with the magazine, every time she returned to New York it felt like she was coming back to something familiar, something that was hers. Today, this place no longer felt like hers.

She set her bags in her room, hung up her coat in the closet and then plugged in the Christmas tree. It was the same white artificial tree that she and Val had put up for years, but Avery felt a stronger attachment to the tree that Forest had brought her and helped her decorate. Two days ago, she had undecorated it, packing away all of the ornaments with care and feeling quite numb as she worked. It seemed a shame to dismantle such a beautiful work, but she didn't know when she'd be back. So she had to tend to the tree. Once it was bare, she had dragged it to the curb so it could be recycled with the rest of the trees in Tinsley Cove.

She'd had the forethought to photograph it before she took it apart.

Not only had she captured it in some of the shots when she'd photographed Mistletoe Cottage, but she'd also snapped pictures with the camera on her phone.

After she turned up the thermostat to take the edge off the chill in the apartment, she made herself a cup of tea and scrolled through the photos of the tree. When she got to one with Forest in it, smiling at her and holding out his arms as if beckoning her into a hug, her heart ached so badly that she pressed a hand to her chest.

If not for the ache, she would feel empty inside.

She wasn't sure which was worse, heartache or feeling empty.

Later that evening, someone rang the buzzer downstairs. Avery thought it might be Val and Eddie returning early, but that didn't make sense. They were meant to be gone until tomorrow afternoon. Who else would it be? Maybe Val had forgotten her keys.

"Hello?" Avery said.

"Hi, Avery, it's me. Forest."

Her heart kicked up and lodged in her throat.

"Forest? What are you doing here? How did you get here?"

"Will you please let me come up so we can talk?"

When the buzzer sounded, Forest pulled open the glass door and stepped into the empty lobby. A set of stairs sat next to a single elevator. Since her place was on the third floor, he opted for the stairs, hoping to burn off some of his nervous energy.

When he got upstairs, he'd barely knocked when Avery opened the door and threw herself into his arms.

After the way they'd left things, he'd been afraid that she wouldn't even see him. The dread in his heart slowly gave way.

He held her for a long moment. When they broke apart, he noticed she was crying.

"Hey, it's okay," he said.

She nodded and drew in a shuddering breath, then motioned him inside and shut the door behind them.

"You're here," she said. "You're supposed to be celebrating Christmas with your family."

"Why would I do that when I want to be with you?" he said. "For once, I'm following my heart and doing what

I want to do." He shrugged. "I was pleasantly surprised that when I leveled with them and shared my plans, they were supportive. I guess I underestimated them."

What good did it do to do for others if he couldn't do it with a happy heart? Resentment was bound to build, and he was living proof of it.

"Won't they resent me for taking you away on Christmas Day?"

He shook his head. "No. They know I love you and they want me to be happy. They want *us* to be happy. I've spent my whole life working to please everyone else. Finally, I'm doing something for myself. For us."

She closed her eyes and shuddered. "I guess I should've stayed until after Christmas, but I felt so caged in, I thought if I didn't get away, I might… I don't even know," she said. "What I do know is I seem to keep making wrong turns with every decision I make. I keep making a mess of things. With Gran—the way I let my job come before her, like we had all the time in the world. The job. My time with you. You are the best guy a woman could dream of, but—"

He held up his hands. "But what? There are no guarantees in life, Avery. That's what makes it all the more important to hold the people you love close while you can. Punishing yourself for this perceived notion of not being there for your gran doesn't fix things, it just perpetuates the feeling of loss. It holds you back from living. Do you think your parents or your grandmother would've wanted that for you? The best way you can celebrate her—all of them—is to live your life to its fullest."

"I know that, Forest. It's just not that easy."

"I don't know how it could be any simpler. I love you. You love me."

She stared at him with eyes that were stormy with emotion.

"Unless, I have this entirely wrong," he added. "Maybe you don't feel the way I thought you did. Maybe I've been so blinded by my feelings I'm way off base."

Tears were flowing down her cheeks again. He wanted so badly to pull her close and tell her everything would be okay, but now he wasn't so sure it would be.

"Tell me you don't love me and I'll go, Avery. I'll walk away right now and not bother you again."

"No, that's not it, Forest. I do love you—with all my heart. That's the problem. I lose everyone I love."

This time, Forest was the one shaking his head. "If you love me and that's the only thing keeping us apart, I'm not going to let that happen."

He pulled a small light blue box from his pocket and dropped down on one knee. "Avery Anderson, I've loved you from the moment I met you. I lost you once when we were too young, but now that you've come back into my life, I'm not going to let you get away. If you'll have me, please make me the happiest man alive and marry me."

Paris, France
Sunday, December 31

Avery took in the lovely view from their Paris hotel room. The French doors opened onto the cutest Juliette balcony that offered a breathtaking view of the Eiffel Tower lit against the inky sky.

"More champagne, Mrs. McFadden?" Forest asked as he walked up behind her and pulled her against him.

"Yes, please," she said, turning around to face him.

Her three-carat solitaire winked at her as if saying "Well done, you two! Well done."

After Forest had proposed in New York, he'd told her that he had planned to do so on Christmas Day at his parents' house. When plans took the turn that they had, he regrouped and brought the ring to New York.

His quiet persistence was one of the many things she loved about this man. For the first time in her life she felt…secure. For the first time in her life she was in love in the purest sense of the word.

Forest refilled her flute. She touched her glass to his and then leaned in to kiss him. She still couldn't believe all that had happened since that proposal.

Three days after Christmas, Avery and Forest had gotten married in the office of the city clerk. While Bunny had not been happy about missing the wedding of her oldest son, they had compromised. The civil ceremony would be just for them—and Avery's roommate, Val, who acted as their witness—but they would have a church wedding later in the year.

They spent their wedding night at the Plaza and the following two days, they toured New York like newlywed tourists—kissing at the top of the Empire State Building… And on the Statin Island ferry… And at the top of the Statue of Liberty… And on the steps of the Met… Then on the third day, they had boarded a plane for Paris, where they would have a three-week honeymoon while Avery did the photographs for the *Carousels of France* coffee-table book.

After getting more details about the assignment from Barry, including a list of the towns where the carousels were located, she'd learned that twenty of the merry-go-rounds were in Paris. The plan was to spend the first week shooting them, and then she and Forest would rent a car and travel to the other locations on the list.

It was likely that she would get all the photos she needed on this trip, which would also double as their honeymoon. If she didn't, she would go back to France. Just because she was married didn't mean that she would lose her career.

Just because she had a career didn't mean that she couldn't let someone in.

Her husband was incredibly supportive and had been quite patient as she'd navigated the intricacies of her feelings about love and loss, and where and how they fit into each other's lives.

He had helped her see that it didn't have to be all or nothing. Career or love. The funny thing was that now that they were married, she didn't feel the need to hide behind her camera. She no longer felt like she had to hide at all.

Now that Avery could see things in a different perspective, it was clear that Gran had given her the greatest gift of all. Because of the extended time at Mistletoe Cottage she had been able to experience the beauty of friendship and community—even if, at times, it had been painful. Avery now realized her social skills were like an unused muscle that was uncomfortable as she exercised it by completing the tasks on Gran's wish list, through the auspices of her two wonderful, willful Secret Santas.

As for Mistletoe Cottage, she and Forest were keeping the house and she would use it as a studio next door to their house, where she'd live with her husband, the man she'd fallen in love with, the man who had never given up on her. He'd broken through her defenses and opened her heart to love. He was her sweet Gran's final, enduring gift to her.

Forest completed her. Together they were whole.

"It's about one minute until midnight," she said. "Do you have your champagne?"

He filled his glass and they stood entwined in each other's arms on the balcony as fireworks exploded over the Eiffel Tower, ushering in a new year for the world and a new life—a second chance—for the two of them.

When the fireworks stopped, Forest handed her an envelope. "I almost forgot to tell you. This arrived while you were in the shower."

She opened the white linen envelope and pulled out the card.

Congratulations, Mr. and Mrs. McFadden!
We wish the two of you the happiest life together.

Now that Christmas is over, our work here is done. We will retire our Santa hats. Avery, we're sure we don't have to tell you that you're never alone because you now have the biggest, best family and it's clear your husband loves you very much. Still, always remember your Gran and your parents live in your heart and we are always close by.
Love,
Hazel Buckminster and Doris Smith
Your Secret Grandmas

* * * * *

Don't miss out on these other
great holiday romances:

Triplets Under the Tree
By Melissa Senate

The Rancher's Christmas Star
By Stella Bagwell

Their Convenient Christmas Engagement
By Catherine Mann

Available now wherever Harlequin Special Edition
books and ebooks are sold!

Chapter One

Hutch Dawson's new nanny stood in the doorway of his home office with his squirming, screeching baby daughter in her arms. "Sorry, but this just isn't working out," she said.

He inwardly sighed but completely understood. His triplets were *a lot*. But maybe if he didn't look up from his computer screen, she'd take pity on him and go back into the living room where he could hear his other two babies crying. It was four thirty and her day ended at five. If he could just have this last half hour to deal with his to-do list.

He had three texts from his cowboys to return. Two important calls, including one from the vet with a steer's test results. And he was in the middle of responding to his brother's passive-aggressive email about the needs of the Dueling Dawsons Ranch.

The woman marched in, holding Chloe out with her legs dangling as though she were a bomb about to explode. Given the sight of the baby's clenched fists and red face, she was about to let out one hell of a wail.

She did, grabbing on to the nanny's ear too.

Mrs. Philpot, with her disheveled bun and shirt full of spit-up stains, grimaced and pried tiny fingers from her ear. "I won't be back tomorrow." She stood at the side of his desk and held out the baby.

This wasn't a big surprise. The previous nanny had quit two days ago, also lasting two days. But Hutch had to have childcare. He had ten days to go before his ex-wife was due back from her honeymoon—he could still barely wrap his mind around the fact that they were divorced with six-month-old triplets and that she'd remarried practically five minutes later. With two of his cowboys away for the holidays, his prickly brother—and new business partner—constantly calling or texting or demanding a meeting, a fifteen-hundred-acre ranch to run and way too many things to think about, Hutch *needed* a nanny.

Chloe let out a whimper between her shrieks, and Hutch snapped to attention, her plaintive cry going straight to his heart. He stood and took his baby girl, Daddy's arms calming her some. The moment Mrs. Philpot was free, she turned and hurried from the room. By the time he'd shifted Chloe against him and went after Mrs. Philpot to talk, use his powers of persuasion, to *beg*, she had on her coat and boots, her hand on the doorknob.

Noooo, he thought. *Wait!*

"I'll double your salary!" he called as she opened the door and raced out to her car in the gravel drive.

Then again, her salary, like the two nannies before her, had already been doubled. The director of
the nanny agency had assured him that Mrs. Philpot,
who'd raised triplets of her own, wouldn't be scared
off by a little crying in triplicate.

A little. Was there any such thing?

"They're just too much for me, dear," Mrs. Philpot
called back. She smoothed a hanging swath of her silver
hair back into the bun, rubbed her yanked-on ear, then
got into her car and peeled away, leaving him staring
at the red taillights disappearing down the long drive.

And hoping for a miracle. Like that she'd turn back.
At least finish the day. Even that would be a big help.

He did not see the car returning.

The other two babies were screaming their little heads
off in their swings in the living room. Hutch was lucky
he was hundreds of acres and many miles away from his
nearest neighbor in any direction. This morning, before
his workday, before the nanny was due to arrive, he'd
dared take the trio into town because he'd discovered
he was out of coffee and needed some and fast. He'd
taken them to Java House, and two of the babies started
shrieking. Compassionate glances of commiseration
from those sitting at the café tables with their lattes and
treats turned into annoyed glares. One woman came up
to him and said, "They could really benefit from pacifiers and so could we."

He'd been about to explain that his ex-wife had gotten him to agree to wean the triplets off their pacifiers
now that they were six months old. He truly tried to
adhere to Allison's lists and rules and schedules since
she really was better at all of it than he was, than he'd
been since day one. Even her new husband, a very nice,

calm optometrist named Ted, was better at caring for the triplets than Hutch was.

He shifted Chloe again, grateful that she, at least, had stopped crying. Whether from being in her daddy's arms or the blast of cold December air, flurries swirling, or both, he didn't know. She wore just cotton pj's, so he stepped back inside and closed the door. In the living room, Carson and Caleb were crying in their swings, the gentle rocking motion, soft lullabies and pastel mobile with little stuffed animals spinning having no effect. Little arms were raised, faces miserable.

What Hutch really needed was to turn into an octopus. He could cuddle each baby, make a bottle and down a huge mug of strong coffee all at the same time. He might have been chased out of Java House but not before he'd bought himself an espresso to go and two pounds of Holiday Blend dark beans.

"Hang on, guys," he told the boys, and put Chloe in her swing. She immediately started crying again, which he should have seen coming. "Kiddos, let me make a quick call. Then I'll be back and we'll see what the schedule says."

He lived by the schedule. His ex-wife was a stickler for it, and Hutch, truly no expert on how to care for triplet babies, regarded it as a bible. Between the trio's general disposition, which was crotchety, to use a favorite word of his late mother, and the three-page schedule, complete with sticky notes and addendums, it was no wonder Hutch had gone through six nannies in six months.

And he really was no better at caring for his own children than he was when they were born. He might be making excuses, but he blamed his lack of skills on the fact that he'd been relegated to part-time father from the moment they'd arrived into the world. His ex had left him for another man—her "soulmate"—when she was five months pregnant. He and Allison had joint fifty-fifty custody, so Hutch had the triplets three and a half days a week, which meant half the time to figure out how to care for them, to discover who they were becoming with each passing day, who liked and disliked what, what worked on which triplet. On his ex's custody days, he'd miss little firsts or milestones, and though just last week she'd Facetimed the trio trying their first taste of solids—jarred baby cereal—it wasn't the same as being there and experiencing it with them.

With his ex away for the next ten days, Hutch was actually very happy to have them to himself. The triplets were here, in his home, on his turf. Hutch's life might have been upended by the breakup of his marriage and the loss of his father just months ago and then everything going on with the ranch, but for the next week and a half his babies would be here when he woke up in the morning and here when he went to sleep. That made everything better, gave him peace, made all the other stuff going on trivial. Almost trivial.

He hurried into his office and grabbed his phone and pressed the contact button for the nanny agency, then went back into the living room, trying to gently shush the triplets, hoping his presence would calm them.

"I'm sorry, I can't hear you over the crying," the agency director said, her tone a bit strained. He had a feeling she'd already heard from Mrs. Philpot that she would not be back tomorrow. The woman had gotten *that* call four times before.

Hutch hurried to his office, closing the door till it

was just ajar. He explained his predicament. "I'll *triple* the salary of whoever can start tomorrow morning," he said. "I'll even double the salary of *two* nannies so that the big job isn't heaped on one person at such a busy time." Emergency times meant emergency measures.

"That's quite generous, Mr. Dawson, but I'm sorry to say that we're plumb out of nannies until after the new year." His heart sank as he glanced at his computer, the blinking cursor on his half-finished email to his brother, his to-do list running in his head. "If I may make a suggestion," she added—kindly, Hutch thought, hope flaring.

"Please do," he said.

"You have quite a big family here in town—all those Dawsons with babies and young children and therefore tons of experience. Call in the cavalry."

Just what his cousins wanted to do when they had families, jobs, and responsibilities of their own and right in the middle of the holiday season. He'd leaned on the generosity and expertise of various Dawsons for the past six months. He needed a dedicated nanny— even part-time.

As he disconnected from the disappointing call with the agency and went back out into the living room, his gaze landed on the tilted, bare Christmas tree he'd ordered from a nearby farm the other day when one of those Dawson cousins noted there *was* no tree. Not a half hour after it was delivered, Hutch had accidentally backed into it while rocking Carson in one arm and trying to push Chloe in the triple stroller since that usually helped her stop crying. Two bare branches hung down pathetically. He'd meant to decorate the tree, but between running the ranch and caring for the triplets once the nanny left, the box of ornaments and garland remained in the basement.

He looked at his precious babies. He needed to do better—for them. No matter what else, it was Christmas. They deserved *better.*

Caleb was crying harder now. Chloe looked spitting mad. Carson just looked…sad. Very sad. *Please pick me up, Daddy*, his big blue tearful eyes and woeful frown said.

"All right, kiddos, I'm coming," he said, rallying himself. He went for very sad Carson, undid the harness and scooped him out. This time, just holding the little guy seemed to help. But no, it was just a momentary curiosity in the change of position because Carson started crying again. He carefully held the baby against him with one firm arm, then got Chloe out and gave them both a rocking bounce, which seemed to help for two seconds. Now Caleb was wailing harder.

Hutch needed a minute to think—what time it was, what the schedule said. He wasn't *off*-schedule; he knew that. He put both babies in the playpen and turned on the lullaby player, then he consulted his phone for the schedule.

> *6:00 p.m.: Dinner. Offer a jar of vegetable baby food. Caleb and Chloe love sweet potatoes. Carson's favorite is string beans. Burp each baby. 6:30: Tummy time. 6:45: Baths, cornstarch and ointment as needed before diapers and pj's. 7:00 p.m.: Story time. 7:45: Bedtime.*

It was five forty-five. Clearly the babies needed something *now.* But what? Were they hungry a little early?

Had soggy diapers? Tummy aches—gas? He tried to remember what he'd read in last night's chapter of *Your Baby's First Year* for month six. But Chloe had awakened at just after midnight as he'd been about to drift off with month six milestones in his head, and then everything went out of his brain as he'd gotten up to tend to her. The moment he'd laid her back down in her bassinet in the nursery, Caleb's eyes popped open. At least Carson had slept through.

The schedule went out of his head as he remembered he still had to return the texts from one of his cowboys and had mini fires to put out. He stood in the middle of his living room, his head about to explode. He had to get on top of everything—the triplets' needs and the to-do list.

Maybe someone would magically respond to his ongoing ad for a nanny in the *Bear Ridge Weekly*. Just days ago he'd updated the half-page boxed ad, which ran both online and in the print edition with an optional border of tiny santas and candy canes to make the job seem more…festive. He quickly typed *Bear Ridge Weekly* classifieds into his phone's search bar to make sure his ad was indeed running. Yup. There it was. The holiday border did help, in his opinion.

Loving, patient nanny needed for six-month-old triplets from now till December 23rd. M-F, 8:00 a.m. to 5:00 p.m. Highly paid position, one hour for lunch, plus two half-hour breaks. See Hutch Dawson at the Dueling Dawsons Ranch.

He'd gotten several responses from the general ad over the past six months, but some candidates had seemed too rigid or unsmiling, and the few he'd tried out in between the agency nannies had also quit. One lasted three days. Now, everyone in town seemed to know not to respond to his ad. *It's those crotchety triplets!*

Caleb was suddenly shrieking so loud that Hutch was surprised the big round mirror over the console table by the front door didn't shatter. He quickly scooped up the baby boy and rubbed his back, which seemed to quiet him for a second. Chloe had her arms up again. Carson was still crying—but not wailing like Caleb. A small blessing there, at least.

The doorbell rang. Thank God, that had to be Mrs. Philpot with a change of heart because it was the Christmas season! Or maybe it was one of those wonderful Dawson cousins, any number of whom often stopped by with a lasagna—for him, not the babies— or outgrown baby items. They could strategize, make a nanny materialize out of thin, cold air. Mary Poppins, please.

He went to the door. It was neither Mrs. Philpot nor a Dawson.

It was someone he hadn't laid eyes on in seventeen years, since high school graduation. She was instantly recognizable. Very tall. The long red wavy hair. The sharp, assessing brown eyes. Plus there had always been something a little fancy about her. Like the cashmere emerald green coat and polished black cowboy boots she wore.

It was Savannah Walsh, his old high school nemesis—really, his enemy since kindergarten—standing there on his porch. In her hand was the updated ad from the *Bear Ridge Weekly*.

It might have been almost twenty years since he'd seen her, but he doubted she was anything like Mary Poppins.

"You might not remember me," Savannah said in a rush of words, her heart hammering away—so loud she was surprised he didn't hear it over all the wailing. "Savannah Walsh? We were in school together." *I had an intense crush on you since the first time I saw you—kindergarten. And every year I secretly loved you more...*

"I'd recognize you anywhere," he said, giving the baby in his arms a bounce. "Even without eyeglasses."

For a split second, Savannah was uncharacteristically speechless. She always had something to say. He *remembered* her. He even remembered that she wore glasses. She wasn't sure he would. Then again, she'd been the ole thorn in his side for years so she was probably unforgettable for that reason.

He looked surprised to see her—and dammit, as gorgeous as ever. The last time she'd seen him up close was seventeen years ago. But the warm blue eyes, almost black tousled hair, the slight cleft in his chin were all the same except for a few squint lines, a handsome maturity to his thirty-five-year-old face. He had to be six-two and was cowboy-muscular, his broad shoulders defined in a navy Henley, his slim hips and long legs in faded denim.

She'd seen him around town several times over the years, always at a distance, when she'd be back in Bear Ridge for the holidays or a family party, and any time she'd spot him on Main Street or in the grocery store or some shop, her stomach would get those little but-

terflies and she'd turn tail or hide behind a rack like a
sixteen-year-old who couldn't yet handle her emotions.

Amazing. Savannah Walsh had never been afraid
of anything in her life—except for how she'd always
felt about this man.

His head tilted a bit, his gaze going to the ad in her
hand. "You're here to apply for the nanny position?"
He looked confused; he'd probably heard along the way
that she was a manager of rodeo performers—even had
a few famous clients.

She peered behind him, where the crying of two
more babies could be heard. "Sort of," she said. "We
may be able to help each other out."

His eyes lit up for a moment, and she knew right
then and there that he was truly desperate for help.
Then his gaze narrowed on her, as if he was trying to
figure out what she could possibly mean by "sort of" or
"help each other out." That had always been their thing
back in school, really; both trying to read the other's
mind and strategy, one-up and come out victorious.

They'd been rivals whether for class treasurer, the
better grade in biology, or rodeo classes and compe-
titions. They'd always been tied—she'd beat him at
something, then he'd beat her. She'd had his grudging
respect, if not his interest in her romantically. She'd
been in his arms exactly once, for two and a half minutes at the senior prom, when she'd dared to ask him
to dance and he'd said, *Okay.* A slow song by Beyoncé.
But he'd stood back a bit, their bodies not touching,
except for his hands at her waist and hers on his shoulders, and he'd barely looked at her except to awkwardly
smile. Savannah, five foot ten and gangly with frizzy

red hair, oversized crystal-framed eyeglasses and a big personality, had been no one's type back then.

"Well, come on in," he said, stepping back and letting her enter.

The baby he held reached out and grabbed her hair, clutching a swath in his tiny fist. Ooh, that yank hurt. Rookie mistake, clearly.

She smiled at the little rascal and covered her eyes with her hands, then took them away. "Peekaboo!" she said. "Peekaboo, I see you!"

The baby stopped crying and stared at her, the tiny fist releasing her hair. Ah, much better. She took a step away.

He looked impressed. "You must have babies of your own to have handled that so well and fast."

For a moment she was stunned that she *had* done so well and she smiled, feeling a bit more confident about the reason she was here. But then the first part of what he'd said echoed in her head—about babies of her own.

"Actually, I don't. Not even one," she added, and wished she hadn't. *Do not call attention to your lack of experience.* Though, really, that was why she was here. To *gain* experience. "I have a three-year-old niece. Clara. She was a grabby one too. In fact, that's why I knew to put in my contact lenses to come see you. Clara taught me that babies love to grab glasses off my face and break the ear piece in the process."

He smiled. "Ah. I thought all my pint-sized relatives would have better prepared me for parenthood, but nope." Before she could respond, not that she knew what to even say since he looked crestfallen, he added, "So you said you're *sort of* here about the nanny job?"

Her explanation would take a while so she took off

her coat, even though he didn't invite her to, and hung it on the wrought-iron coatrack. For a moment all the little snowsuits and fleece buntings and man-size jackets on the various hooks mesmerized her. Then she realized Hutch was watching her, waiting for her to explain herself. Thing was, as she turned to face him, she really didn't want to explain herself. What was that saying, *all talk and no action*? Act, she told herself, like she had with the peekaboo game to free her hair from the itty fist. Then talk.

She turned her focus to the baby who'd resumed crying in Hutch's arms. Even red-faced and squawking, the little boy was beautiful. That very kind of observation was among the main reasons she was here. "Well, aren't you just the cutest," she said to the baby. "Hutch, why don't I take this little guy, and you go deal with the loudest of the other two and then we'll be able to talk without shouting." She smiled so it would be clear she wasn't judging the triplets for being so noisy. Or him.

He still had that look of confusion, but he let her take his son from his arms. As she cuddled the baby the way her sister had taught her when Clara was born three years ago, rubbing his little back in gentle, wide circles, he calmed down a bit and gazed up at her with big blue eyes.

"You wanna hear a song?" she asked him. "I'm no singer, but here goes." She broke into "Santa Claus Is Coming to Town." "He's making a list, he's checking it twice, he's gonna find out who's naughty and nice…"

Hutch paused from where he'd been about to pluck a baby in pink-and-purple-striped pj's from the swing area by the sliding glass doors and stared at her in a kind of puzzled wonder.

But she barely glanced at him. Instead, her attention was riveted by the sweet, solid weight in her arms, the blue eyes gazing up at her with curiosity. As the baby grabbed her pinky and held on with one heck of a grip, something stirred inside her. She almost gasped.

She'd been right to come here. Right to propose her outlandish idea. If she ever got around to it. She was stalling, she realized, afraid he'd shut her down and show her the door.

It was really her sister Morgan's idea. And it had taken Savannah a good two hours to agree it was a *good* one. She had no idea what Hutch would think.

She glanced at the baby she held, then at the other two. "Is it their dinner time?" she asked. "Maybe they're hungry?"

"Dinner is at six but I suppose they could eat ten minutes early." He paused. "That sounds really dumb— of course they should eat early if they're hungry. I'm just trying to follow the holy schedule."

Hmm, was that a swipe at the ex-wife she'd heard about from her sisters? "I know from my sister how important schedules are when it comes to children," she said with a nod. She'd once babysat Clara when she was turning one, and the list of what to do when was two pages long. "I'm happy to help out since I'm here."

His gaze shot to her, and he seemed about to say, *Why* are *you here*, but what came out of his mouth was, "I appreciate that. Their high chairs are in the kitchen."

She followed him into the big, sunny room, a country kitchen but with modern appliances. A round wood table was by the window, three high chairs around it. She'd put her niece in a high chair a time or two, so she slid the baby in and did up the straps. The little guy must know the high chair meant food or Cheerios because he instantly got happier. "What's this cutie's name?" she asked.

With his free hand, Hutch gave himself a knock on the forehead. "I didn't even introduce them. That's Caleb. I have Chloe," he said, putting her in the middle chair. "And I'm about to go get Carson." In twenty seconds he was back with a squawking third baby, who also immediately calmed down once he was in the chair. Hutch went to the counter and opened a ceramic container and scooped out some Cheerios on each tray. The babies all picked one up and examined it before dropping it on their tongues.

"Are they on solids?" she asked, remembering that was a thing at some point.

He nodded. "Jarred baby food. Their schedule has their favorites." He pulled out his phone and held it so she could see the list, then went to the cabinet and got out three jars and then three spoons from the drawer.

"Bibs?" she asked, recalling seeing it on the schedule next to dinner: *Don't forget the bibs or their good pj's will get stained.*

"Oh right," he said, and pulled three bibs from a drawer. He handed her one and quickly put on the other two. "Since you've made buddies with Caleb, maybe you could feed him while I do double duty with these two."

She smiled and took the jar he handed her. Sweet potato. And the tiny purple spoon. He sat back down and opened up two other jars, spoon in each hand, dipped and into each little mouth they went at the same time.

The kitchen was suddenly remarkably quiet. No crying.

She quickly opened up the sweet potato and gave Caleb a spoonful. He gobbled it up and tried to grab the spoon. "Ooh, you like your dinner. Here's another bite." She could feel Hutch's gaze on her as she kept feeding Caleb.

"I definitely recall hearing somewhere that you're a manager of rodeo performers?" Hutch said, dabbing Chloe's mouth with her bib.

"Yes. I'm off till just after Christmas, taking a much-needed vacation. I'm staying with my sister Morgan while I'm in town."

"But you're sort of here about the nanny job?" he asked, pausing from feeding the babies. Chloe banged a hand on the tray, sending two Cheerios flying.

"I... Yes," she said. "I'll get this guy fed and burped and then I'll explain."

He nodded and turned his attention back to Chloe and Carson.

As she slipped another spoonful of sweet potato puree into the open tiny mouth, she wondered how to explain herself without revealing her most personal thoughts and questions that consumed her lately and kept her up at night.

She could just launch into the truth, how she'd been at her youngest sister's bridal shower earlier today, which she would have enjoyed immensely were it not for her least favorite cousin, Charlotte. Charlotte, also younger than Savannah and a mom of three, had peppered her with questions about being single—long divorced—at age thirty-five. *Don't you want a baby? And don't you want to give that baby a sibling? Aren't you afraid you'll run out of time?*

Savannah's middle sister, Morgan, happily married

with a three-year-old and a baby on the way, had pro-
tectively and thankfully pulled Savannah away from
their busybody cousin. And what Savannah had admitted, almost tearfully, and she was no crier, was that
yes, she *was* afraid—because she didn't know what she
wanted. She'd been divorced since she was twenty-five.
Ten years was a long time to be on her own with every
subsequent relationship not working out. She'd put her
heart into her career and had long figured that maybe
not every woman found their guy.

Over the years she'd wondered if she measured her
feelings for her dates and relationships against the
schoolgirl longing she'd felt for Hutch Dawson. No
one had ever touched it, not even the man she'd been
briefly married to. That longing, from grade school
till she left Bear Ridge at eighteen, was part of the
reason Morgan had shown her Hutch's ad in the *Bear
Ridge Weekly*.

The other part, the main part, was about the babies.
The family.

She just had to explain it all to Hutch in a way that
wouldn't mortify her and would get him to say: *the
job is yours*.

"I have a proposal for you," she said.

Chapter Two

Savannah held her breath as Hutch looked over at her, spoonfuls of applesauce and oatmeal midway to Chloe's and Carson's mouths.

"A proposal," he repeated, sliding a glance at her. "I'm listening."

Since no words were coming out of her mouth, he turned his attention back to the babies, giving them their final bites of dinner. Then he stood and lifted Chloe out of the high chair, cuddling her against him and gently patting her back. One good burp later, he did the same with Carson.

Maybe Hutch realized she could use a minute before she blurted out her innermost burning thoughts. She definitely did, so she focused on Caleb and his after-dinner needs. She'd never been able to get a good burp out of her niece when she was a baby. Savannah was on the road so often, traveling with her clients, or at home three hours away in Blue Smoke, where one of the biggest annual rodeos was held every summer, that she didn't really see Clara as much as she wanted. Savannah had a bit of experience at childcare. But it was just that. A bit. And when it came to babies, that experience was three years old.

She'd watched how Hutch had handled burp time, so she stood and took Caleb from the high chair, put him against her shoulder and gently patted his back. Nothing. She patted a little harder. Still nothing.

Her shoulders sagged. How could she expect Hutch to give her a job involving baby care when she couldn't even get a baby to burp!

"Caleb likes three fast pats dead center on his back," Hutch said. "Try that."

She did.

BURP!

Savannah grinned. "Yes!" The little boy then spit up on her fawn-colored cashmere sweater, which probably wasn't the best choice in a top for the occasion of coming to propose he let her be his nanny till Christmas. At least she wore her dark denim and cowboy boots, which seemed perfectly casual.

Hutch handed her a wet paper towel. "Sorry."

"No worries. That I don't mind is actually an important element of why I'm here."

"Right," he said. "The proposal." He stared at her for a moment. "Let's take these guys into the living room and let them crawl around. They're not actually crawling yet but they like to try. Then I want to hear all about this proposal of yours."

She had Caleb and he took both Carson and Chloe.

She followed him into the living room, and they sat down on the huge soft foam play mat decorated with letters and numbers. The babies were on their hands and knees and sort of rocked but didn't crawl. They were definitely content.

She sucked in a breath. *Okay,* she told herself. *Come out with it.* "I'm kind of at a crossroads, Hutch."

He glanced at her. "What kind of crossroads?"

"The kind where I'm not sure if I want to keep doing what I'm doing or…something else."

"Like what?" he asked, pushing a stuffed rattle in the shape of a candy cane closer to where Carson was rocking back and forth. The boy's big eyes stared at the toy.

Here goes, she thought. "I'm thirty-five and long divorced. Married life, motherhood has all sort of passed me by. I have a great job and I'm suited to it. But lately, I've had these…feelings. Like maybe I do want a family. I'm not the least bit *sure* how I feel, what I truly want."

His head had tilted a bit, and he waited for her to continue.

Why was it so hard to say all this? "My sister happened to see your ad while she was looking for a date-night sitter in the local paper's help wanted section. She thought maybe I could get a little clarity, find out what family life is like by helping you out with the triplets till Christmas."

"I see," he said. And that was all he said. She held her breath again.

For a moment they just watched the babies, Carson batting the stuffed rattle on the mat, Chloe still rocking on her hands and knees, Caleb now on his back trying to chew his toe.

"I don't have any experience as a nanny," she rushed to say, the uncomfortable silence putting her a bit off balance. Clearly, since she wasn't exactly selling herself here. "I've cared for my niece, as I've said, here and there over the past three years. More there than here. I want to see what it feels like to care for a baby—babies. To be involved in a family."

"Like an experiment," he said.

"I guess so." Her heart sank. She was sure *experimenting* with his children wasn't going to be okay with him. Why had she thought he might consider this?

"And no need to pay me for the ten days, of course, since we'd be helping each other out." Savannah was very successful and didn't look at this as a temporary job; it was a chance to find out if motherhood really was what she wanted. For that, *she'd* pay. Her heart hammered again, and she took a fast breath to calm down a bit. "I'm sure you want to think it over." She hurried over to the coatrack and pulled her wallet from her coat pocket, taking out a business card. She walked back over and knelt down to hand it to him. "My contact info is on there."

He looked at it, then put it in his back pocket. "Can you start immediately?" he asked. "Like now?"

She felt her eyes widen—and hope soar. "I'm hired?" Had she heard him correctly?

"I can't do this alone," he said. "And I can't take off the next several days from the ranch. I need help. And here you are, Savannah Walsh. If there's one thing I remember about you it's that you get things done. And—" He cut himself off.

Well, now she had to know what that *and* was about. "And?" she prompted gently.

"And…okay, I'm just going to say it. I used to think, man, that Savannah Walsh is all business, works her tail off, but then I experienced firsthand that you have a big heart too. That combination qualifies you for the job. And like I said, the fact that you're here. Wanting the job. Many nannies have given up. I insist on paying you, though. And a lot."

She was still caught on the middle part of what he'd said. About his experiencing that she had a big heart. There could only be one instance he was referring to— that bad day at a rodeo competition when he'd come in third and his father had gone off on him, and she— who'd come in second—had tried to comfort him. She was surprised it had stuck with him all these years later, but she supposed those kinds of things did stick with people. When you were going through something awful and someone was in your corner.

"Of course, we were big-time rivals back then," he rushed to say. "So we might not get along even now."

She smiled. "I'm sure we won't, if it's like old times."

He smiled too. "Though we had a couple of moments, didn't we?"

She almost gasped. So he remembered the other incident too. The dance at the prom. All two and half minutes of it. Had *that* stuck with him?

"Plus it's been a long time," she said. They were different people now; they'd lived entire lives, full of ups and downs.

"A long time," he repeated.

"I can't promise I'll be great at the job," she said, probably too honestly. "But I'll try hard. I'll be responsible. I'll put my heart and brains into everything I do when I'm with your children, Hutch."

"I appreciate that," he said. "And you have two hands. That's what I need most of all."

Happy, excited chills ran up and down her spine. "Well, then. You've got yourself your holiday season nanny."

A relief came over his expression, and she could see his shoulders relax. He was desperate. But in this case, it worked in her favor.

"Look, Savannah," he said. "Because I know you, I mean, we go way back, and this is a learning experience for you and a severe need for me, would you consider being live-in for the ten days? The triplets are pretty much sleeping through the night, if you consider midnight to five thirty 'the night.'"

Live-in. Even better. "That would certainly show me true family life with babies," she said. "So yes. I'll just get my bags from my sister's and be back in a half hour."

"Just in time for the bedtime routine," he said. "I'm pretty bad at that. And I have a lot of unfinished business from today that I still need to get to, so having your help will make it go much faster. I can't tell you how lucky I feel that you knocked on the door, Savannah."

Ha. We'll see if you're still feeling lucky tomorrow when it's clear I don't know a thing about babies. Times three.

She extended her hand. "And truly, I won't accept pay."

"How about this—I'll donate what I'd pay you to the town's holiday fundraiser for families who need help with meals and gifts and travel expenses."

She smiled. "Perfect."

He gave her hand a shake, holding on for a moment and then covering her hand with his other. "Thank you."

"And thank you," she said a little too breathlessly, too aware from the electric zap that went straight to her toes that her crush on Hutch Dawson was far from over.

"Well, guys," Hutch said to the triplets, each in their own little baby tub in the empty bathtub. "That is what's known as a Christmas miracle."

He still could barely believe he'd gotten so lucky—though lucky was of course relative. Savannah Walsh might not have experience with babies but she was here. Or would be in about ten minutes. To help. And oh man, did Hutch need help.

Carson banged his rubber duckie, and Chloe chewed her waterproof book with the chewable edges as Hutch poured warm water over the shampoo on Caleb's head, careful not to let it get in his eyes. A minute ago, Chloe had dropped her head back at the moment Hutch had gone to rinse the shampoo from her hair, and water and suds had streamed down her face. She'd wailed for a good half minute until Hutch had distracted with peekaboo—Savannah's earlier go-to. One of his cousins—Maisey, who ran the childcare center at the Dawson Family Guest Ranch, had given him five pairs of goofy glasses to make peekaboo work even faster. He'd grabbed the plastic glasses with their springy cartoon puppy cutouts, and Chloe was indeed transfixed and had stopped crying. He had a pair in practically every room in the house.

Carson batted his hands down, splashing lukewarm water all over his siblings, who giggled.

"All right, you little rug rats, bath time is over. Let's get you dry and changed."

He lifted each baby with one hand, drained their tub with the other, then wrapped them in their adorable hooded towels, a giraffe for Caleb, a lion for Chloe and a bear for Carson. He plopped them down in the portable playpen he'd bought just for this purpose—to get all three babies from the bathtub to the nursery at the same time. It was probably the baby item he used most often; he transported them all over the one-story ranch house with ease.

He got each baby into a fresh diaper and pj's, and now it was time for their bottles. Then it would be story time, then bedtime. Hopefully Savannah really would be back to help with that.

The doorbell rang. Perfect. She was back a little early and could help with bottles. He'd gotten okay at feeding two babies at once, but he didn't have *three* hands.

He wheeled the playpen to the door, but it wasn't Savannah, after all. It was Daniel, his brother. Or his *half* brother, as Daniel always corrected him. Tall like Hutch, with light brown hair and the Dawson blue eyes, Daniel lived in town with Olivia, his wife of twenty years. When he and his brother inherited the ranch from their father three months ago, Daniel had surprised Hutch by taking down his CPA shingle in town and coming aboard full-time as chief financial officer, which Hutch had been initially glad about since it freed him up to focus on the day-to-day of managing the ranch. But his brother disagreed with a lot of Hutch's plans for the Dueling Dawsons Ranch—too apt a name, as always. Hutch had been the foreman for a decade—he knew the fifteen-hundred-acre ranch inside and out—but family feuds had plagued the Dawsons on this property since his great-grandfather and great-uncle had bought the land more than a century ago. He and Daniel did not break the pattern.

The one thing Daniel did not seem interested in was pursuing the list of "Unfinished Business" that Lincoln Dawson had left tacked up on his bulletin board. There were only two items, both doozies. But Hutch intended to cross them off by Christmas. Somehow, he thought his father would truly rest in peace that way. And Hutch by association. God knew, Daniel needed some peace.

"I'm leaving for the day," Daniel said, shoving his silver-framed square eyeglasses up on his nose. "And still no response to my email about your list of costly initiatives for the ranch," he added, shoving his hands into the pockets of his thick flannel barn coat. He wore a brown Stetson, flurries collecting on top and the brim.

"I was actually in the middle of answering when disaster struck," Hutch said, stepping back so Daniel could come in out of the cold. "The new nanny quit on me."

"Another one?" Daniel raised an eyebrow, stopping on the doormat, which indicated he wasn't staying long—good thing. "Is it you or the triplets? Probably both," he said with a nod, answering that for himself.

Ah, Daniel. So supportive, as always.

"I was just about to make up their bottles," Hutch said, angling his head toward the playpen. "If you can feed one of the babies, I can do two and we can talk."

Daniel scowled. "I'm long done feeding a baby." Hutch mentally shook his head. Daniel and Olivia were empty nesters; their eighteen-year-old son was in college two hours away near the Colorado border. "We'll talk in the morning. Or are you going to be trapped here with them and not out on the ranch, taking care of business?"

Keep your cool, hold your tongue. That was Hutch's motto when it came to dealing with his brother. His half brother.

"*Trapped* isn't the word I'd use," he said, narrowing a glare on Daniel. "And I have a new nanny already. She's starting tonight, as a matter of fact. She'll be a live-in through Christmas Eve."

"Good. Because you need to get your share of the work done."

Keep your cool, hold your tongue...

"I'll see you at 6:00 a.m. in the barn," Hutch said. "We can talk about the email and the sheep while taking on Mick's and Davis's chores."

"I don't see why cowboys had to get ten days off," Daniel groused.

Had Hutch ever met someone more begrudging than Daniel Dawson? "Because they've worked hard all year and get two weeks off. They both had the time coming to them."

"It's bad timing with our father being gone."

"Yeah," Hutch said, picturing Lincoln Dawson. He'd been sixty-two when an undiagnosed heart condition took him from them. Maybe he'd hidden the symptoms; Hutch wasn't sure, and Daniel had kept his distance from their dad as he had his entire life. Lincoln had worked hard, done the job of a cowboy half his age. He'd hated administrative work and trusted few people so he'd offered Hutch the foreman job ten years ago, when Hutch had been fresh out of an MBA in agricul-

tural business, about to take a high-paying job at a big
cattle ranch across town. Hutch had shocked himself
by saying yes to his father's offer at half the salary and
fewer perks. *Maybe I'll finally figure you out, Lincoln
Dawson*, he'd thought.

But he hadn't. And Daniel hated talking about their
father, so he'd never been any help.

Daniel reached for the doorknob. "Six sharp."

"You could acknowledge your niece and nephews,"
Hutch said unexpectedly, surprised it had come out of
his mouth. But he supposed it did bother him that his
brother barely paid them any attention. He was their
uncle.

"Don't make this something it's not," Daniel said,
without a glance at the triplets, and left.

Hutch sighed and rolled his eyes. "Your uncle is
something, huh, guys?" he directed to his children. "*A
piece of work*, as your late grandmother would have
said. "Or as your late grandfather would have said suc-
cinctly, *difficult*."

His brother had always been that. When Daniel
was four, Lincoln had walked away from his family
to marry his mistress—Hutch's mother. A year after
their marriage, Hutch was born, and Hutch could recall his brother spending every other Saturday at the
ranch for years, until Daniel was twelve or thirteen and
said he was done with that. Their dad hadn't insisted,
which had still infuriated Daniel and also his mother;
Hutch had known that from screaming phone calls and
slammed doors between the exes.

What Hutch did know about his father was that he'd
loved his second wife, Hutch's mom, deeply. The two of
them had held hands while eating dinner at the dining

table. They'd danced in the living room to weird eighties new wave music. They'd gotten dressed up and had gone out to a fancy meal every Saturday night without fail. The way his father had looked at his mother had always softened Hutch's ire at very-difficult-himself Lincoln Dawson; Hutch had given him something of a pass for what a hardcase he'd been with Hutch and Daniel and anyone else besides his wife. Hutch's mother had died when he was eighteen, and in almost twenty years, Lincoln had never looked at another woman as far as Hutch knew. But the loss had turned his father even more gruff and impatient, and Hutch had threatened to quit, had quit, about ten times.

Your mother wouldn't like the way I handled things earlier, Lincoln would say by way of apology. *She'd want you to come back.*

Hutch always had. He loved the Dueling Dawsons Ranch. The land. The work. The livestock. And he'd loved his father. He'd been gone three months now, and sometimes his absence, the lack of his outsize presence on the ranch, gripped Hutch with an aching grief.

There were just some things that stayed with a person— the good and the bad. When Hutch's ex-wife had sat him down last year and tearfully told him she was leaving him for Ted, a distraught, confused, scared Hutch had packed a suitcase and turned up at the ranch. His father had taken one look at his face, at the suitcase, and had asked him what happened. Lincoln had called Allison a vile name that Hutch had tried to put out of his memory, then told his son he could stay at the ranch in his old room, take some time off work as the foreman if he needed and went to make them spaghetti and garlic bread, which Hutch had barely been able to eat but appreciated. They'd sat at the table in near silence, also appreciated, except for his father twice putting his hand on Hutch's shoulder with a, *You'll get through this.*

Whenever things with his dad had gotten rough, he'd remember that Lincoln Dawson had been there for him when it really mattered. He also liked how his father had bought the triplets a gift every Monday, the same for each, whether tiny cowboy hats or rattles or books, when Allison would drop them off. Lincoln would give her the death stare, then dote on the triplets, talking to them about ranch life. Then in another breath, he'd flip out on Hutch for how he handled something with a vendor or which pasture he'd moved the herd to.

He's never going to be any different, Daniel had said a few times the past couple of years when Lincoln must have started feeling sick or weakened but had refused to see a doctor and had brushed off questions about his health. *Stop chasing his approval already.*

Hutch often wanted to slug his brother, but never so much as during those times when he'd accuse Hutch of exactly that. Chasing his approval. He'd had it—his father had made him his foreman, hadn't he? Daniel would say it was more than that, deeper, but Hutch would shut that down fast.

Five minutes later, the doorbell rang again, and he shook off the memories, shook off his brother's visit and attitude. Savannah was back. His shoulders instantly unbunched. There was something calming about her presence, a quiet confidence, and he liked the way she looked at the triplets. With wonder and affection.

He liked the way she looked, period. Had she always been so pretty? He hadn't really thought of her that way back in school, given their rivalry. But he did remember being surprised by his reaction when she'd taken his hand in solidarity after that rodeo competition their senior year. A touch he'd felt *everywhere*. His father had screamed his head off at Hutch about a minor mistake he'd made that had cost him first and second place, and Savannah had heard the whole thing. She'd walked up to him and took his hand and just held it and said, *You didn't deserve that. You were great out there as always.* The reverberation of that touch had distracted him for a moment, and he wanted to pull her to him and just hold her, his rival turned suddenly very attractive *friend*. But he'd been seventeen and humiliated by his father's tirade and wanted the ground to swallow him so he'd run off without a word, shaking off her hand like it had meant nothing to him.

He wondered if she even remembered that. Probably not. It was a long time ago.

He went to the door and there she was, her long red hair twisted into a bun—smart move—her face scrubbed free of the glamorous makeup she'd worn earlier. She wore a down jacket over a T-shirt with a rodeo logo and faded low-slung jeans. He swallowed at the sight of her. Damn, she was beautiful.

"The doorbell reminded me that I need to give you a key," he said, reaching for her bags. He took her suitcase and duffel and set them down by the door, then reached into his pocket for his key ring and took off one of the extra house keys. "I'll give you a quick tour and show you your room, and then we can give the triplets their bottles."

She smiled and put the key on her own ring, looking past him for the triplets, first at their swings, then at the playpen, in which the three were sitting and contentedly playing with toys. "Let me at those adorable littles." She rushed over to the playpen and knelt down beside it, chatting away to the babies about how she was here to help take care of them.

As she stood and turned back to him, she seemed so truly happy, her face flushed with excitement, that he found himself touched. This was a completely different setup than he was used to; she wasn't working for him, he wasn't paying her. She was here to get experience, to have some questions answered for herself.

It occurred to him that they should probably talk about that setup—expectations on both sides, how she wanted to structure the "job," the hours he'd need to devote to the ranch, the triplets' schedule, details about each of them, such as their different personalities, likes and dislikes, what worked on which baby. They should also talk about nighttime wakings; at least one triplet woke up at least once a night and would likely wake her up. He wanted to ensure that he wouldn't be taking advantage of her being a live-in.

He suddenly envisioned Savannah coming out of her room at 2:00 a.m. to soothe a crier in nothing but a long T-shirt. He blinked to get the image out of his head. He seemed to be drawn to her—there was just something about her, something winsome, something both tough and vulnerable—and they did go back a ways, which made her seem more familiar than she actually was. But Hutch had had his entire world turned upside down and sideways and shaken—by the divorce, by being a father of three babies that he loved so much he thought he might burst sometimes, by his father's loss and the sudden onslaught of his brother. He couldn't imagine wanting anything to do with the opposite sex.

Or maybe I could, he amended as a flash of Savannah in just a long T-shirt floated into his mind again.

Nah, he thought. He really doubted that even sex could tempt him to step back into the romance ring. Not after what he'd been through.

Suuure, said a very low voice in the back of his mind where reality reigned.

Chapter Three

Savannah liked her room. It was a guest room next door to the nursery. There were two big windows, soothing off-white walls with an abstract watercolor of the Wyoming wilderness, a queen-size bed with a fluffy blue-and-white down comforter and lots of pillows, a dresser with a round mirror, a beautiful kilim rug, and a glider by the window. Perfect for taking a crying baby into her room in the middle of the night to soothe without waking up the other two.

Hutch, with the baby monitor in his back pocket, was putting her suitcase and duffel by the closet. Being in here, her room for the ten days, with him so close was doing funny things to her belly. "This was my room growing up. The furniture was different then, but that's the window I stared out every day, wondering where my life would take me." He walked over and looked out. He'd had a view of a stand of evergreens and the woods beyond and part of the fields.

"It took you right here," she said, thinking about that for a moment. Full circle. "Did you even consider that then? That you'd be the foreman on this ranch?"

"Absolutely not. My father wasn't the easiest man to get along with. But not long after I left for college to study agricultural business—with the intention of having my own ranch someday—I lost my mom. When my dad offered me the foreman's job, the idea of coming home called to me. She loved this ranch. I always did too."

"I grew up in town," she said. "But I've always wanted to live on a ranch. I'm a rodeo gal at heart."

"Well, for the next week and a half, you'll be woken up by a crowing rooster long before a crying baby or two or three, so that might get old fast. You should visit the barn. We have six beautiful horses."

She smiled. "I'll plan to. So what's on the schedule? I'm excited to jump right into my first official task as Christmas season nanny."

"It's time for their last bottles. Usually I feed two at once, then the third, but now we can split that up."

"I see what you mean about needing an extra set of hands," she said. "It must have been really hard these past six months, being on your own once the nannies were done for the day. I guess you had to figure it out as you went?"

"Yup, exactly. I'm a pretty good multitasker, though, something necessary to be a good ranch foreman. You know what the hardest part has been? When I don't know how to soothe one or two or all three, when they're crying like they were earlier when the former nanny quit on me. When I don't know how to make it better and nothing works. I feel like a failure as a dad." He frowned, and it was clear how deep the cuts could go with him.

"Oh Hutch," she said, her heart flying out to him. "I'll bet it's like that for any parent of even just one baby. They don't talk, they can't tell you where it hurts or what they want, and you love them so much that it just kills you."

"Exactly," he said. "For someone who doesn't have experience with babies, you definitely get it."

She felt herself beam. She wasn't entirely sure how she "got it"; she supposed it was just human nature to feel that way about something so precious and dependent on you.

"Let's go feed them, and we can talk about how to arrange this," he said, wagging a finger between them. "How it'll all work. I really don't want to take advantage of you being here, living here, and the *reason* you're here. It's a tough job, Savannah."

"I'm a tough woman," she said. Except she didn't feel that way here in Hutch's house, in his presence. She felt…very vulnerable.

"You were a tough girl," he said. "Kept me on my toes."

She laughed. "Well, tough might have kept me from—" Ugh, she clammed up in the nick of time. Was she honestly about to tell Hutch Dawson that she was afraid her cousin Charlotte's assessment of her earlier at the bridal shower was right, that who Savannah was made her unappealing to men—*intimidating* and *too successful* were the actual words her cousin had used today.

Oh please, Savannah had thought, but she'd heard that her entire life. She'd been five foot ten since she was thirteen and no slouch, literally or figuratively, so she'd been standing tall a long time. And yes, she was straightforward and could be barky, and she was damned good at her job. It was true that she could make some people quake because of her stature in the industry at this point. But that was business, and her profession demanded *tough*. She'd never gotten very far with men, though. She'd get ghosted or told it just wasn't working out after a week or two of dating.

Or seven months of marriage. *I'm not one of your clients*, her new husband had said so many times that she'd started doubting herself—who she was, particularly. *You're trying to manage me*, he'd toss at her. *Maybe if you didn't work such long hours or travel so much, I wouldn't have cheated.*

With a friend, among others, no less. Savannah hadn't been sure he had been cheating until her "friend" had confirmed it and said the same thing her husband had: *If you devoted yourself to your marriage instead of your career...* At twenty-five she'd had an ex-husband, an ex-friend and dealt with her doubly broken heart by devoting herself even more to her career. She was in a male-dominated industry, but her voice, drive and determination had carried her to the top. She took reasonable risks, demanded the best of her clients and for them, but cared deeply about each one. Yeah, she was tough.

To a point, she reminded herself. Lately, she'd find herself tearing up. She'd been in a grocery store a few days ago and the sight of a young family, a dad pushing the cart with a toddler in the seat, the mom walking beside him with a little girl on her shoulders and letting the child take items off the high shelves for her—Savannah had almost burst into tears in the bread aisle of Safeway.

Do I want that? she'd asked herself, perplexed by her reaction. Why else would she have been so affected? She'd written off remarriage and happily-ever-after, having lost her belief and faith in either, in the fairy tale. Her parents had had a wonderful, long marriage. One sister was happily married and the other was engaged and madly in love with her fiancé. Savannah knew there were good men out there, good marriages. But she'd always been…tough. And maybe meant to be on her own.

She didn't know how to be any different. It was her natural personality that put the fear of God into the men and women rodeo performers she managed, from up-and-comers with great potential to superstars, like her most famous client, a bull rider who'd quit fame and fortune to settle down with the woman he loved and the child he'd only recently discovered was his. She'd spent some time with the happy family the past few months, and Logan Winston's happiness, a joy she hadn't seen in him ever before, made her acknowledge a few hard truths about herself. That she was lonely. That she did have a serious hankering for something more—she just wasn't sure what, exactly. A change, but what change? She should talk to Logan about it while she was in town.

Hutch was leaving the room so she shook off her thoughts and followed, excited to get started on her new role—for the time being, anyway. A life of babies and Hutch Dawson.

In the kitchen, she stood beside him as he made up the bottles, watching carefully how he went about it so she could do it herself. Back in the living room, he set the three bottles on the coffee table, then grabbed a bunch of bibs and burp cloths from the basket on the shelf under the table, and finally, wheeled the playpen over to the sofa.

"I'll watch you for a moment," she said, sitting down. "See how you hold the baby, hold the bottle, just so I know how to do it all properly."

"It's a cinch. Maybe the easiest part of all fatherhood—and the most relaxing, well, except for watching them sleep. There's just something about feeding a baby, giving him or her what they need, all in the grand comfort of your arms."

"I always felt that way when I watched my sister feed Clara," she said, recalling how truly cozy it looked, how content mama and baby had always appeared.

He picked up Carson and settled him slightly reclined along one arm, then reached for a bottle and tilted it into the little bow-shaped mouth. Carson put his hands on the bottle and suckled away, Hutch's gaze loving on his son.

"Got it," she said. "Should I grab another baby for you?"

"Sure, take your pick."

"I'll save Chloe for myself since I got time with Caleb earlier." She scooped the little guy from the playpen and settled him on Hutch's right side. When he shifted Caleb just right, she handed him a bottle. In no time, he was feeding both babies.

My turn! She picked up Chloe, who stared at her with huge blue eyes. *Oh, aren't you precious,* she thought, putting Chloe along her arm and grabbing the third bottle. "Hungry?" she asked. She slipped the nipple into the baby's mouth, and it was so satisfying as Chloe started drinking, her little hands on the sides of the bottle. Savannah gazed down at her, mesmerized. When she glanced up, she realized Hutch was watching her. Her. Not how she was holding Chloe or the bottle. *Her.*

Could he be interested? Hutch Dawson, guy of her dreams since she was five, star of her fantasies since middle school? He was the one thing she'd ever wanted that she hadn't gone for, her fear—of rejection and how bad it would hurt—and lack of confidence when it came to personal relationships making her anything but tough.

"This is great," he said with a warm smile. "Having the extra two hands."

Oh. That was what the look of wonder was about. How helpful she was. He wasn't suddenly attracted to her. It wasn't like she'd changed all that much physically since high school, and he'd never given her a second glance back then.

"Having you here for the bedtime routine will be a huge help," he added. "I've really never been good at it. One of the triplets always fights their drooping eyes and fusses, then another fusses, then one starts crying… What takes Allison and Ted fifteen minutes takes me an hour."

"Allison and Ted?" she asked, glancing at him. She darn well knew who Allison was—his ex-wife. Savannah remembered her from school. Petite, pretty, strawberry blonde and blue eyed. A cheerleader. Hutch Dawson's type. They'd dated on and off but had always been more off as Savannah recalled. She knew a little bit about the divorce from her sister. Apparently Allison had reconnected with an old flame from college on Facebook. And actually walked away from her marriage at five months pregnant. According to Morgan, Allison had been shunned by some and lauded by others—*How could you?* vs *Life is too short not to follow your heart.*

All Savannah could think was how absolutely awful it must have been for Hutch.

"My ex-wife," he said. "And her new husband. You might remember Allison Windham from school. Then she was Allison Dawson for a year, but now she'll be Allison Russo. Sometimes I can't wait until the triplets are old enough for people to stop gossiping about how I'm divorced with babies. Some folks know the sob story but most assume *I* left, even though my ex is the one living in my former house with another man. You should see some of the stare downs I get in the grocery store."

"Ugh, that's terrible," she said. "How unfair. To have your life turned upside down and to get the blame."

He shot her something of a smile. "Small town, big gossip."

"Yeah, I remember. It's one of the reasons why I was excited to leave for bigger pastures. I do love Bear Ridge, though."

"Yeah, me too." They glanced at each other for a moment, and she felt so connected to him. They came from the same place, had the same beginning history in terms of school and downtown and the Santa hut on the town green. She'd passed it several times since she'd arrived, her heart warmed by the sight of the majestic holiday tree all decorated and lit up in the center of the small park, the red Santa hut with the big candy cane chimney, the families lined up so that the kids could give Santa their lists.

She wondered if Hutch had envisioned himself standing with his family in line, the triplets in the choo choo train of a stroller she'd seen by the door, his wife beside him. Had he been blindsided by her affair? In any case, he must have been devastated when his ex had told him she was leaving.

She glanced down at Chloe, just a tiny bit left in her bottle, and then the baby turned her head slightly.

"That means she's done," Hutch said. "You can burp her and set her in the playpen, and then grab Carson—he's done too."

Savannah stood and held Chloe up vertically against her, about to pat her back.

"I'd set a burp cloth on your shoulder and chest," he said. "You don't want spit up all over that cool shirt."

She glanced down at her *Blue Smoke Summer Rodeo 2019* jersey. Years old and soft and faded. She'd worn it specifically for the job—no worries in getting dirty and grabbed and pulled out of shape. But she'd still prefer spit up on the burp cloth and not her. She shifted Chloe and bent a little to pick up a cloth, arranging it on her shoulder, hanging down on her chest.

She gave Chloe's back a good three pats and a big burp came out. "Success!" Savannah said. "What a great baby you are," she whispered to Chloe. "An excellent burper."

She set Chloe in the playpen and reached for Carson. Was it her imagination or did Hutch's gaze go to the sliver of belly exposed by her shirt lifting up as she leaned over? He handed over Carson and she repeated what she'd just done, but getting a burp out of this guy was taking longer.

How many times had she told her clients—and in

talks to various groups and schools—not to think one great performance meant another? You had to work for it—always. She adjusted Carson in her arms and gave up two more pats with a bit more force, and out came a big, satisfying burp.

"I've got this!" she said, unable to contain her excitement. "I was afraid you'd regret taking me on as a student nanny, but I'm feeling a lot more confident."

He smiled. "Good. Because you're doing great."

"You hear that, Carson?" she said, running a finger down the baby's impossibly soft cheek. "I'm doing great!"

Once all three babies were in the playpen, Hutch stood. "If you'll keep watch over them, I could use a solid twenty minutes to finish up today's work—just some administrative stuff, texts and calls and emails."

"Sure thing," she said.

As he left the room, she felt the lack of him immediately.

My crush on your daddy will never go away, I guess, she said silently to the triplets as she wheeled the playpen over to the sliding glass door. There was a pretty pathetic Christmas tree with one strand of garland hanging down along with two branches. The entire tree was tilted as though someone had backed into it. She had a feeling that someone was Hutch with two babies in his arms. She'd help him get the tree decked out. Since the babies weren't crawling, there were no worries about safety-proofing for Christmas yet.

"Well, guys," she said. "How am I doing so far? Not too bad, right?"

Carson gave her a big gummy smile, two tiny teeth poking up.

I sure do like you three, she thought, giving Caleb's

soft hair a caress. She'd been here, on the job, for barely an hour and she was falling in serious like with everything to do with the triplets. And Hutch Dawson all over again.

Hutch sat at his desk in his home office, half expecting Savannah to appear in the doorway with a crying baby with a firm grip on her hair or ear and say, *Sorry, but I've already realized that this isn't the life for me, buh-bye*—and go running out the door.

But he'd gotten through three calls, returned all the texts and had made himself mental notes for tomorrow's early-morning meeting with his brother in the barn—and no appearance in the doorway. No quitting. No *crying*.

Blessed silence.

His office door was ajar and every now and then he could hear Savannah's running commentary. She'd wheeled the babies in the playpen into the nursery and changed them one by one, choosing fresh pj's, which he knew because she was chatting away. *Stripes for you, Caleb. Polka dots for Chloe, and tiny bears for Carson. Oooh, another rookie mistake, guys, Caleb almost sprayed me!* She'd laughed and then continued her commentary all the way back down the hall to the living room.

Now she was talking to the triplets about the Christmas tree and how she and her sisters used to make a lot of their ornaments when they were little as family tradition. From what he could tell, she'd wheeled the playpen over by the tree and was picking up each triplet to give them turns at being held and seeing the lonely, bare branches.

"Oooh, that's what I get for letting you get too close to my ear," he heard her say on a laugh to one of the triplets. "Strong girl," she added. "Peekaboo! I see you!"

He smiled as he envisioned her playing peekaboo with one hand to get her ear back. He'd have to tell her about the goofy glasses.

"Okay, now it's Carson's turn," she said.

This was going to work out just fine, he thought, turning his attention back to his brother's email. Ten minutes later, he was done, turned off his desk lamp and went to find Savannah and the babies.

They were sitting on the play mat, and she was telling them a story about a fir tree named Branchy who no one picked for their home at Christmastime.

"Buh!" Caleb said, batting his thigh.

Carson shook his stuffed rattle in the shape of a bunny.

Chloe was giggling her big baby laugh that always made Hutch laugh too.

Savannah turned and grinned. "They like me! Babies like me!"

He realized just then how nervous she'd probably been about how they'd respond to her. They'd managed to chase off professional nannies, including one who'd raised her own triplets. So he understood why a woman who'd never spent much time around babies would worry how she'd fare with three "crotchety" six-month-olds. She'd probably expected them to cry constantly and bat at her nose.

They did do a lot of that kind of thing. But they were also like this. Sitting contentedly, giggling, shaking rattles. If not exactly listening to her story, hearing it around them, enjoying her melodic voice.

"I'd say so," he confirmed, and she beamed, her delight going straight to his heart. "It's bedtime for these guys."

As if on cue, Carson started rubbing his eyes.

Then Caleb did.

Chloe's face crumpled and she let out a loud shriek, then started crying.

Savannah picked up Chloe and held her against her chest, rubbing her back, which helped calm the baby.

Hutch picked up both boys, Carson leaning his head against his father's neck, one of Hutch's favorite things in the world, and Caleb rubbed his eyes.

Savannah's phone rang, and she shifted Chloe to pull it from her back pocket. She glanced at the screen. "Ugh, business," she said, continuing to rub Chloe's back as she bounced her a little. "Savannah Walsh," she said into the phone. "Ah, I've been waiting for your call. No, those terms are *not* acceptable. That's right. No again. Oh well, no deal then. Have a nice night. What's that? You'll come up the five thousand? Wonderful. I'll expect the contract by end of business tomorrow." Click.

He watched her turn the ringer off and then chuck the phone on the sofa.

"Sorry," she said. "I just realized I shouldn't have taken that call. I'm on duty here."

"Of course you should have taken it. Your life off this ranch still exists. You do what you need to. And that was very impressive to listen to. Hopefully you'll rub off on me and I'll be tougher when it comes to negotiating at cattle and equipment auctions."

She eyed him. "Were you always a nice guy? I don't remember that."

Hutch laughed. "Nice enough. But competitive with you. Now, I'm just relieved we're both Team Triplets."

She grinned. "Team Triplets. I like it. And I don't want my life to interfere with my time here. In fact, I just realized that for certain. I'll have my assistant, who already has a few clients of her own and is ready to be an agent in her right, handle that contract. I want to focus on the reason I'm here."

Chloe rubbed her eyes and her face started scrunching.

Savannah cuddled Chloe closer. "You better watch out, you better not cry," she sang softly. "You better not pout I'm telling you why. Though, that is what babies do, isn't it, you little dumpling. But Santa Claus *is* coming to town, and he's making a list."

Chloe made a little sound, like "ba," her gaze sweet on Savannah's face, then her eyes drooped. She let out a tiny sigh and her eyes closed, her little chest rising and falling.

"Aww, she fell asleep!" Savannah said. "Huh. I'm not too shabby at this, after all. They're all changed and ready for their bassinets."

"You really are a Christmas miracle," he said.

Her face, already lit up, sparkled even more. He led the way into the large, airy nursery with its silver walls decorated with tiny moons and stars, a big round rug on the polished wood floor, the bookcase full of children's titles, two gliders by the window. His father had ordered the three sleigh-shaped wooden bassinets, each baby's name stenciled and painted on it. Every time he looked at the bassinets, at the names, he'd forget all the crud that Daniel kept bringing up and he'd miss his dad, his grief catching him by surprise. People were never just one thing.

Savannah was a good example of that. If he'd seen her walking down Main Street yesterday in her cashmere coat, barking a negotiation into her cell phone, he'd never imagine her as someone who'd sing Christmas carols to a crying baby, whose eyes would light up at a crabby little girl falling asleep in her arms. People could always surprise you, he knew.

"I'm praying for my own Christmas miracle that I can transfer Chloe to her crib without waking her," she said. "What are my odds?"

"She's iffy," he said. "You just never know. Carson's more a sure bet—heavy sleeper. Caleb always wakes up the minute his head touches a mattress. At my house, anyway."

Savannah glanced at him for a moment, seeming to latch on to that part about "his house." She started quietly singing "Santa Claus Is Coming to Town" again, then carefully lowered Chloe down, gently swaying just a bit. The baby's lower lip quirked, and when she was on the mattress, she simply turned her head and lifted a fist up to her ear, eyes closed, chest rising and falling.

"I did it!" Savannah whispered.

But then Chloe's eyes popped open and she started fussing.

"Scratch that. I didn't do it." Savannah's shoulders sagged.

"Told you she's iffy," he said. "She likes having her forehead caressed from the eyebrows up toward her hairline. And she likes your song. You could try both."

Savannah brightened and reached down to caress Chloe's forehead, singing the carol, and the baby girl's eyes drooped, drooped some more, and then she was asleep. "Phew," she whispered.

A half hour later, both boys were finally asleep in their bassinets, Caleb indeed taking longer than Carson. Hutch had the urge to pull Savannah into his arms for a celebratory hug, but a fist bump seemed more appropriate.

"Our work here is done," he said, holding up his palm. "I could use coffee. You?"

She grinned and did give him a fist bump. "Definitely. And we can talk about the grand plan for my time here."

As they tiptoed out of the nursery, the urge for that embrace only got stronger. Because they were Team Triplets, and it felt so good to have someone on his side, someone who wouldn't quit on him, someone he could talk to?

Or was it all of the above *and* because he was attracted to Savannah Walsh?

It was choice B that made her just as scary as she'd been seventeen years ago.

Don't miss
Triplets Under the Tree
by Melissa Senate,
available November 2023 wherever
Harlequin® Special Edition
books and ebooks are sold.

www.Harlequin.com

#3019 A MAVERICK'S HOLIDAY HOMECOMING
Montana Mavericks: Lassoing Love • by Brenda Harlen
'Tis the season...for a holiday reunion? Rancher Billy Abernathy has no interest in romance; Charlotte Taylor's career keeps her far away from Montana. But when the recently divorced father of three crosses paths with his runaway bride from long ago, a little bit of mistletoe works magic...

#3020 HER BEST FRIEND'S WEDDING
Bravo Family Ties • by Christine Rimmer
Through the years Sadie McBride and Ty Bravo have been rivals, then enemies—and in recent years, buddies. But when a Vegas wedding party leads to a steamy no-holds-barred kiss, will they risk their perfectly good friendship with something as dangerous as love?

#3021 MARRY & BRIGHT
Love, Unveiled • by Teri Wilson
Editor Addison England is more than ready for a much-earned promotion. The problem? So is Carter Payne, her boss's annoyingly charming nephew. Competition, attraction and marriage mayhem collide when these two powerhouse pros vie for *Veil Magazine*'s top job!

#3022 ONCE UPON A CHARMING BOOKSHOP
Charming, Texas • by Heatherly Bell
Twyla Thompson has kept Noah Cahill in the friend zone for years, crushing instead on his older brother. But when a bookstore costume contest unites them as Mr. Darcy and Elizabeth Bennet—and brings unrealized attraction to light—Twyla wonders if Noah may be her greatest love after all.

#3023 A FAMILY-FIRST CHRISTMAS
Sierra's Web • by Tara Taylor Quinn
Sarah Williams will do anything to locate her baby sister—even go undercover at renowned investigation firm Sierra's Web. She knows her by-the-book boss, Winchester Holmes, would fire her if he knew the truth. So falling for each other is not an option—*right*?

#3024 MARRIED BY MISTAKE
Sutton's Place • By Shannon Stacey
For Chelsea Grey, the only thing worse than working next door to John Fletcher is waking up in Vegas married to him. And worse still? Their petition for annulment is denied! They'll keep fighting to fix their marriage mistake—unless knee-weakening kisses and undeniable attraction change their minds first!

HARLEQUIN
PLUS

Try the best multimedia
subscription service for romance
readers like you!

Read, Watch and Play.

Experience the easiest way to get
the romance content you crave.

Start your **FREE TRIAL** at
<u>www.harlequinplus.com/freetrial</u>.